WHALE
of a
CRIME

A Gray Whale Inn Mystery #7

Karen MacInerney

Gray Whale Press

Published 2017 by Gray Whale Press
Copyright 2017 by Karen MacInerney
Print design by A Thirsty Mind Book Design

Dedicated to my mother, Carol Swartz, and my sister, Liza Potter, with love.

ONE

"Red sky in morning, sailor's warning." I'd heard it a thousand times, but as I stood staring out at the cloudless sky suspended like a blue bowl over the Gulf of Maine, I reflected that the day had turned out perfectly after all.

Boy, was I wrong.

Of course, I didn't know that at the time. I was aboard the *Summer Breeze*, savoring the feel of the wind and the salt spray in my face and enjoying the rhythm of being aboard a schooner as it rode over the waves. The sun was warm on my face, and being out on the open water was invigorating. I loved the sea; something about it always energized me.

I was playing hooky from the Gray Whale Inn for the afternoon and joining my guests on a whale-watching outing. I had booked the inn for the week, and I was providing breakfast, lunch, and dinner to the ten guests who had signed up for the Northern Spirit Tours excursion. Even though it had been a beautiful summer on Cranberry Island, the inn had been so busy I hadn't had much time to enjoy it. Today was going to be a welcome respite.

As I opened my eyes and took in the sun on the

sparkling Gulf of Maine, a short, rather squat woman lumbered over to the rail and stood beside me. "I didn't much care for the frittata you cooked this morning. Are there any snacks?"

I turned and gave Doreen a thin smile. She'd only been here for twenty-four hours, and she was already a top contender for the "most irritating guest" award.

"There's some fruit in the galley if you're really hungry, but I'm afraid that's all I've got until lunch."

"I get low blood sugar," she complained. "It's important for me to have access to food."

"Maybe I'll send some muffins tomorrow," I suggested.

"Just as long as they're gluten-free," she reminded me, and marched off to talk to the first mate about something else.

I looked back at the water, trying to recapture the mood, but it had evaporated.

"I can see why you decided to move here."

I turned to see Alex van der Berg, the handsome tour naturalist. This was the tour's second time at the Gray Whale Inn, and my best friend Charlene was absolutely delighted. She and Alex had gone out to dinner a few times during the July tour, and now that Alex was back, my friend was practically a fixture at the inn. It was a good thing her niece Tania was able to run the Cranberry Island General Store and handle the mail, or half the island would be out of milk and behind on their bills.

To be honest, I could see why. Not only did Alex

have sun-streaked blond hair and an appealing grin, but he had a great personality to match. It was a good thing I was married to a handsome man, or I might find myself sorely tempted. "You've got a pretty terrific job yourself," I pointed out. "You get to go all over the world."

"I do," he agreed. "But sometimes it would be nice to settle down."

I gazed back across the water to where the inn nestled at the end of the island. "It has been wonderful living here," I said.

"Even with certain guests?" he asked, glancing toward where Captain Bainbridge was now grilling first mate Martina Garza, who was looking very uncomfortable. I wasn't surprised; I knew a big investor was on the tour, and the crew were trying very hard to make everything look as perfect as possible.

I laughed. "Adds spice," I said. "Might want to remind the captain of that when you get the chance."

"He's been in a bad mood the last few days," Alex admitted. "He and Martina haven't been getting along."

"Probably the stress of having the investor on board," I said.

"Martina's having heartburn about buying a second boat, I think," he said.

"They're co-owners, aren't they? It's a big investment," I replied, remembering how nervous I'd been when I plunked down my savings to buy the

Gray Whale Inn. "But the tours seem to be going well."

"They do," he said. "The plan is to do winter tours in the south, where the whales migrate during the winter months."

"Makes sense," I said.

"The new boat even has sleeping quarters and a full kitchen," he said. "If you're ever looking for a winter job, they might be in the market for a cook."

"Tempting," I said, "but the inn runs year-round these days. Besides, I'm not sure I could cook in a kitchen the size of a shoebox."

"Worth thinking about," he said. "It's awfully cold here in January."

"True," I said, mulling over the idea. Maybe I would talk to John about it…

All of a sudden, the engine slowed. I listened; a moment later, the distinctive hissing sound of a whale breathing came to my ears.

"They're here," Alex said, pointing to where a gray fin slid through the blue waves. The whale released a plume of vapor from its blowhole before submerging again.

"It's a humpback," he said, turning to address the other passengers with a smile. They hurried to the side of the boat, cameras at the ready. "With any luck, they'll be bubble netting."

"Oh, I'd love to see that," I breathed. I'd often read about how humpbacks swam in circles, forming nets of bubbles around their prey, then came up through the center of the net, breaching the surface. As we watched, the rest of the passengers crowded to the side of the boat.

"We can't get closer than 100 yards," Alex said as the boat slowly moved closer to the whales. There were at least three of them. "They seem to be hanging out," he added. "Maybe we'll get lucky."

As we watched, the first mate Martina steered the boat closer to the breathing whales. Alex glanced over toward the captain, who was directing Martina to move the schooner closer to the whales as the would-be investor stood at his right arm.

"Martina," he called. "Back off a bit. We're getting too close."

"It's fine," the captain said.

"Really," Alex said. "We have to back off. It's not safe for the whales."

The captain narrowed his eyes at the naturalist, then countermanded him. "It won't hurt them if we get a little closer." Martina looked between the naturalist and the captain, and acceded to the captain's wishes.

"Isn't that illegal?" I asked Alex under my breath.

"It is," he said. "And bad for the whales. If I didn't need this job so much, I'd report him."

His eyes scanned the water, his jaw tight. I followed his gaze. "What's that?" I asked, noticing something trailing in the wake of one of the whales.

"Fishing gear," he said. "Bad news. I think it's caught up in it."

"Oh, no," I said. A murmur went through the crowd; I wasn't the only one who had seen it.

"Is that normal?" Jan, one of the guests on the tour, asked.

"No," he said. "In fact, it can be fatal. Not only does the gear make it harder for the whale to get to the surface to breathe, but it can get caught up on other gear and drown it."

"Drown it?" I asked.

He nodded. "They need to get to the surface to breathe. If they can't…"

"That's terrible!" Jan said, echoing my thoughts. The edges of her brown eyes crinkled in worry; I knew she fostered cats back home in Iowa and had a soft spot for animals. "We need to do something about it!"

"Ideally we'd be able to remove the gear, but I'd need a smaller boat…we're not set up to do that. Plus, I think we need to notify one of the conservation agencies." As we watched, the whale surfaced again, dragging what looked like at least 25 feet of tangled fishing gear behind it. "Poor thing," Alex said.

A moment later, a flurry of small bubbles began popping on the surface of the water, about fifty feet away from us. "Look," Alex said, pointing to the silvery ring. "Bubble netting!"

A moment later, an enormous humpback whale exploded from the surface of the water, landing with a loud smack. The tour group broke out in spontaneous applause.

"That was amazing!" Jan said, mouth agape.

"Did you get a picture?" Herb, a stout, red-faced sixty-something man asked Gayla, his wisp of a wife.

"I think I missed it," she said.

He sighed. "It happens one time, and you miss it."

"Here," she said, shoving the phone at him. "If you're so good, you get the next shot."

I stifled a grin.

As we stood there, another whale leaped into the air, coming down with a huge splash.

"Incredible," Jan breathed.

"Did you get the shot?" Gayla asked Herb.

"What?" he asked, still staring at the spot where the whale had disappeared back into the water. "Oh...I'll get the next one."

"That was absolutely magnificent," Jan said, still watching the water.

I had to agree with her; the sight of the massive whale leaping through the air, the salt spray gleaming in the sunshine, had taken my breath away. But I was more worried about the whale with the fishing gear attached. Would we be able to help it before it got caught up in one of the thousands of lobster trap lines that cluttered the Gulf of Maine?

I certainly hoped so.

John was deep into dinner preparations when the captain dropped anchor offshore from the inn; I could smell garlic sautéing in butter from the boat, and even though I'd eaten a lobster roll and several cookies for lunch, my stomach was rumbling. I went ashore with the first group of guests, and hurried up to the kitchen to help.

John stood at the stove, sautéing mushrooms in garlic. My husband, I reminded myself, touching the ring on my left hand as if making sure it was true. With his sandy hair, green eyes, and lean, athletic frame, he looked like an L.L. Bean cover model. A sculptor who worked with wood, he had a delicious woodsy scent that was even better than the lovely aromas emanating from the pan on the stove. I walked up behind him and touched his shoulder. "Hi," I said. "It smells delicious."

John turned and smiled at me. "You're back! How did it go?"

"It was terrific," I told him as he kissed me on the cheek. "We saw a pod of humpbacks bubble netting," I told him.

"You did? That's incredible!" he said.

"Yes, but one of them has a bunch of fishing gear attached to it. Alex is going to call a few people he knows and see if he can organize something to help free it."

"Poor thing," he said. "I hope they manage to figure something out."

"Me too," I said. "It looked awful."

"Did the guests have a good time?"

"All except Doreen," she said. "She spent the morning talking about her low blood sugar, and most of the afternoon complaining that there aren't any gray whales off the coast of Maine."

"I always did wonder why you named the inn that," John said. "With your background, I figured you'd know better."

I poked him playfully. "Just because I have a background in wildlife conservation doesn't mean I can't have flights of fancy," I said. "There was something about the gray color of the shingles that made it feel right. Besides, the Gray Whale Inn sounds a lot better than the Humpback Whale Inn."

"You have a point," he conceded as I grabbed a chocolate cookie out of the cookie jar on the counter.

"Where's Charlene?" I asked.

"She's on her way," John said. "She's been calling every half hour to see if you were back yet. By the way, we may have a new neighbor; she said there was someone looking at Cliffside yesterday, and there's a rumor there's a contract on it."

Cliffside was an imposing house with a commanding view of Cranberry Island's small harbor. It had sat vacant for some time...some islanders said because it was overpriced, and others said it was because the scent of herring from the lobster coop was a bit too close for comfort. "It's been on the market for how long, now?"

"Years," John said. "It's a big house; you could have a family reunion in it and still have free rooms."

"I hope it's someone nice," I said. The last owners had been anything but. "Thanks for cooking, by the way. Why don't I set the tables, and then I'll come back and give you a hand with the last minute stuff?"

"Thanks," he said. "It was on my list, but I haven't gotten to it yet."

"Believe me, I understand," I said. "Where's Gwen?" I asked. My lovely niece, who had been staying with me for the past few years helping out at the inn while working on her budding art career, usually helped out in the evening, but she was nowhere to be seen.

"Adam's cooking her dinner tonight," he told me. Adam, her fiancé, was a local lobsterman and Princeton grad. They were very happy together... even though I knew my sister wouldn't approve. Gwen had just called and broken the news to her last week. It hadn't gone over well.

"Where's your mom?" I asked. My mother-in-law Catherine was also remarkably absent.

"Oh, gallivanting with Murray, as usual," he said. To our surprise, Catherine had paired off with local irritant Murray Selfridge not long after moving into what used to be John's carriage house. We'd expected the romance to die down, but it had been almost a year and they were still going strong. I still wasn't sure how I felt about it, but since Catherine seemed happy, it really wasn't my business.

"With all this romance, it's amazing any work is getting done," I said.

"I can work and kiss at the same time," John said. "Try me."

I laughed. "Let me get the tables set, and I'll take you up on it."

"Promise?"

"Absolutely." As I turned and opened the door to the dining room, angry voices pulled me up short.

"I told you it's a bad idea. We're already in debt. What happens if we can't sell the cabins at that price? We haven't ever done anything in that market."

"It'll work out," the other voice responded. "We can get our passengers so much closer to the whales than the normal cruise ships...they'll pay for the privilege."

"Alex is a problem," the first voice said. "He was causing trouble with the passengers today."

"Then we'll get rid of him," he said.

"What if he complains to the Coast Guard?"

"He won't," the voice responded in a tone that made my skin crawl. "I promise."

TWO

"I'm investing everything I have in this. If you hadn't managed to pull strings, we would have taken a bath last time…"

"You worry too much. I have everything under control."

"You'd better," came the voice, with a note of warning that made my hackles rise. I chose that moment to push through the door noisily; I was curious to see who was talking.

"Oh, hi!" I said brightly as I rounded the corner. It was Captain Bainbridge and Martina, the first mate. "I didn't realize anyone was in here," I lied. "I hope you like beef stroganoff; John should have it ready in about fifteen minutes."

"Great," Captain Bainbridge said. His had been the "under control" voice, I realized; it was the first mate, Martina, who had been sounding the alarm bells. "It was so nice having you out with us today, Natalie," he said. "And the lobster rolls were terrific!"

"I'm glad you liked them," I said. "It was amazing to see the bubble netting. But I'm still worried about that whale with the fishing line attached to it. Is there anything we can do?"

"Martina here is getting in touch with some of the scientists to see what we can do," the captain said, clapping a hand on his first mate's shoulders. It may have been my imagination, but Martina looked surprised.

"Well, there are a lot of lobstermen on the island who would be happy to lend a hand, I'm sure," I said. "Keep me posted."

"Thanks," Captain Bainbridge said.

"I should probably get the tables set," I said. "There's a bottle of wine on the sideboard if you'd like," I said, "and it looks like John put out some smoked trout dip and crackers."

"We don't drink on duty, I'm afraid," the captain said. "But I'm sure the guests will be pleased."

"Thanks again for staying with us," I said. "It's been a lot of fun; I'm hoping I can sneak out for one of the tours later this week."

"We'd love to have you," the captain said. "And the food and rooms have been terrific. So much better than docking at Bar Harbor."

"I'm glad you think so," I said, wondering if getting a bigger boat might mean they wouldn't need the inn. Then again, Alex had said they were planning on running tours in the south; would they have two boats running in different places, or move them around?

"We should probably clean up before dinner," he said.

"I'll let you go, then," I told them. "See you soon!"

They both strode away, and if they resumed their conversation, it wasn't where I could hear it.

Either John's cooking was particularly delicious, or the guests were particularly hungry; they devoured his stroganoff, plowed through his bread pudding, and raved about his cooking. Between serving and cleaning up, it was almost 10:00 by the time we finished up and headed to bed.

"This full-service thing is a lot of work," John said as we headed up the stairs to our room.

"Particularly when half your staff is off gallivanting with their boyfriends," I said. I looked down at the carriage house; the windows were still dark. "Looks like your mom isn't back yet."

"Looks like it. It's late for her," he said. "We haven't seen Charlene and Alex, either."

"I wonder if the tour is okay with him leaving for the evening so often?"

"Not a lot of wildlife to identify in the dining room," he pointed out.

"I'm sorry I left you all alone today, by the way," I told him as I followed him into our suite. When I'd first moved here, I never dreamed I'd be sharing my room with the handsome island deputy who lived in the cottage house down the hill at the time. "If I'd known you'd be on your own, I wouldn't have gone."

"And you wouldn't have seen a humpback whale breach," John said, turning to embrace me as I closed the door behind us.

"Which was absolutely amazing," I admitted. They were so close to the schooner I felt like I could reach out and touch them. "There was a baby with them" I said. "She kept leaping around. I sometimes forget they're out there, just a couple of miles from the inn...it was an amazing reminder of all the lives going on around us." I kissed him. "I still feel like I abandoned you, though."

"It was fine. I told Gwen and my mother to go; I knew I could handle it."

"You're amazing," I said.

"It's your turn for breakfast, though," he reminded me with a grin.

"If you're very nice tonight," I said, "I might bring you breakfast in bed."

"How about a midnight snack now?" he asked, pulling me into his arms and giving me a long kiss.

I'd liked being single, I thought as I melted into his embrace, but there were definite benefits to sharing your life with a man like John Quinton.

I woke up in the middle of the night, flailing at the covers and breathing hard. The dream faded as I reoriented myself in our bedroom; I'd imagined I was tangled up in the fishing gear we'd seen attached to the whale that morning and being dragged down to the bottom of the ocean. A breeze blew through the open window, ruffling the curtains, and my orange tabby Biscuit made a discontented noise from the bottom of the bed. As my breath began to steady, I heard a faint meowing sound from outside.

Biscuit heard it, too; I could feel her body tense. We both listened for a moment; it came again. It was very high-pitched and small, and a little bit shaky.

I glanced at the clock; it was 2 a.m. I got up and wrapped my robe around me as I padded to the door, trying not to wake John. Biscuit didn't follow me—which wasn't a surprise, since she wasn't exactly what you'd call an athletic feline specimen.

Moonlight flooded the kitchen when I got to the bottom of the stairs, where I paused for a moment, trying to orient myself to the sound. It seemed to be from the porch behind the kitchen. I let myself out the door, being as quiet as possible, and shut it behind me. There was silence for a moment, interrupted only by the sound of the waves, and then the mewling started again.

It was coming from the corner of the porch, where a tiny kitten, faintly illuminated by the light of the moon, huddled under a rocking chair. "Oh, poor thing!" I breathed.

I walked toward it slowly, trying not to scare it, and crouched down. "It's okay, baby," I said as I reached out to touch its soft head. The little thing trembled under my touch. Gently, I put my hand under her and scooped her up. Even though it was only in the 60s outside, the little body felt cold.

"Where's your mom?" I asked as I cradled the

kitten in my arms, tucking her into my robe. I didn't have a ton of experience with kittens, but I knew enough to know she was too young to be separated from her mother. Although she was shivering, the plaintive mewling turned into a rumbling purr. I stood outside for a moment, listening in case she—I don't know why, but I knew she was a she—had siblings nearby, but she seemed to be alone.

"Let's go get you warmed up," I said, carrying her inside. When I got inside, I shifted her to the crook of my left arm and grabbed my laptop, pulling up a page on caring for kittens.

I was doing the right thing for starters—warming her up—and gauged her age to be about six weeks. Once she was warm, I would see if I could get some food into her. If I was right about her age, she should be able to manage some canned food, which was a good thing, since I didn't have any kitten milk on hand. I closed the laptop and leaned back in my chair, stroking the kitten's head and wondering where she had come from. She settled down into a rhythmic purring, which faded slowly as her breathing became soft and regular. I closed my eyes for a moment, focusing on the little body nestled into me, and must have fallen asleep with her.

A noise jolted me awake. The kitten woke, too; I could feel her stir in my robe. I swallowed hard when I realized someone was at the kitchen door. As I watched, a dark form let itself into my kitchen, closing the door with a thunk. My mouth was dry and my heart was pounding, but I had to say something.

"Can I help you?" I asked.

The figure jumped about three feet into the air. "Natalie?"

"That's me. Who are you?"

"Alex," he said. "What are you doing up? You scared me to death."

"Likewise," I said dryly.

"I was just getting home from dinner with Charlene. I was trying not to wake anyone."

"Late dinner," I said. "Why didn't you come in the front door?'

"Sorry about that; it was locked," he said, "and I left my key in my room."

"No worries," I said, the adrenaline still draining from my system. "I'm glad it's just you."

"What are you doing up?" he asked.

"I found a kitten on the back porch. I was going to warm her up and feed her, but she fell asleep." I reached into my robe and touched her little paws; they were no longer cold, and the shivering had stopped long ago. I was planning to ask Jan how to take care of her in the morning; I was worried I might do something wrong. "Know anything about kittens?"

"Unfortunately, no," he said. "My knowledge is limited to wild fauna, I'm afraid." He yawned. "If you don't mind, I'm going to head up to bed. I'm supposed to go help get the boat ready at six tomorrow."

"What's today's expedition, again?"

"The seals," he said, "and more whales if the group

wants to look for them."

"I'll be sorry to miss it," I said.

"You saw the main show today," he said.

"Do you think you'll be able to help that whale who's caught up in gear?"

"It can be tricky," he admitted, "but if we can get a GPS tracker on her and some floats, we'll have a decent chance. I'm hoping to hear back tomorrow morning."

"The captain seemed to be getting a bit close to the whales," I said.

"Yes," he said shortly. "It's a real problem. That's how whales get hurt."

"And boats," I suggested.

"Sometimes, yes," he said. "Well, I'm going to head to bed. Good luck with the kitten."

"Thanks," I said as I got up, cradling the kitten in my arms, and fished in the pantry for a can of cat food. I put a little wet food on a plate and watched as she sniffed at it. I was waiting for her to eat when there was the sound of another door opening and closing.

"Be back in a moment," I whispered to the kitten, and walked over to the kitchen door, thinking the inn was rather active for 2:30 a.m.

"Hello?" I called.

There were footsteps; unless it was my imagination, they paused for a moment, then resumed at a faster pace, hurrying up the stairs. A moment later, a door upstairs opened and closed. An insomniac out for a late-night walk? I knew it wasn't Alex; his room was on the first floor. I looked out toward the back of the inn, but there was nothing other than the moonlight on the water, and the dark shape of the *Summer Breeze* bobbing in the distance.

I turned back to the kitchen and the kitten, wondering who had been out for a late-night walk.

The alarm went off way too early the next morning. It had been almost four a.m. by the time I got back upstairs, and I was exhausted. The kitten had eaten a little bit, which was encouraging, and then fallen back to sleep in my arms. I wasn't sure what Biscuit would think of her, but I was afraid she'd get too cold if I left her on her own, so I carried her up with me and tucked her up against me when I climbed under the covers. Biscuit hadn't moved from her spot at the foot of the bed. Her hackles rose, and she let out a little growl, but quieted when I stroked her head. She did make a point of moving to John's side of the bed. I couldn't see in the darkness, but I had the feeling she was giving me a nasty look from her beautiful green eyes.

Now, as the morning sun streamed through the window, Biscuit was curled up at John's feet, and the kitten was a tiny gray ball nestled under my chin. She had a little white patch on her chest and a matching spot on her forehead, with white whiskers that contrasted beautifully with her fur. She opened her blue eyes slightly as I shifted, then curled up tighter, like a fluffy pill bug.

Although I hated to disturb her, I had breakfast to prepare. I tucked her into the blankets, keeping an eye on Biscuit, and quickly brushed my teeth and dressed, monitoring Biscuit to make sure she didn't try any funny business.

About fifteen minutes later, I tucked the kitten into a blanket near the radiator in the kitchen, turned the heat on low—it was a little chilly in the kitchen—and got to work on breakfast.

The morning's menu was a spinach frittata, apple caramel muffins, a fruit salad, and sausage links. The group would be stopping at a lobster pound on Mount Desert Island today, so I didn't need to worry about lunch. As the kitten curled back up into a ball, I reached for my recipe binder—but it wasn't there.

Had John misfiled it last night? I wondered. I opened a few cabinets and drawers with no luck, and then reached for one of my back-up cookbooks until I found something similar. I'd ask John when he came downstairs; in the meantime, I found an apple streusel muffin recipe that looked like it would fill the bill.

I chopped up a few granny smith apples, looking out the window as I worked. It looked like it was going to be a beautiful day for the tour group. The sun was gilding the tops of the mountains of Mount Desert Island, and the water was calm and blue. A deep peace enfolded me as I paused to gaze out the window of my kitchen at the beauty on my doorstep; I was so grateful for the beauty of my surroundings, and the people in it.

As the smell of baking muffins filled the kitchen, I poured myself another cup of coffee—I was still a bit groggy after last night's interrupted sleep—and reached for a cantaloupe. I had just halved it when there was a knock on the kitchen door.

I turned around and swore under my breath.

It was my sister, Bridget, looking like she was in the mood to commit murder.

THREE

"Bridget," I said, almost dropping the cantaloupe. I rinsed my hands, dried them and hurried to the door. "I wasn't expecting you!" I said as she swept into my kitchen rolling an ominously large black suitcase behind her. She wore a tan trench coat, black slacks, and an expensive-looking silk blouse. "Are you in town for business?" I asked, as if she would have a case on Cranberry Island.

"Of course not, Natalie," she said, giving me a perfunctory hug. "Where is my daughter?"

"Still asleep, I think," I said, hoping that Gwen was upstairs in her room, and not at her fiancé's house. "This is a surprise visit," I said. "What brings you here?"

She arched a dark eyebrow. "What do you think?"

I gave her a winning smile. "Wanted to check out the inn? Take a vacation in Maine and visit family?"

"I want to talk my daughter out of this ridiculous idea you've talked her into, of course."

"Ah," I said, and turned back to the cantaloupe, gripping the knife perhaps a bit more firmly than necessary. "What ridiculous idea would that be?"

"Getting married to a lobsterman," she said. "A

lobsterman you helped her try to pass off as a shipping magnate, if I recall."

"I never said anything about Adam being a shipping magnate, Bridget," I said, even though I hadn't exactly corrected her when she leapt to that assumption. "And Gwen's decisions are entirely her own. I love her, but she's in charge of her own life. Not me."

"No, you're not in charge of her life," Bridget said. "You're her aunt, not her mother."

Since Gwen was in her early twenties, her mother wasn't exactly in charge of her life, either, but I decided not to mention that. This conversation wasn't going in a good direction, I realized. Maybe caffeine would help. "How about a cup of coffee?" I suggested.

"Black, please."

"I remember," I said, and poured her a mug. As I handed it to her, I reflected on how much she and her daughter resembled each other; they had the same mass of curly dark hair and the same willowy figures. Their personalities, on the other hand, could not be less similar.

"When did you get in?" I asked as I sliced the melon into wedges.

"I got in late last night. It was too late to catch the mail boat, so I stayed in Bar Harbor and took the first boat over this morning."

"I wish you'd let me know you were coming," I said as I scooped seeds out of the cantaloupe. Where was I going to put my sister? I wondered. Every room was booked, and my mother-in-law, Catherine, was living in the carriage house.

"Well, I'm here now," she said, taking a sip of her coffee. "When does Gwen usually get up?"

"It varies," I said vaguely as I sliced the cantaloupe into chunks. "So," I said, hoping to change the subject yet again. "How's work?"

"Busy as always," she said. She sighed. "Sometimes I wish I had more of a menial job, like yours. It gets tiring thinking all the time."

I gritted my teeth as I brought the knife down on the cantaloupe a bit harder than strictly necessary. "Oh, there are plenty of challenges, I assure you," I told her.

"Yes," she said. "I guess it must be tough getting up and cleaning toilets every day."

I was saved from having to strangle her by the arrival of Gwen through the kitchen door.

"Hey, Aunt Nat," she said as she closed the door behind her. "Do you need a hand with…" As her eyes lit on her mother, she broke off and let out a short noise that sounded a little like a scream.

"Good morning, Gwen," my sister said.

"Mom," she choked out. "What are you doing here?"

Bridget gave her a tight smile. "I came to spend some time with my daughter, of course."

Gwen walked over and gave her mother a stiff hug. "You didn't tell me you were coming."

"I had a last-minute change in schedule."

"Where are you staying?" Gwen said.

My sister blinked at her. "Why, here, of course."

"But the inn is totally full," she said.

"Really?" Bridget turned to me. "I thought business was slow."

"Actually, it's been really busy."

She turned to Gwen. "Well, I guess I can bunk with you."

At the look of horror on my niece's face, I said, "Maybe we can put you up in the carriage house with Catherine."

My sister looked puzzled. "Who's Catherine?"

"My mother-in-law," I reminded her.

"Oh, yes. I remember," Bridget said. "Has she found a job yet?"

Gwen and I exchanged tortured glances. "She's helping me out at the inn, actually," I said. "Which is a big help, since we've been booked solid since the summer season began."

"I'm going to run upstairs for a moment," Gwen said. "I'll be back to help in a bit," she told me.

"Take your time," I told her. "I've got it under control." The breakfast part, anyway. I wasn't so sure about Bridget.

I kept a steady patter of questions going as I added strawberries and blueberries to the sliced cantaloupe and began chopping veggies for the frittata. It was a self-defense strategy I'd picked up when we were kids, and it still worked. By the time Gwen came back downstairs, Bridget had told me all about the most recent multi-million dollar corporate lawsuits she'd won, as well as her plans for a second home in Hawaii.

"What can I do?" Gwen asked as she tied an apron around her slender waist. At that moment, the kitten made a small mewing sound. "Oh, my goodness," Gwen said, spotting the kitten. "How adorable. Who is this?"

"I found her under the porch," I said. "I'm hoping Jan can tell me what to do with her."

"She is so sweet," Gwen said, forgetting about her mother as she bent down to rub the kitten's head.

"Isn't that against the health code?" my sister asked.

"Why don't you set the tables in the dining room, Gwen?" I suggested.

To my surprise, Bridget stood up. "I'll come help," she announced.

"No," Gwen said sharply. "I mean, I've got a system," she added lamely.

But Bridget was undeterred. "Then I'll come keep you company."

As Gwen walked out of the kitchen looking like a condemned woman, I reflected that it was going to be an interesting week.

I had no idea exactly how interesting, though... the day had only just begun.

Breakfast was well received—I made a mental note to add the muffin recipe to my binder, as they disappeared almost instantaneously—but only two-thirds of the crew turned up in the dining room. Bridget sat in the kitchen the entire time, watching with tight lips and never offering to help, but I managed to ignore her and focus on the tasks at hand. Jan came in and took a look at the kitten, pronounced her old enough to eat canned food, and wondered about her family. "She was on the back porch?"

"Yes," I said.

"Have you seen any other cats around?" she asked as she stroked the kitten's head.

I shook my head. "She just showed up this morning," I said.

"Well, she's old enough to survive without her mother, but keep her warm and keep an eye on her. I'd get her to the vet to get her tested, too."

"The mobile vet should be here this week," I said.

Jan nodded. "Good," she said, and smiled at me. "I'm so glad you're taking care of her. If you hadn't taken her in and warmed her up last night, she might not have made it."

"Thanks," I said, as we walked back to the dining room. "And thanks for taking a look at her."

"Anytime," Jan said, beaming, as she returned to her seat.

I scanned the room; everyone was down except for the captain, which was unusual. He was usually the first one up.

"Where's Captain Bainbridge?" I asked Martina as I refilled her coffee.

"I don't know," she said, looking worried. "I knocked on his door twice, but he didn't answer. I was hoping he went out to the boat early, but the skiff is at the dock."

"Maybe he went out for a morning walk?" I suggested.

"Maybe," she said, but she looked unconvinced. She glanced at her watch. "We're supposed to head out at 8:30," she told me. "If he's not here in ten minutes, we're going to have to go out without him."

"I'm sure he'll turn up," I said.

"I hope so," she told me.

As I headed back to the kitchen, Gayla stopped me. "What kind of coffee is this?" she asked, blinking at me through thick glasses. There was an intensity to her that was interesting, but inconvenient at the moment; I often felt as if I were a bug under a microscope, for some reason.

"French Roast," I said. "I have it roasted specially for the inn."

"Where?" she asked. "I'd love to have this at home."

"I'd be happy to send some with you," I said.

"It would be so much easier if I could get it directly, though," she said.

"I'll get you the info after breakfast," I said.

"By the way, how did you manage to organize getting the tour group here?"

I put on what I hoped was a pleasant expression and tried again. "I'd love to chat, but I've got to help out in the kitchen. Maybe later?"

"I'm free after breakfast," she said.

"Unfortunately, I've got to take care of the rooms. Maybe this afternoon?"

She didn't look pleased with that answer, but I didn't have a choice; with a full inn, I couldn't afford the time. Besides, I still had to figure out what to do with my sister.

Eight-thirty came and went, and there was no sign of Captain Bainbridge. Martina stood up and put on a big smile, but I could see the worry in her eyes. "Everybody ready to go see some seals?"

"What about the captain?" asked Stacy, the young, dark-haired reporter who was doing an article on Northern Spirit Tours—and who I suspected had a crush on the handsome Bainbridge, since she'd been following him around since she arrived.

"He'll join us later," Martina said. "Let's head down to the boat."

I grabbed the basket of cookies and fruit I'd prepared for a late morning snack—lunch wasn't until 1:30—and followed them down to the dock. There were a few murmurs about the captain, but Martina and Alex were putting a bright face on things, and simply assured everyone that he'd be back.

I handed Martina the basket and leaned against the dock, chatting with Alex and the remaining group as Martina headed out with the first group.

"What are you going to do without the captain?" I

asked Alex in a quiet voice.

"I've been on boats since I was a kid. I'm licensed; we'll be fine," he assured me, and I relaxed. The last thing I wanted was to send my guests out on an understaffed boat.

As the skiff returned for the second round of passengers, I lingered at the dock, enjoying the cool, beautiful morning—and, to be honest, putting off going back to face my sister. The sun gleamed on the wooden boat, and I found myself wishing I were joining them. Heck, I'd rather do a tour of Maine landfills than go back and deal with my sister and Gwen this morning.

I could hear the sound of the winch pulling up the anchor chain; they were about to cast off. I was about to turn back to the inn when there was a scream. I peered at the boat; there appeared to be something large and floppy attached to the chain. I squinted and shaded my eyes, and then sucked in my breath.

It looked like they'd found Captain Bainbridge.

FOUR

I ran back to the inn.

"What's wrong?" my sister asked as I rushed into the kitchen. "I need to talk to John," I told her, and hurtled up the steps.

My husband was still sound asleep with Biscuit curled up at his feet. "John," I said, shaking his shoulder.

"I thought you were doing breakfast," he said sleepily.

"Breakfast is over," I informed him. "I think they just pulled Captain Bainbridge up with the anchor."

John's green eyes flew open, and he sat straight up. "What?"

"I think it's him, anyway; I just saw it from a distance. He didn't come down to breakfast this morning, and when they pulled up the anchor, there was...what looked like a body attached."

He leapt out of bed and reached for his jeans. "I'm going out to take a look," he said. "Will you call the police?"

"Of course. My sister's here, by the way," I said as he rummaged in a drawer for a T-shirt.

He looked shocked for the second time this

morning. "What?"

"She showed up while I was making breakfast. I'm sure it's about Gwen."

He sighed. "Well, if you're right about Captain Bainbridge, at least we'll have an excuse for being busy."

"Not much of a silver lining," I said.

"I know," he grimaced, pulling a green T-shirt on over his head as he reached for the doorknob. "I'll head out and secure the scene if you'll call the police on the mainland."

"Got it." A moment later I followed him downstairs.

"This must be your husband," Bridget said as we came into the kitchen. "He's more handsome than I expected."

"Thanks," I said dryly.

"Nice to meet you," John replied politely, not breaking stride. "I'd love to stop and say hi, but there's an emergency."

"I'll bet you have a lot of maintenance issues in an old house like this," Bridget said, misunderstanding the nature of the emergency.

He gave her a tight smile and opened the door as I reached for the portable phone. I followed him out to the porch so that Bridget couldn't listen in, and dialed as I stared out at the schooner. I was guessing they'd either dropped the anchor again or somehow levered the body onto the deck; in any case, it was no longer hanging off the side of the boat. Five minutes later, the dispatcher assured me someone was on the way, and I headed down to the dock.

The guests looked like they'd seen a ghost when I tied up alongside the *Summer Breeze*, right next to John's skiff *Mooncatcher*. When I climbed onto the deck, it was a very different scene from yesterday. A body-sized lump lay under a big piece of canvas. A length of chain and the curve of an anchor protruded from beneath the edge of the cloth, and I didn't want to think about what else was under there. Something glinted in the sunlight; a hairpin. I stooped down to pick it up on instinct, then realized it was a crime scene and let it be.

John stood nearby, examining the schooner's gunwale.

"What happened?" I asked.

"The captain," Martina told me, looking pale and shaken. "He must have gotten caught up in the chain and gone under."

"But how?" asked Stacy. "The anchor line is on the side of the schooner, and the skiff was moored at the dock. Unless he swam out here and was planning to swim back to shore, there's no way it's possible."

"Maybe he was climbing the anchor chain to get into the boat and got caught up in it," Gayla suggested.

"He got his leg tied to the chain two feet above the

anchor," Stacy said. "Pretty impressive feat, since it was at least sixty feet down."

She had a point. The guests started glancing around at each other, as if suddenly realizing there might be a murderer among them.

"Why don't we let the detectives figure things out," John suggested. "In the meantime, if you'd like to go back to the inn, I'm sure Natalie and Martina can escort you. He gave me a level look; I knew he wasn't leaving anyone alone with the body unattended until the mainland police arrived.

"Excellent idea," Alex, who had been uncharacteristically quiet, said. He was pale, but forced a grim smile.

"I'm staying here," Martina said stubbornly.

"Then Natalie can transport everyone," he said, looking at me.

"I'll help," Alex said.

"Thanks," I said, relieved. "I've got tea, coffee, and cookies back at the inn—and something stronger, if anyone feels the need for it. I'm so sorry it's been such a...terrible morning."

At the promise of cookies, the mood brightened at least a fraction, and within five minutes, we had the first group in the two boats and were heading back to the inn.

Once everyone stepped out onto the dock, I joined them on the walk up to the inn while Alex went back to retrieve the last few guests. The normally talkative group was somber as I led them into the dining room and hurried into the kitchen to make another pot of coffee and load up a plate with cookies.

"What's going on?" Bridget asked as I scooped coffee into the coffee maker.

"Someone got caught up in the anchor chain and drowned, I think," I told her as I put the last scoop in and turned the machine on.

"Yikes. Good thing it didn't happen on inn property, or you might be sued. You're not affiliated with this company legally, are you?"

"Mom," Gwen said as she closed the dishwasher. "Someone just died." She looked pale. "Was it anyone from the island?" she asked.

"It was Captain Bainbridge," I said.

"The captain? What a terrible accident," Gwen breathed. "I can't believe it."

Bridget looked like she was about to say something, but before she could open her mouth, I said, "Gwen, could you please put on the kettle? I'm going to take the coffee that's left in the thermos out, along with some cookies."

"Of course, Aunt Nat."

"You really think cookies are going to make things better?" Bridget asked.

"Do you have another suggestion, Mom?" Gwen said.

"I was just saying…"

"Well, don't," Gwen said, her cheeks flushing with anger.

I busied myself with the cookies and hurried out

of the kitchen, happy to leave a very uneasy mother-daughter detente behind me.

The mood in the parlor was not much better than the mood in the kitchen. Gayla and Herb sat close together on the love seat. The first mate and Stacy were still on the boat, along with gluten-free Doreen, thankfully. Jan sat by the window in a wingback chair, looking out at the schooner in the distance. Alex tried to entertain the two kids of the family from Minnesota with a game of Go Fish, but all they wanted to do was look out the window at the boat.

"Do people usually fall off boats and get caught up in the anchor?" Liam asked.

"No," his mother said, looking shaken. "It was a freak accident."

"Would you like some cookies?" I asked the kids, hoping to distract them from the morning's gruesome discovery.

Lizzie wrinkled her nose. "Is there coconut in them?"

"No," I said. They're chocolate chip.

"One each," their father admonished as Lizzie reached for a plate.

"How's the kitten?" Jan asked as the kids bit into their cookies.

The little girl brightened. "Kitten?"

"I found one on the back deck when I came down to make breakfast," I told her. "Would you like to see it?"

"What color is it?" she asked.

"Gray, with a little bit of white," I said. "Stay here, and I'll bring her out." Their mother gave me a grateful look, thankful for the distraction from difficult questions.

I went back into the kitchen, where stony silence still reigned, and picked up the drowsy kitten, nestling her into my arms. "Are you putting me up with Gwen?" Bridget asked as I reached the door.

"Let me talk with Catherine first," I suggested. "There's more room in the carriage house."

"What do you want me to do with my suitcase?" she asked.

"Why don't you leave it at the base of the stairs. If you need to change, you're welcome to go upstairs and use our room," I told her. "It's the door on the left. It's a gorgeous morning for a walk, if you'd like to explore the island," I suggested, hoping to give Gwen a reprieve.

"I think we need to catch up a bit first," she replied, casting her daughter a critical look. "And I need to meet this boyfriend of yours."

"Fiancé," Gwen corrected her.

"Do you even have a ring?" Bridget asked.

"It's right here," Gwen said, holding up her left hand.

"Oh, that's all? No wonder I didn't see it."

I gave Gwen a pitying look and pushed through the door to the kitchen. At the rate my sister was going, there might be a second death at the inn before the week was out. I wasn't sure who was going to be responsible: me, or her daughter.

As soon as the kitten hit the parlor, the body on the schooner was forgotten—at least by the children. "He's so small!" Lizzie breathed, eyes wide.

"It's a she, actually," Jan said, smiling.

"Do you keep that cat in the kitchen?' Gayla asked with a sniff of disapproval.

"I just found her on the back porch last night," I said. "She's staying near the radiator to keep warm."

"Is that health code?" her husband Herb asked. Nan, the wealthy investor from New York, was eyeing me with interest.

"I'm just keeping her in a basket by the radiator while I figure out what to do with her," I said.

"You're going to keep her, aren't you?" Lizzy asked. "Or maybe," she added, turning back to her mom, "We could take her home with us!"

"I don't think our other cat would like that very much," their mom said. "She is very cute, though. As if on cue, the kitten opened her eyes.

"They're blue!" Lizzie said. "Just like mine!"

Yvette and I exchanged looks.

"We don't want to take her away from her home," her mother said.

"But she doesn't have a home. Miss Natalie said she just found her this morning!"

"We're not taking her home," Yvette said, looking to her husband for support. Carson, however, was on the other end of the living room, staring out the window, evidently still transfixed by the schooner; he hadn't said a word since they got back to the inn. I felt bad for Yvette. It was clear the burden of parenting fell on her...and the captain's discovery must have been a real shock for the kids.

"How long have you had the inn?" asked Nan, reaching for a cookie and studying me. Although her investment company had made her a multimillionaire, she was simply dressed in jeans and a T-shirt, and her silver hair was cropped. Her eyes had a bright intelligence to them, and I got the feeling not much slipped by her. Ever since she'd arrived, I had the feeling she was inspecting everything about both the schooner and the inn. Although I was comfortable with the level of service I was providing, something about her was unnerving. Between Nan and Stacy, I was feeling a little bit like a paramecium under a microscope. And with the addition of Bridget's surprise visit and the captain's unfortunate anchor accident to the mix, the week was shaping up to be less than relaxing.

Still, I put on what I hoped looked like an easy smile as Lizzie petted the sleepy kitten. "I opened the inn a few years ago," I said.

"Did you have a hospitality background?"

"Actually, I worked in the Parks and Recreation Department in Austin," I told her.

"Risky move," Nan said.

I smiled. "It's worked out better than I could have dreamed," I said. With the exception of the dead captain, that was. I turned to Yvette. "Can you hold her for a moment?"

"I'd love to," she said, scooting back on the couch so that I could put the kitten on her lap. "She's so soft. She looks like a little mouse."

"That's what you should call her," Liam said. "Mousy!"

"No," Lizzie argued. "That's a terrible name for a cat."

"Ratty?" Liam suggested as I stood up.

"How about Felicia?" Alex suggested.

Lizzie scrunched up her face. "Felicia?"

"Short for *Felis catus*," Alex told her. "It's the scientific name for cat."

"I like it," Lizzie said. "She kind of looks like a Felicia."

I shot Alex a grateful look for defusing the argument and said, "Coffee, anyone? Tea is on the way, too."

"I'll take some, thanks," Nan said.

"Do you have hot chocolate?" Liam asked. "With marshmallows?"

"That's so much sugar, though, sweetheart," Yvette said, then glanced out the window and seemed to change her mind. "I guess it's okay as a special treat," she said. Anything to keep the kids' mind off the boat.

"So how do you think the captain got stuck in the anchor chain?" Liam asked.

"He must have gotten his foot caught somehow," Yvette said. "A terrible accident."

"But the chain was outside the boat," Lizzie said. "How do you get your foot caught if the chain isn't on the boat?"

She had an excellent point.

"And how did he get out there, anyway?" Liam asked as I handed a cup of coffee to Nan. "Did he swim?" The adults exchanged uneasy glances; we had all thought of the same thing privately.

"Maybe," his mother said. "How are your cookies?" she asked, trying to switch the focus of the conversation.

"At least he still had his eyes," Liam said. "I hear sometimes the fish eat them."

"Liam!" Yvette chided him.

"That's gross," Lizzie announced, and I had to agree with her.

"Who's going to teach me to fish if the captain's dead?" Liam asked.

"I will," Alex said. "Now," he added, trying to return their attention to the game. "Do you have a red two?"

I headed back to the kitchen to check on the tea as they resumed their game. Bridget must have gone upstairs to change; to my relief, only my niece was there. The water had boiled, and Gwen was pouring it into the teapot.

"How's it going out there?" she asked.

"Well, Liam's wondering why the fish didn't eat the captain's eyes, and he wants to name the kitten Ratty," I said. "But Alex managed to distract them, and I have a hot chocolate order. Any hot water left in the kettle?"

"Enough for two hot chocolates," she said.

I grabbed a few packets of hot chocolate mix and some marshmallows. "How's it going in here?" I asked.

"My mom wants to meet Adam," Gwen said.

"Do you want to do it here?" I asked.

She shook her head. "I figured we'd go to Spurrell's Lobster Pound. She might be more likely to behave in public."

"I wouldn't bet on it," I said with a grin.

"What do we do if she can't bunk with Catherine?" Gwen asked, looking like a spooked horse. "If we have to share a room, I'm not sure we'll both make it through the week. I don't even know how long she's staying."

"She didn't tell me, either, but we'll figure something out," I said.

"I'd stay with Adam, but..."

"Best not, under the circumstances," I agreed. "Maybe you can go hide out at Charlene's and give up your room," I suggested as I emptied the hot chocolate packets into two mugs.

"I don't want to abandon you," she told me.

"I'm battle-hardened," I reminded her. "I spent eighteen years with her, remember?"

"So did I," she commiserated.

"She loves you," I told her. "She just wants what's best for you."

"No," Gwen corrected me. "She wants what she thinks is best for me. There's a difference."

I sighed. "Do the best you can," I told her.

"I'm trying," she groaned as I stirred marshmallows into the hot chocolate and put the mugs on a tray.

"Have you seen Catherine this morning yet, by the way?" I asked her as I retrieved the cream pitcher from the refrigerator.

"She's usually up by now, but I haven't seen her."

"Would you run down and knock on her door?" I asked. "We need to figure out the schedule for the day...and I need to see if she's okay with Bridget bunking with her."

"Happily," she said.

"I might ask her if she can take your mom for a tour of the island, too, while you're at it. You and I can take care of the rooms."

Gwen's face broke into a smile. "You're brilliant, Aunt Nat," she said as I added the teapot and some cups onto the tray. "I'm going to go now, before she comes down."

"Gwen?" came Bridget's voice from upstairs.

"Go now!" I whispered, and Gwen tiptoed out the back door as I hefted the tray and headed toward the parlor.

"Gwen!" my sister called again as I pushed through the swinging door.

It was going to be a very long week.

FIVE

The police arrived a little over a half an hour later, and I kept everyone supplied with cookies and beverages as one of the detectives took statements from all of the guests. I glanced out the window at the schooner; a police launch had tied up next to it, and the antique boat was now crawling with crime scene investigators.

My mother-in-law had come to Gwen's and my rescue. I'd debriefed her on what was going on, and she'd not only offered to let Bridget stay in the carriage house, but volunteered to take her out on Murray's boat for the day. I wanted to kiss her, but thought it might be better to wait until Bridget wasn't standing in the same room with us.

John was busy helping out on the schooner, so I refilled the coffee, tea and cookies and headed up to take care of the rooms, shuddering as I passed the captain's room, which was busy being sorted through by a team of investigators. From what I'd gathered, they were treating his death as a homicide. To be honest, unless he really had swum out to the *Summer Breeze* by himself and tied himself up to the anchor chain, it was the logical conclusion.

But who would want him dead? I wondered.

As I remembered the argument between the naturalist and the captain the previous day, I had an uneasy feeling. I hadn't been the only one to witness the harsh words between them. I thought also of the conversation between the captain and the first mate—and the captain's veiled threat toward Alex. Had he threatened him last night, only to have the tables turned by his intended victim? I realized with a sick feeling that I'd seen Alex coming into the inn at two in the morning. Was it possible that Charlene's new beau was a murderer? I knew I had to tell the investigators what I'd seen and heard. But should I tell Charlene as well?

I was going to start at the end of the hall, but decided instead to start with Alex's room. If he was a dangerous man, I needed to tell my friend. I grabbed my bucket of cleaning supplies and unlocked the door to his suite, praying there would be nothing incriminating in the naturalist's room.

I let myself in and shut the door behind me. The room smelled faintly of his cologne, and the curtains were drawn shut, the bed a tangle of sheets and quilt. I opened the curtains to let sunlight into the room, then did a quick scan of the desk and the dresser. Despite the unmade bed, the rest of the room was neat and orderly; his razor and hairbrush were neatly lined up on the bathroom counter, and his damp towel hung on a hook.

A half dozen field guides were stacked on the

desk, along with a notebook. I glanced over my shoulder and opened the notebook; it was lined with dates, times, locations, and names. I was confused until flipped through to yesterday's entry and saw both the time of day and a number. This must be a record of the whales he had seen, I realized. I closed the book and was putting it back into its place when I noticed a folded page sticking out of the back of the book. I opened it; it was an article on a Japanese whaler and its encounter with the *Sea Shepherd*, an anti-whale-hunting boat, a few years back. I scanned it quickly and tucked it back into the notebook, wondering why he'd printed the article, and continued my survey. There was nothing incriminating, thank goodness, and I felt a little bit better as I straightened the sheets on the bed, did a quick cleanup in the bathroom, and headed to the next room.

The police had completed with their initial inquiries by the time I finished up the rooms, and it suddenly occurred to me that with the discovery of Bainbridge's body, the group's reservations at Jordan Pond House were probably not going to happen.

That meant I had a dozen people to feed, and nothing to feed them, unless I wanted to pirate my dinner plans. Evidently the same thought had occurred to Martina; as I put up my cleaning supplies and turned to go find her, she knocked on the kitchen door, looking worried.

"I just realized our lunch plans are off!" she said.

"Me too," I said, opening the fridge. "And I haven't picked up the order for tomorrow's lunch yet," I said, and turned to her. "Let me call Spurrell's and see if they can get a dozen people in," I suggested.

"Good thinking," she said. "I'm sorry... it's just..." Her eyes welled up. "I can't believe Carl is gone. And they think someone murdered him."

I reached out to touch her shoulder. "I'm so sorry," I said gently. "It must be a shock."

"And now I have to keep everyone busy for the next four days. The investor is probably going to get cold feet, and I don't even have access to the schooner...besides even if I do, I'm down a crew member."

"What about Alex?" I asked. "He has a license, doesn't he?"

"That's true," she said. "I hadn't thought about that."

"In the meantime, is everyone free to go this afternoon? Maybe I can find a lobster boat they can go out on—see how a lobsterman works."

"Great thinking," she said.

"I'll see if I can get in touch with my niece's fiancé. Let me make a few phone calls, and I'll let you know."

"You're a lifesaver," she told me. "I can't thank you enough."

Ten minutes later, I had secured two tables at Spurrell's Lobster Pound and had Adam motoring back toward the island, along with a friend who'd agreed to help us out. John wasn't available, so Gwen drove some of the group over in the van while Alex and I took the young family in my skiff, the *Little Marian*; John's skiff was still out at the schooner. Fortunately, I had extra kids' life jackets in the storage closet, so we got Liam and Lizzie fitted out.

"We're not going to get caught on the anchor, are we?" Lizzie asked, a concerned look on her face, as I helped her into the skiff.

"Of course not," I said. "But you will get to see how lobsters are caught. You'll probably see some crabs, too—and maybe even a sea cucumber."

"What's a sea cucumber?" Lizzie asked.

"You'll see," I told her. "You can tell me how many lobsters you counted when you get back!"

"I still think the kitten should be named Ratty," Liam piped up.

Carson sighed, and Yvette gave me a long-suffering look. I grinned to myself and started up the engine, giving the schooner a wide berth, although my eyes were drawn to it. There was no way the captain had gotten his leg tied up in that anchor chain.

Which meant somebody, most likely somebody at the inn, had murdered him.

The phone was ringing when I got back to the

kitchen. "Can you believe it?" Charlene asked breathlessly when I picked it up.

"You've heard?"

"Of course I've heard," she said. Nothing happened on Cranberry Island that Charlene, as postmistress and gossip hub, didn't hear about. "It's so terrible!"

"I know," I said as I sat down at the kitchen table. "How did things go with Alex last night?"

"He is amazing," she said, her voice suddenly dreamy. I smiled; the male population of Cranberry Island was going to be sorely disappointed that my curvy, caramel-haired friend had been snapped up by an outsider.

"I figured it was going well. You guys sure were out late," I said.

"Not that late," she told me. "He went back to the inn before midnight."

"That's funny," I said, feeling my stomach lurch. "He didn't get back to the inn until after two."

Charlene was quiet for a moment. "Well, it is a bit of a walk," she said.

Not two hours, I thought to myself. If he wasn't coming back from Charlene's house, what exactly was Alex doing out at two in the morning? My thoughts turned to Captain Bainbridge, and my stomach lurched. "Charlene," I said. "You know the captain was probably murdered last night."

"Murdered?" she asked. "I thought it was an accident."

I described the circumstances of Bainbridge's death.

"That's horrible," she breathed.

"I hate to ask this," I said, looking out the window at the *Summer Breeze*, "but did Alex say anything about his relationship with the captain?"

"Wait," she said. "You don't think..."

"I don't know. But there are two hours unaccounted for last night."

"No way, Natalie," she said flatly. "He had nothing to do with it."

"Even so," I told her. "What do you know about their relationship?"

"Well..." she hesitated. "He was angry that the captain took the schooner so close to the whales," she admitted. "But that's hardly a motive for murder."

"Did he say anything else about him? Anything that might help figure out who might have wanted him dead?"

"I know there was a squabble between the captain and the first mate," she said. "From what I could tell, she wasn't totally on board with buying a second boat."

I was about to tell her about the conversation I had overheard between the captain and the first mate, but there was a yowling noise from the end of the kitchen. "I've got to go," I said...

"What's that noise?"

"Biscuit just discovered the kitten," I said.

"Kitten?"

"I'll tell you later," I said, hanging up the phone as I grabbed my chunky orange tabby. I'd put the kitten in the laundry room before I left, but evidently someone had left the door ajar. The kitten had ventured back to the radiator, and had had the misfortune to settle into Biscuit's favorite spot.

Biscuit growled in my arms, her tail tripling in size. I carried the tabby upstairs and locked him in our bedroom, then came down and relocated the kitten to the laundry room. I reassured her, stroking her soft head, and she started purring immediately, sounding like a miniature outboard engine. She seemed remarkably unconcerned, thankfully, but I wasn't encouraged by the tenor of the two cats' encounter, and mewled as I closed the door behind her and headed back up to release Biscuit, who stalked to the radiator and reclaimed her spot, giving me a miffed look through slitted green eyes.

I had just washed my hands and was looking for a recipe—the guests had emptied the cookie jar—when Catherine and Bridget came in. I stifled a groan; with all the excitement, I'd almost forgotten my sister was in town.

"How'd it go?" I asked, applying what I hoped was a bright smile.

"It's not a very big island, is it?" Bridget asked.

"Lots of beautiful views though," Catherine said. "And Gwen has such a way with them... I can't wait for you to see her paintings."

"It's a good hobby," Bridget said, "but I can't help

but think she's wasting her talents."

My mother-in-law flashed me a look that was something between amusement and exasperation. "If you'll excuse me," she said, "I'm going to head down to the carriage house. Do you need anything here, Nat?"

"I think we're good for now," I said. "I took care of the rooms this morning, and I'm about to make cookies."

"I'll do room duty tomorrow," she told me. "Need help with dinner?"

"If you could help with setting up and serving, that would be great," I told her.

"I'll be here at 5:30," she said. "What are they doing with the guests today, by the way?"

"Adam is organizing an excursion for them," I said.

Bridget's narrowed her eyes. "You mean the Adam Gwen wants to marry?"

"Yes," I told her. "What's your plan for the day?" I asked in a bright voice, trying to change the subject.

But Bridget was not so easily dissuaded. "What a great opportunity to get to know this boy who wants to be my son-in-law," she said. "I think I may join them."

"You can't," I blurted. The last thing I needed was for my sister to badger Adam with half the tour group on board. "I mean, there isn't room on the boat. Besides, I was hoping we'd spend some time together and catch up," I said. "It's been what...five years?"

My mother-in-law shot me another look that was something between pity and mirth. "I'm headed down to the carriage house," she said. "Let me know if you need anything, Nat."

"Thanks, Catherine...and thanks so much for showing my sister around."

"My pleasure," she said, looking slightly relieved as she headed for the door.

As she closed the door, my sister settled herself at the kitchen table and fixed her eyes on me. "What do you know about this Adam boy?"

"He's a very nice young man," I said, reaching for my recipe binder and realizing that it was still missing. I'd have to ask John what he'd done with it, I thought as I selected another cookbook from my collection. I had been planning on making Blackout Brownies, but I'd have to do something different.

"Does he really have a degree from Princeton?" my sister asked.

"Yes," I said, and decided it was best not to tell her that he'd tossed it into the Gulf of Maine when he bought his lobster boat, the *Carpe Diem*. "Tell me about California, Bridget. It sounds like the law practice is really going well," I said as I leafed through the recipes looking for something delicious. I needed something gooey and comforting, I decided—not just for my guests, but for me. Between the horrible tragedy on the boat and Bridget's unexpected visit, I needed a little bit of chocolate therapy.

I stopped when I hit a recipe for chocolate chip bars—and then remembered I had a jar of salted caramel sauce in the pantry. What if I made salted caramel chocolate chip bars—with milk chocolate instead of semisweet? My mouth was starting to water already.

"Natalie!"

I looked up from the cookbook. "What?"

"Didn't you hear me?'

"Sorry," I said. "I was looking at a recipe," I said, scanning the ingredients list and heading for the pantry. If I put a layer of caramel in the middle of the bars...

"Anyway," she said. "Real estate prices are completely insane in California. Of course, it's an excellent investment, but the taxes are just terrible. I probably pay as much in taxes as you do for your whole mortgage!"

"That's terrible," I said mechanically as I gathered flour and sugar from the pantry and grabbed the bottle of vanilla extract I'd made with bourbon and vanilla beans. As she prattled on, I made occasional noises, concentrating on the soothing ritual of baking. I did it every day, but it never grew old. As my sister regaled me with news of her latest cases, I focused on the task at hand, creaming the butter and sugar, adding eggs and dry ingredients, and stirring in a mix of milk and dark chocolate chips, half-listening as I worked. I wasn't sure how it was possible that we were so different, but I suppose it made sense;

our parents were opposites, too. Where my sister had always been voted most likely to succeed, I'd spent my childhood out tramping around in the fields and woods, making disastrous experiments in the kitchen, and reading Nancy Drew mysteries while sucking on butterscotch drops. I was wondering how to incorporate that lovely butterscotch flavor into a cookie when Bridget said, "That's why I've decided Gwen's coming back to California with me."

I looked up from the chocolate-chip-studded batter. "What?"

"I'm taking Gwen home with me," she said.

"Have you talked to her about that?"

"I will this evening," I said. "She needs a break from all of this."

"She just spent almost a year in California," I said, putting down the spoon and looking at my sister. "She finished her degree and decided to come back."

My sister's face darkened. "Her degree was in art, not business."

"Yes. She chose art. And she's good at it...you'll see when she shows you the studio."

Bridget looked like she could have chewed a bullet and spit it out. "Gwen's my daughter, Nat. Not yours."

I took an involuntary step back at the fury in her voice. "I know. I've never claimed to be her mother. But what does that have to do with whether or not she decides to go to California?" I asked.

"Everything," my sister spat. "I know you fancy

yourself some kind of... I don't know," she said, waving a dismissive hand, "second mother to Gwen, but the truth is, she's my daughter."

"I've never questioned that."

"Are you sure? I know you always wanted kids, and never had a chance to have one of your own, but Gwen is my daughter, Natalie. Not yours."

I set down the spoon, my face flaming. "Excuse me?"

"You're overstepping your bounds," my sister told me, her own cheeks pink. "You've been doing it ever since she set foot on this godforsaken island. When I said she could come for a few months, I didn't mean you could take over her life."

"This is ridiculous. Talk about overstepping bounds..." I was so angry I almost couldn't speak. "Take over her life? Bridget, she chose to stay!"

"You derailed her, Natalie." My sister's nostrils flared. "She had a future. A real future! She was smart, she had good grades, all the right extracurricular activities...she could have had a successful life!"

I stepped back as if my sister had slapped me. "Successful?" I said. "She's an artist, Bridget. She's doing what she loves."

"There you go again. Filling her head with...nonsense."

I took a deep breath. "I think you need to leave my kitchen now," I said, in as calm a voice as I could muster.

"Fine," she said, standing up. "But this conversation isn't over."

SIX

I bit my tongue as she turned and stalked to the back door, head high. Anger flared in me, and I wanted to say all kinds of things in response...but anything I said could reflect back on Gwen, and she had it hard enough already.

When the door closed behind my sister, I let out a long, slow breath and stabbed the spoon back into the batter, swearing under my breath. I couldn't believe Bridget had just accused me of trying to steal her daughter.

I shouldn't be surprised, I told myself as I spread the batter in the brownie pan. Bridget had been appalled when I quit my job to buy the inn. The thought of her daughter making beds and helping clean up after other people's breakfasts must be horrifying; she'd been prepping Gwen for a career in either law or business ever since she was born, and the service industry certainly wasn't on her list of acceptable professions. She and her husband had spent tens of thousands on private schools, music lessons, and tutoring to groom their daughter for big things.

Had I led Gwen astray? I wondered. It was true, I

thought as I spread caramel over the batter, that she probably would have followed a different path if she hadn't come to help me out at the Gray Whale Inn. She certainly wouldn't be engaged to a lobsterman and painting watercolors for a living.

Was there a grain of truth in what my sister had said? Had I derailed my niece's career trajectory? She was bright, talented, vivacious…would her gifts be wasted here on Cranberry Island? I felt a stab of self-doubt as I sprinkled fleur de sel—French sea salt—over the caramel and then spread the second half of the batter into the pan before tucking it into the oven. I was happy here…but I'd already had a career when I chose to make the move, and had lived another life. Gwen was just beginning hers. Would she look back in ten or twenty years and wish she'd taken a different path?

These unsettling thoughts were swirling around in my head when John walked in through the back door.

"Hey," I said, putting down the bowl I was washing and rinsing my hands. "What's going on out there?"

He sighed. "Homicide, I'm afraid."

Even though I wasn't at all surprised, my stomach contracted. "I figured."

He glanced behind him toward the door. "What's up with your sister?" he asked.

"She thinks I'm trying to be Gwen's mom and mucking it up," I said.

"Because she didn't go to business school? She

made that decision before she ever came here."

"Because she's throwing her life away to do menial work in a backwater," I said. "At least that seems to be my sister's opinion of the situation."

"Wow," John said, coming over, arms open, and pulled me into a hug, fitting my head into the crook of his neck and putting his chin on my head. I inhaled his masculine, woodsy scent and felt something inside me relax. "I'm so sorry, Nat. Did she really say that?"

"More or less," I said into his T-shirt clad chest, loving the feel of his strong arms around me. I stayed that way for a moment, then gave him a squeeze and stepped back, looking up at him. "Do the police have any suspects?"

"Detective Fleming has been tight-lipped," he said. "They seemed very interested in the rest of the crew, though."

"I was worried about that," I said.

"What do you mean?"

"Charlene's pretty into Alex," I said. "But I heard him arguing with the captain yesterday...and last night, when I came down to get the kitten off the back porch..."

John blinked. "Kitten?"

"She's in the laundry room; she's really cute. She was just meowing on the back porch last night. Didn't I tell you?"

He kissed me on top of the head. "We didn't really have time to talk this morning," he pointed out. "The day kind of started out with a bang."

"And not the good kind," I agreed.

"No." He kissed my head again. "At any rate, last night, when you were getting the kitten I haven't heard about off the back porch…"

"Oh, right. It was after 2 a.m., and Alex came in the back door. He said the front door was locked."

"Late night with Charlene?"

"That's what I thought, but when I talked to her this morning, she said he went home at midnight. Someone else was moving around, too…on the second floor. I heard a door close."

"Busy night at the inn," he observed.

"I know. And yesterday, I heard a conversation between the captain and the first mate." I relayed what they'd said about "taking care" of Alex.

"Are you thinking Bainbridge tried to do something to Alex, and Alex acted out of self-defense?"

"It's a possibility," I said. "But tying a man to an anchor a pretty nasty way to do someone in. Not really a crime of passion. And it's not like it looked like an accidental death."

"It seems someone hit Bainbridge over the head first," he said. "He was probably unconscious when he went down."

"I'm glad of that—I hope he didn't suffer too much. But that makes more sense; if he were conscious, it'd be hard to keep him still long enough to tie the chain around his leg." I shivered. "I hope he didn't feel anything."

"Me too," he said. "Horrible way to go."

We both looked out at the deceptively serene blue water. It was beautiful, but everyone on the island also knew it could be deadly.

"I guess we need to tell the detectives about Alex," I said.

"We do," he said.

"Charlene won't be happy."

"If she's dating a murderer, none of us will be happy," he pointed out.

I sighed. "She's got the worst luck."

"Hey," John said. "At least Alex is still alive." He had a point; many of Charlene's previous beaus had met untimely deaths.

"At least so far," I said. "But is it better to date a killer than a victim?"

John gave me another squeeze. "Let's hope he's neither."

Gwen arrived just as I finished spreading the last bit of caramel on the top of the bars. I smiled at her as I reached for the milk chocolate chips.

"Where's my mother?" she asked as she crept into the kitchen, her art bag over her shoulder.

"I don't know," I said. "Maybe the carriage house?"

"Her shoulders sagged. "Hallelujah," she said, and heaved her bag onto the table.

"She's not very happy with me," I said as I

sprinkled the chips over the top of the caramel. Once they melted, I'd swirl them in. The bars would be too gooey for the cookie jar, but I had a cake plate that would work just fine.

"Why not?"

"She thinks I'm responsible for you not earning a business degree and getting engaged to a lobsterman," I said. "I'm a bad influence; I've ruined your life."

Gwen snorted. "You're kidding me, right?"

"Unfortunately not," I said as I swirled the melting chocolate into the caramel. "But she got me thinking. Are you sure this is the life you want?"

"You mean, instead of working in a law office or a corporation, suing people or organizing ad campaigns?" she asked dryly. "Aunt Nat, you gave me the opportunity to spend time with you when I needed time to figure out what I wanted in life."

"Yes," I said. "But did I talk you into staying?"

"Of course not!" She fished in her bag and pulled out a watercolor pad. "Look what I did this morning," she said, flipping through four gorgeous sketches of scenes on the island. My eyes lingered on a watercolor of Adam's lobster boat chugging out from the dock. The colors leapt off the page; my niece's talent had blossomed these past few years.

"They're beautiful," I said. "You just keep getting better."

"I do," she agreed. "I have work I love, in a community I adore, and I'm engaged to the most amazing man I've ever met. Why would I want anything different?"

"You've just worked so hard over the years," I said. "I want to be sure you've thought this through. Remember, I had a career in Austin before I came here."

She rolled her eyes. "You're as bad as my mother," she said. "Can't you just accept that this is my choice?"

"I do," I told her quietly. "I just want to make sure you've thought about it."

She slapped her watercolor book closed and shoved it into her bag. "How come nobody believes me when I say this is what I want? It's my life, not my mother's," she said. "So I'll thank you to butt out."

"Gwen..."

"I'll be here to help with dinner," she said. "See you later." Before I could answer, she headed back out the door, slamming it in her wake.

I was doing a terrific job in the family relations department, I thought morosely as I watched her march up the road, away from the inn.

Despite the challenging start to the day, the tour group's outing appeared to be a success.

"That clam chowder at Spurrell's was the best I've ever had," Jan told me as I put the cake plate of cookies and a pot of tea out on the dining room sideboard. "And I can't imagine working out on the water every day...it's so beautiful!"

"That herring is a bit stinky, though," Doreen said. "I could hardly eat my lunch. Besides, those lines are dangerous; think what would happen if you got caught on one of them?"

"Did you have to bring that up?" Yvette asked her, giving her children a pointed look.

Doreen pressed her lips together and didn't respond.

"Can they each have a chocolate caramel bar?" I asked Yvette.

"Sure," she said.

"Hot chocolate?" Lizzie asked.

"Only if your mom approves," I told her.

"You can choose one; a cookie, or hot chocolate," she advised them. They both went for the caramel bars.

"Did you have a good outing?" I asked Stacy as she reached for a cookie. I was very happy with how they'd turned out; the mix of milk chocolate and butter and salt was addictive.

"It was an interesting day," she said. "I enjoy seeing how life really is for the people who live here."

"And the sea cucumbers are gross," Liam announced. "They squirt water if you squeeze them."

"Did you know they're related to starfish?" Alex asked. I found myself studying him, wondering if he was the one who had tied that chain around the captain's leg and thrown him into the water.

"Really?" Lizzie asked.

"They're both from a family called *Echino-*

dermata—it means spiny skin." He smiled at her, and once again, I could see why Charlene had fallen head over heels for him.

"Cool!" Lizzie said, taking a big bite of cookie.

I stood up and caught Martina's eye. She was smiling, but it looked brittle. I walked over to her and asked quietly, "Are you going to have access to the boat again tomorrow?"

"I think so," she said, glancing out the window at the schooner. "They said they were finishing up tonight; I'm going to have to go and clean everything up tonight, though."

"Do you have someone to crew for you?"

"Alex can help," she said. "And Adam's got a friend he's going to send to help crew. He's a nice man."

"I know," I told her. "He's going to marry my niece soon."

"Lucky girl," Martina said.

I smiled. "He's a lucky guy, too. They make a great couple," I said, regretting the way my conversation with Gwen had ended earlier. Had I been too interfering? I wondered. I started to have a bit of empathy for my sister. It was hard enough being an aunt; I couldn't imagine being a mother. My eyes strayed down to the carriage house; I hadn't seen Bridget since the morning. Was she still down the hill, or had she headed out for the day?

"Everything okay?" Martina asked.

"Oh, fine," I told her. "Lots going on. Dinner at seven okay?" I asked.

"Perfect," she said. "That will give everyone an hour to decompress. I'll head out and clean up the boat after dinner."

"If you need help, I can probably come out and give you a hand."

"Thanks...if it looks like it's too much, I may come find you." She sighed. "I just can't believe he's gone," she said, and I could see her eyes welling up."

"Were you two close?" I asked.

"We had our disagreements—who didn't? But we'd worked together for five years." She nodded. "Yes. We were close. With Carl gone, I just don't know what I'm going to do about the business..."

"Surely you can manage on your own?"

"I don't know," she told me. "Plus, I don't know who inherits his share of the company."

"You didn't work that out beforehand?"

"I don't think so," she said. "We're both in our forties...it just never occurred to us that we'd have to face something like this. He was so young," she said, and began to cry, then took a deep breath. "We should talk about this later," she said. "I still have to be on. I can't afford to think about it right now." She reapplied the brittle smile, wiped her eyes, and turned back to the group. "You're welcome to relax until dinner. Tomorrow, we'll do the itinerary we planned for today—including lunch at Jordan Pond House."

"Any word on Captain Bainbridge?" Stacy asked, while Nan looked on with interest.

"I'm sure the police will let us know as soon as they have any information," she said in a stilted voice. "Anyway, I'm headed out to get the boat ready for tomorrow. See you at dinner!"

Alex watched her as she headed for the back door. Did she really not know what the terms of the captain's will were? I wondered. Or was that just a smoke screen?

I surveyed the group of people gathered in my dining room. Someone had tied that chain around the captain's leg and tipped him into the ocean. Had it been someone in this room?

Or had the captain had other enemies I knew nothing about?

SEVEN

By the time I finished serving dinner, it felt like I'd been up for a week. The shrimp scampi had been a big hit, as had the key lime pies I'd thawed; I'd gotten limes on a sale a few weeks back and baked a few extras.

As I cleaned up the kitchen, I found myself wondering how Adam and Gwen were holding up; they had invited my sister over for dinner at Adam's house. Emotions were obviously running high for both Bridget and my niece; I felt sorry for Adam. Talk about trial by fire!

After drying the last of the dishes, I reached for my cookbook—my binder still hadn't resurfaced—and started leafing through, looking for another version of the blueberry muffin recipe I'd planned to make in the morning. As I flipped through the pages, I found myself wondering how I could have handled both Gwen and Bridget differently. Was Gwen right to take me to task for trying to interfere with her life? Or did Bridget have a point—had I played a part in limiting my niece's options for her future? There didn't seem to be a right answer. I checked the fridge to make sure I had bacon and eggs and enough blueberries for the muffins. When I was satisfied that I was prepared for the morning, I grabbed the Tupperware with the rest of the caramel-chocolate-chip bars so that I could refill the cake plate on the dining room sideboard.

Alex was still sitting in the parlor, which surprised me; I'd expected him to go and see Charlene. After arranging the cookie bars on the cake plate, I walked into the parlor and sat down on the wingback chair across from him. Everyone else had gone to their rooms, and he was leafing through a book on the history of Cranberry Island I'd left on the coffee table.

"This is an interesting book," he said. "I had no idea the island has been inhabited for so long."

"Oh, yes," I said. "If you haven't had family here for at least 200 years, you're still kind of an outsider. How's everyone doing after this morning, do you think?"

"It was a shock for them," he admitted. "Heck, it was a shock for me."

"I'll bet. How long had you known Captain Bainbridge?" I asked.

"We go back about three years," he said. "I started to crew for him when he started the tour company. I work part time as a nature photographer, part time as an on-board naturalist."

"Nice work," I said.

"It is," he said, "But it's not very centered. I feel like I live out of a suitcase all the time. Sometimes I think it would be nice to have a real home base."

"I'll bet," I said. "Was the captain as into conservation as you are?"

He laughed. "Not exactly. Although I'm guessing you knew that, based on how close he got to that pod of whales yesterday."

"Profit over protection?" I asked with a grin.

"You don't know the half of it," he answered.

"What do you mean?"

"Nothing," he said, waving his hand as if he were erasing his words. "We just had some different opinions on some things."

"Like what?" I asked.

"Like what the point of whales is," he said. "I view them as having intrinsic value. He viewed them as a source of income."

"Which is why he got so close to them yesterday,"

"Exactly," he said. "It's illegal; it was risky, not just for the whales, but for his business."

"What do you mean?"

"You don't do things like that with a journalist on board," he said.

"I thought she was just doing a travel piece?"

"Why do a travel piece when you can do an exposé?" he asked with a crooked grin.

"You think?"

"I don't know." He shrugged. "I'm just speculating. I've known enough journalists to know it's better to be careful."

"What made him choose Cranberry Island, anyway?" I asked.

"I got the impression he'd been here once before," he said. "But he never said anything about it."

I made a mental note to ask Charlene what she could find out. "Did he often have disagreements with people?" I asked.

He gave me a shrewd look. "In other words, do I think he made enemies who might want him dead?"

"I guess you could put it that way."

"He is…I mean, was…a rather strong personality," he admitted, then gave me a curious look. "You seem awfully interested in what happened to the captain."

"Well, it's a bit upsetting to find a guest tied to an anchor," I said. "I'd like to know if one of my guests is a murderer." Including you, I added silently.

He was about to respond when there was a thunk in the hall. "What's that?"

"The resident ghost?" I joked, but got up and walked to the front hall.

Footsteps scurried down the hall. I didn't get there in time to see who it was, but I did get there in time to see a door close.

It belonged to Stacy Cox—the journalist.

Maybe Alex was right, I thought as I stared down the hall, and she wasn't just doing a fluffy travel piece after all. If that was the case, I had to be extra careful to make sure everything at the inn was in order.

"See a ghost?" Alex asked.

"Nope," I said, and was about to tell him who I suspected was listening—but at the last moment, decided against it. "No Charlene tonight?" I asked, changing the subject.

"I told her I probably needed to be available to smooth things over with the tour group," he said.

"Smart call," I said. "Looks like everyone's turned in early."

"I hope the kids are okay. It bothers me that they had to see that."

"They do keep talking about it," I said.

He sighed. "I guess it's part of life. Still..." He got up and stretched. "I think I'm going to turn in, too," he said.

"You did have a late night last night," I agreed.

He met my eye for a moment, and I felt a twinge of...something. I broke off eye contact. "I'd better go check on the kitten," I said.

"Is she doing okay?"

"So far, so good," I said. "I just don't know what I'm going to do with her."

"Maybe you can talk Charlene into taking her," he said.

"Maybe," I said, then wished him a good night and headed back to the kitchen, secretly glad my friend wasn't out with a possible murderer.

Unfortunately, when I walked into the kitchen, both Biscuit and Bridget were waiting for me in the kitchen. My orange tabby was hissing at the laundry room door, her tail fluffed up like a bottlebrush. My sister, at the kitchen table, didn't look much more inviting.

"How was dinner?" I asked.

"Fine," she said shortly.

I sighed and changed topics. "Did you make it out to the gallery?"

"I did."

"What did you think?" I asked.

"I don't know how she sells anything there. It seems to me that a store on Mount Desert Island would get a lot more traffic."

I grimaced as I opened the pantry and reached for a can of cat food. There was no pleasing Bridget, and I didn't feel like trying. In fact, I didn't feel like doing anything other than going to sleep.

"Did you get moved into the carriage house?" I asked, trying to keep the conversation on neutral topics.

"Yes. Catherine got me set up with a cot," she said.

"I'm sorry we don't have any rooms available; if you'd told me you were coming, I would have blocked one out." I thought about Captain Bainbridge's room. The investigators still had it closed off; I didn't know when it would be free, and I didn't know how my sister would feel about moving into a dead man's room.

Fortunately, at that moment, John came down the stairs. "Hey, Natalie. Hi, Bridget," he said, and walked over to give my sister a polite hug. "Sorry we didn't get a chance to chat earlier today; it's been a hectic day."

"It sounds like it," she said as she released him.

"Are you enjoying the island?" he asked.

"It's certainly a change from California," she said.

"How's the law practice going?" John asked, sitting down across from her and leaning his elbows on the table, giving her the benefit of his green eyes. "You do corporate law, right?"

"I do!" She was smiling for the first time since she'd arrived. John winked at me, and I mouthed a "thank you" to him as she launched into an animated description of her latest case. I put a dish of cat food down for Biscuit and then slipped into the laundry room, which was kept nice and toasty by the dryers, to check on my new feline charge. The little gray kitten was all curled up in the fleece blanket I'd nestled into the corner of the room, and started purring like an outboard motor when I reached to touch her soft head. The mobile vet was scheduled to visit the island in the next few days; Jan had told me she seemed healthy, but that I should have her checked out anyway. I felt bad that she'd spent the day alone, but she looked like she'd spent most of it napping—and besides, I didn't trust Biscuit.

I put down the food next to her water bowl. She stood up and stretched, then walked over and started eating. I could hear my sister's voice from the next room, and said a small prayer of thanks for John. Next time I talked with Charlene, I'd ask her to find out if anyone was missing a kitten, I thought. Biscuit would be very pleased to see this little one disappear.

Which was kind of how I felt about Bridget.

We were five years apart, and we'd never been close. Bridget had always been driven to be the best of everything: she accepted nothing less than the highest possible grades, and her heart had been set on law school from the moment she out-argued the neighborhood bully over who was next on the swings in the school playground. She was smart, savvy, deeply driven, and loved corporate America…unlike me. The thought of working in an office building gave me hives.

And now, I thought as I stroked the kitten's head, I was enjoying the kind of life I'd dreamed about during the years in my cubicle at the Texas Parks and Wildlife department. A life that my sister obviously considered a failure. Although I was living my dream and had built a successful business on my own terms, the judgment stung a little bit—a throwback to those years in high school when my teachers seemed so puzzled that I wasn't making the grades my sister had.

How come it was so hard to leave childhood behind? I wondered as the kitten finished eating and crawled into my lap, still purring. She looked up at me with those beautiful blue eyes and curled up in a ball, her breathing slowing as I stroked her head. As the kitten dozed, I leaned back against the dryer, listening to the murmur of Bridget's voice and feeling thankful I wasn't in the kitchen with her. It had been a hectic day; this was the first quiet moment I'd had since waking up.

I had leaned my head back and closed my own eyes when I heard a dripping sound. I sat up and scanned the laundry room—the faucet was off, and there didn't appear to be any water coming out from under the washing machine. I set the kitten down and stood up; as I walked across the laundry room, a drop of water hit my arm.

I looked up just as a piece of the ceiling caved in right over my head.

EIGHT

I burst out of the laundry room into the kitchen, the kitten in my arms. "There's a leak," I told John.

"In the laundry room?"

"Above it," I said. "The ceiling is starting to cave in."

"Let's go," he said. Leaving Bridget in the kitchen, we raced to the stairs.

It wasn't too hard to figure out the source of the problem. When we got to the second floor, water was leaking out from under the door at the end of the hall.

"This doesn't look good," I said as John rapped on the door. Nobody answered. He knocked again, and when there was no response, he unlocked the door with the skeleton key and opened it.

My heart sank as water gushed out into the hallway.

Gayla and Herb were nowhere in evidence, even though the king-sized bed was mussed. John splashed over the floor to the bathroom, with me—literally—in his wake.

Water cascaded over the side of the claw foot tub; someone had wrapped a washcloth around the overflow drain and let the tub run.

"What do we do now?" I asked as John turned off the water and opened the drain.

"Start mopping up," he said with a sigh.

"It might be easier if we had something to bail with," I pointed out.

"Actually, you're right. Why don't you go down and get towels and a bucket? I'll dam up the bedroom door with these towels."

"So glad we have such a dream job," I said as I headed toward the door.

"Very relaxing," he agreed as he followed me with an armload of towels.

"What's wrong?" Bridget asked as I hurried through the kitchen.

"Can you hold her for me?" I asked, plopping the kitten into her lap without waiting for an answer. "One of the guests let a bathtub overflow," I said as I slipped into the laundry room and grabbed a bucket and a plastic dustpan—good for scooping, I figured.

"That's got to be just terrible for the floors," she said. "You'll have to worry about mold, too."

"Thanks for the encouragement," I said as I grabbed an armload of towels and headed back toward the stairs.

John had dammed up the doorway and was scooping up water with towels and a coffee cup by the time I got back upstairs.

"Here's a bucket," I said. "And a dustpan."

"Good thinking." I handed him the bucket and

began scooping up water with the dustpan, emptying it into the draining bathtub.

"Thanks," he told me as he dumped a bucket full of water into the tub. "What are we going to do with Gayla and Herb for tonight? We're totally booked up."

"Are the police done with the captain's room?"

"There's no crime scene tape, and they seem to have finished with it, but do you think they'll want to stay there?" he asked.

"They're the ones who overflowed the tub," I said. "Besides...unless you're willing to give up our bedroom, we really don't have a choice."

He sighed and kept mopping. "I hope the floors will be okay," he said.

"I hope the ceiling doesn't completely collapse," I said. "Part of this is over the kitchen."

He grimaced. "We need to call the insurance company."

"On the plus side," I said, "if they give us a hard time, at least we have a lawyer in the house."

Before John could respond, there was a loud exclamation.

It was Gayla, standing at the doorway. "We had the do not disturb sign up," she said. "What are you doing in here?"

"Looks like you forgot you turned the tub on," John said as he dumped another bucket of water into the bathtub. "Natalie realized it when water started coming through the ceiling in the laundry room.

Gayla blinked. "Oh, I'm so sorry. I must have started it and forgotten. Well, no harm done, right?"

"Let's hope not," John said diplomatically.

"There's no way we can sleep here tonight," Herb said. "We should probably switch rooms."

"I'll get the Eider room made up for you," I said.

"Isn't that the captain's room?"

"I'll go get everything taken care of," I said, ignoring the question. There really weren't any other options; they'd have to take it or leave it. "It'll be ready in about a half hour."

"I really don't feel comfortable staying in a dead man's room," Gayla said, shivering.

"Well," John said, "I guess we can make up a couch in the parlor…"

Gayla and Herb exchanged looks. "It'll have to do, I suppose," he said tersely.

"There are cookies downstairs if you want to snack while you're waiting," I told them, wishing Gwen was around—or Catherine. I glanced out the window at the carriage house, but the lights were out; John's mother must be out with Murray again. I was glad romance was blooming on the island, but I wouldn't mind if it took a brief break so I could get some help around the inn.

"Fine," Gayla said.

"If you'd like, I can transfer your things," I said.

"No," Gayla barked, looking alarmed. "I mean, I'd hate for you to go to the trouble."

"It's no trouble," John said. "It's the least we can do."

"No," she said firmly. "Thirty minutes?"

I nodded.

"Let's go get a snack, Herb," she said. He hurried to the desk and grabbed a sheaf of papers, then lumbered after her, shooting a nervous glance back at us.

When they were out of earshot, John looked at me. "What was that all about?"

"I don't know," I said, looking after them. "But now I'm curious about why they don't want us to move their things."

"Natalie." John gave me a look.

I sighed and continued bailing, but that didn't stop me from being curious.

By the time we finished getting the room cleaned up and faced the laundry room. The ceiling had fallen in in a few places, and was sagging. The kitten was curled up in her fleece blanket; she looked up and meowed at us when we walked in.

"She's so tiny!" John said.

"I know. Jan thinks she's about six weeks old." She meowed again and stretched, then walked over to rub her side against John's ankles.

"We can't leave her in here tonight," he said, glancing up at the ceiling.

"Biscuit doesn't like her, though."

"Well," he said, bending down to scoop the kitten up, "she's going to have to adjust." The kitten started purring as he scratched her head. "What's your name, little girl?"

"We haven't named her yet," I said. "I vetoed 'Ratty,' but 'Felicia' is still in the running."

"She looks like a 'Smudge' to me," John said, tucking her into the crook of his arm and turning to me. "Ready to call it a night?"

"I haven't gotten anything ready for tomorrow," I said.

"It'll keep," he told me, and kissed me on the forehead. "It's been a long day; let's hit the sack. I'll get up early."

"What exactly are you planning to do with that kitten?" I asked, looking down at the furry ball in the crook of his arm.

"We're taking it up to bed," he said.

"I'd close your closet door if I were you," I warned him. "Unless you want Biscuit to pee in your shoes."

"You think?"

"I wouldn't risk it," I said. I needn't have worried about John's shoes, though; the moment Biscuit spotted the kitten, her tail tripled in size and she let out a hiss that sounded like steam erupting from a tea kettle.

"Biscuit, sweetheart," John said, bending down. "It's only a kitten." The kitten mewled, and Biscuit's paw slashed out at her.

"Biscuit!"

She gave me a baleful look from her green eyes, then streaked out of the room and down the stairs.

"Well, that solves one problem, I suppose," I said.

He sighed. "Murdered guests, overflowing bathtubs, angry pets...what a week."

"And my recipe binder is missing," I remembered. "Have you seen it?"

He shook his head. "Last time I saw it, it was on the shelf where you always keep it."

I sighed. "Maybe your mom borrowed it."

John gave me a look. "You're kidding me, right?"

"Good point," I said. Since Catherine specialized in low-fat low-carb everything, our recipe overlap was minimal. "I'm sure it will turn up. And at least the day is over. Tomorrow's got to be better, right?"

"At least the day can't get any worse," he said.

No sooner had the words left his mouth than the phone rang.

"Are you sitting down?"

It was Charlene. "What's wrong?" I asked, looking over at Biscuit, who was eyeing me balefully from next to the radiator. As I talked, I walked to the laundry room and peeked in; no more of the ceiling had fallen yet, but it looked like a large section was ready to go at any moment. I tiptoed in to open a window to help it dry out; the last thing I needed was a moldy laundry room.

"Emmeline just called to tell me that someone

bought Cliffside today," she said as I pushed the window up, letting in a gust of chilly air.

I walked back into the kitchen and closed the door to the laundry room, hoping the ceiling would last the night. Compared to everything else that had happened, I didn't see why I should be concerned about Cliffside. "After all these years, it's about time," I said. "What's the emergency?"

"Rumor has it they're not planning to use it as a residence, Nat," she said.

"Hmm. What does the grapevine say buyer has in mind?"

"I don't know for sure, but word is someone from the mainland was looking at it the other day," she said. "She's a commercial architect."

"Did she say what her client was planning?"

"No," she said. "She said the project was 'classified.'"

"Well," I said, "there's not much I can do about it, is there?" Despite my cheerful words, I felt a pit in my stomach. The inn was just now really hitting its stride; how much would a competitor on the island cut into our business?

"I guess there's nothing you can do, but I just have a bad feeling about it." Charlene sighed. "And then there's that terrible thing happened to the captain. Have you heard anything else?"

"I'm assuming it's being treated as homicide, since they had investigators all over the place and talked to everyone on the tour, but I haven't heard anything else."

"That must have been awful," my friend said. "And I heard the kids were on the boat when they pulled him up."

"Yes," I said. "Their mom has been trying to distract them all day."

Charlene pursed her lips. "You know...he looked so familiar to me. I can't place it, but I'm almost sure I met him before."

"He did run another tour out of the inn," I reminded her. "I know you spent the whole week looking at Alex, but surely you at least glanced at Bainbridge."

"That's not it," she said. "I know him from somewhere else. Maybe he summered here or something...I just can't place him."

"I always wondered how he picked Cranberry Island as a tour base," I said. "On the other hand, it's going to be hard to ask him now."

She sighed. "Alex was so upset about it tonight," she said.

"I thought he and the captain didn't get along."

"They had their differences," she said. "But it's upsetting when someone you're close to dies—even if you don't see eye to eye on everything."

"How are things going with him, by the way?" I asked.

"Oh, he's marvelous," Charlene said. "He knows all the scientific names for everything, and he loves animals, and he's just so...rugged. Plus," she added, "he's a great kisser."

"I'll have to take your word on that," I said.

"You've got a handsome guy of your own, Natalie," she said. "You have to leave some for the rest of us."

"I'm quite happy, thank you very much. By the way," I said, as Biscuit slitted her eyes at me, "do you know anyone who's missing a gray kitten?"

"No," she said. "Did you find one?"

"On the back porch," I said. "I'll bring a photo over; maybe you can post it on the board and ask around."

"Will do," she said. "How are things going over there?"

"Well, other than the sudden death of Captain Bainbridge, one of my guests flooded a room, and the ceiling is now caving in in my laundry room," I said, "and my sister showed up on the doorstep and is accusing me of ruining her daughter's life. And my recipe binder is missing. But other than that, things are going great."

"Sheesh," she said. "Can it get any worse?"

"I'm kind of afraid to ask that question." After all, that's what John had asked just before Charlene called.

"Maybe I'm wrong about Cliffside," she suggested. "I mean, it's been on the market for so long."

"Even if you're not," I said, "there's not much I can do about it. And maybe it'll hit a different market."

"Besides," she told me, "you've got such a great

network; you've really built up your list of clients, and you've got a terrific reputation."

"You're right," I said, taking a deep breath. "Assuming I don't go broke fixing the water damage."

"That's what insurance is for, right?"

"Here's hoping," I said, and glanced at my watch. "I've got to get up at six…can we check in in the morning?"

"Sure," she said. "And I'll see if I can find anything else out about Cliffside."

"Thanks, Charlene," I said.

"And if you have any cookies for the register, I wouldn't say no."

"I should have made a double batch yesterday; I wasn't thinking. If I bake more, I'll make extra," I told her. I usually kept her stocked with cookies to sell to island visitors, but the inn had been so busy it had fallen off my mental list.

"Eli is going through sugar withdrawal," she said.

I laughed. Eli was a friend, and the local boatwright who had given me my skiff. His wife Claudette refused to let him have sugar; he kept himself supplied by buying my cookies on the sly. "Tell him to stop by the inn and I'll get him hooked up," I told her.

"He'll be thrilled," she said, and we hung up a moment later. As I headed back upstairs to John, Biscuit gave me a baleful look from her spot by the radiator.

"It's only temporary," I told her, but she didn't seem convinced.

The kitten spent the whole night curled up between John and me, and followed us to the stairs when we got up at dawn to start breakfast.

"I still think we should call her Smudge," he said.

"It suits her," I said, watching as the little creature looked up at him and meowed.

"Think Biscuit will be better behaved?" John asked as she attempted to negotiate the top step.

"I wouldn't bet on it," he said as he scooped her up and carried her down the stairs.

Sure enough, the moment she spotted Smudge, Biscuit's tail puffed out and she hissed.

"Let's put her in the laundry room," I said. When I opened the door, I changed my mind; half the ceiling was on the floor. "Uh oh."

John came up behind me and winced. "Not good," he said. "On the plus side, at least it's not in the kitchen."

"We need to call the insurance adjustor today," I said. "I hope the floors survive."

"Who starts a tub and walks away from it, anyway?" John asked.

I was about to answer when there was a knock at the back door. "Who is it?" I asked.

"Detective Fleming and another officer," John

said.

"Uh oh," I said, as he went to get the door.

"Good morning," John said as he opened the door. "You're here early. Can we get you some coffee?"

"Thanks, but we won't be here long," the detective replied.

"What's up?" I asked.

"Is Alex Van Der Berg here?"

"Unless he went down to the *Summer Breeze* early, I think he's still in his room," I said. "Why?"

"We have a warrant for his arrest," the detective said.

NINE

I blinked at her. "Arrest? For what?"

"For the murder of Carl Bainbridge," she said. "Can you take me to his room?"

I stared at her open-mouthed, as John said, "I'll show you the way." My husband shot me a grim look as he led the detective and her partner through the swinging doors to the rest of the inn, still holding the kitten against his chest.

Poor Charlene, I thought, staring out at the police launch that was tied up to the dock. As I scooped coffee into the grinder, I wondered what it was that had implicated Alex. Had he really murdered the captain? And if so, why?

The coffee was brewing when the police came back downstairs with a rumpled-looking Alex in tow.

"Are you sure you don't want coffee?" I asked.

"No, thank you," the detective said.

"Tell Charlene it wasn't me," Alex said, looking wild-eyed and a bit scared. "I promise."

"I'll tell her," I said. "Anything else?"

He sighed. "Just tell her...tell her I love her," he said.

"I will," I told him, feeling my heart wrench for

my friend. "Do you need help finding an attorney?"

"He can call from the station," Detective Fleming said. "We've got to head out."

"But what are we going to do about the tour?" I asked—as if they would release a murder suspect to make things more convenient for me. I definitely needed that second cup of coffee.

Detective Fleming shrugged. "I'm sure you'll figure something out," she said as she escorted Alex through the back door. John and I stood and watched as she and her partner led him to the police launch.

"This is not my favorite week," I said as they walked down to the dock, Alex sandwiched between them.

"No, it hasn't been one of our better ones," John agreed. "When are you going to call Charlene?" he asked, still stroking the kitten.

"After breakfast," I said. "Unless she calls me first; you know how news travels." I looked out at the schooner, which was bobbing in the water. "I wonder why they think he killed him?"

"I'm going to see if I can find out," John said grimly. "Right after I call the insurance adjustor."

"I'm kind of afraid to go upstairs and look at the floors," I said. "Do you think we should wake up Martina?"

"Let's take one thing at a time," my handsome husband suggested. "Let's put this kitten back in our bedroom and get started on breakfast. Once we have that under control, we'll go tell Martina."

"You're right," I said, taking a deep breath. "I wish I could find my recipe binder. I guess we'll just have to wing it."

Despite the sunshine pouring through the windows, the mood in the kitchen was dark as we worked that morning. As John assembled a strata, I whipped up a sour cream coffee cake and put it into the oven, then cut up a cantaloupe and hulled strawberries for a fruit salad.

"What do you think Martina is going to do without Alex to help out?" I asked as John tucked the strata into the oven next to the coffee cake.

"Maybe Adam can help out," he suggested.

I put plastic wrap over the fruit salad and washed my hands. "I'll go knock on her door," I said, and gave John a kiss before heading out the kitchen door.

Martina was on the second floor of the inn, in the Lupine room. I could hear her moving around even before I knocked; she opened the door almost immediately. As usual, her dark hair was pulled back into a tight bun, and her polo shirt was tucked into khaki pants, a brown belt around her trim waist.

"Everything okay?" she asked.

"Alex was arrested this morning," I said.

She drew in her breath, and a series of emotions flickered over her face, so rapidly that I couldn't parse them. "No! Because of what happened to Carl?"

"I'm afraid so," I said.

"But that's crazy!" Martina said. "He never would have hurt the captain."

"They took him to the mainland a little while ago. John and I have breakfast underway, but I know you can't operate the boat solo. Do you want me to see if I can find someone on the island to help?"

"Oh, my God. I hadn't even thought of that." She took a deep breath. "Do you think you can?"

"We're surrounded by lobstermen," I said. "And half the island has worked in the tourism industry at some point. I'm sure I can find someone."

"Thanks so much," she said. "It won't be the same, but at least we'll be able to go out." She sighed. "This tour has turned out to be a nightmare. First Carl, and now this..." She looked haggard. "I just can't believe he's gone."

"I know," I said, reaching out to touch her shoulder...but part of me was wondering how she really felt. How upset was she that the captain was gone? And was she upset--or relieved--that Alex was arrested? "I'll go down and see what I can do," I said.

"Thank you," she said. "I'll be down in a minute."

John was setting up the dining room and the smell of coffee cake had started to fill the kitchen when I picked up the phone a few minutes later to call Gwen's fiancé. I knew he had traps to pick up, but I couldn't think of who else to call.

"I can't take a second day...and I don't know any other lobstermen who'd be willing, but what about Eli?" Adam asked when I called him a few minutes.

"Adam, that's a terrific idea. Why didn't I think of that?"

"I just saw him down at the store," he said. "If you call, I'll bet he's still there."

"Then I'd have to tell Charlene," I said.

"If you don't tell her, she'll find out from someone else, and she'll never forgive you."

I sighed. "You're probably right. How are things going with Gwen's mom, by the way?"

"As well as anticipated, unfortunately," he said.

"That's what I figured," I said.

"On the plus side," he said, "Alex told me yesterday that he'd been in touch with two of the whale conservation societies. They've sent tracking equipment to College of the Atlantic and to the co-op, and they're sending a vessel up. The Coast Guard has promised to help, too—and the lobstermen have offered to do what they can."

"I just hope we can find her again," I said.

"Or that we find her in time," Adam said. "I'll have to call and let them know I'm the new point of contact. I'm going to call over to College of the Atlantic and see if there's been another sighting," he said. "Even just tracking the whale would be helpful."

"That's a terrific idea," I told him. "In the meantime, I'm going to call Charlene."

"Good luck with that," he said.

"Thanks," I said before hanging up. I looked out the window at the schooner, its lines sleek and beautiful, its masts dark against the blue sky, then took a deep breath and dialed the store.

Charlene answered, of course.

"What's up?" she asked, sounding cheerful. She hadn't heard the news.

"First, is Eli there?"

"Yeah," she said. "I told him he could come by the inn, but he's still complaining that there aren't any cookies behind the counter."

"I'll whip up a batch this week. Tell him not to leave yet," I said.

"Okay," she said, and passed the message on to Eli while I waited. "Why?" she asked when she got back on the phone.

"Are you sitting down?" I asked.

"Uh oh. What's wrong?"

"The police arrested Alex this morning," I told her.

"No," she breathed, sounding like someone had sucker punched her. "They talked with me yesterday, and asked questions about what we did last night, but I thought it was just routine. Oh, God...They really think he had something to do with Bainbridge's death?"

I swallowed. "He didn't come straight back from your house the other night," I told her.

She was quiet for a moment. "How do you know?"

"I was downstairs at 2 a.m., and that's when he came in."

"You mean..." she paused for a moment. "Natalie," she said in a low voice, "You don't think he killed the captain, do you?"

"I don't think anything," I said, although in truth the thought had crossed my mind more than once. "I'm just telling you what I know."

"I know he didn't do it, Nat," she said, her voice passionate. "We have to prove it."

"Are you sure?" I asked. "You haven't known him very long."

"I'm positive," she said. "He's not a murderer. He and Bainbridge may have had their differences, but he never would have done something like that."

I wished I felt as certain, but if Charlene felt that strongly about it, I had to support her. If nothing else, maybe we could find out what had really happened— whether Alex was guilty or not. "Okay," I said. "First, will you ask Eli if he can come help out with the *Summer Breeze* today?"

"Oh. I didn't think about the tour. With Alex gone..."

"Martina's on her own," I finished.

"Hang on," she said. I waited while she conferred with Eli and got back on the line. "He'll do it for a batch of your chocolate chippers. Actually, he'll do it for nothing, but he does love your cookies."

"He's got a deal," I said, smiling. Presuming I could find my recipe binder, that was. "I've got to go take care of breakfast, but can you come over later on today?"

"Tania takes over at two," she said. "I'll come over then, if that works. We have to get Alex free," she said.

"I'll be here," I told her, hoping that Charlene was right, and that there was some other explanation for Alex's 2 a.m. arrival—and wondering exactly how fractious relations between the captain and the naturalist had been.

Stacy Cox was full of questions over breakfast that morning, and I began to wonder if perhaps the slant of her article had changed. How much would the Gray Whale Inn figure into the article? I wondered. I wasn't thrilled with having the inn linked with the captain's death.

"How many times have they based the tour here before?" she asked as I refilled her coffee.

"This is the second time," I said, glancing over at Martina, who was sitting with Nan McGee doing her best to put on a happy face. A murder and an arrest were not exactly what most investors were looking for when considering plunking down a bunch of cash. I wished Martina luck; from the look on Nan's face, I was guessing it was going to be a tough sell.

"This isn't the first time there's been a murder associated with the inn, is it?" she asked.

Before I could answer, Gayla piped up. "I heard there were a few others. And we ended up having to stay in the poor dead captain's room. I think he may be haunting it; I heard all kinds of bumps last night." As Stacy wrote down everything she said, she gave an exaggerated shudder. "It's like the inn is cursed or something."

Stacy looked like a dog on a scent. "Cursed?"

"I've heard there was a ghost here even before the latest murder," Gayla said.

"Is it murder, then?" Stacy asked, looking at me. "Have they arrested someone?"

"I saw the police taking that naturalist away this morning," Gayla said, and I resisted the urge to cram the coffee cake on her plate into her mouth to shut her up. At the rate things were going, the PR article I'd been hoping for was going to turn into a nightmare.

"Is there any crew left?" Stacy asked, her eyebrows rising.

"Martina will be captaining," I said, "and we have a first mate on his way."

"How much experience does he have?"

"He builds boats for a living," I told her. "And he's been on the water since he was born. No one knows these waters better than he does."

"Huh," she said, but didn't sound convinced. "Back to these murders," she said. "Who else has died here?"

"Can we talk about that later?" I asked; this was the last thing I wanted to discuss in the breakfast room.

"How about this afternoon when we come back in?" she suggested.

"I'll see how it goes," I said, not to anxious to commit to an interview. "I have to go refill the coffee…need anything else?"

"I'm fine for now," she said.

I hurried back into the kitchen, relieved to be away from Stacy, but a little nervous about what Gayla would tell her in my absence. How did she know about the inn's history? I wondered. "I don't like the direction this news article is going," I told John as I scooped more coffee into the coffeemaker.

"Why?"

"With everything that's been going on, I'm afraid it's going to be more of an investigative journalism piece than a travel article. Gayla's in there telling her about the other murders that have happened, and how the inn is cursed."

He sighed. "Want me to go in and intercede?"

"You can try, but I'm afraid Stacy's going to take the opportunity to quiz you; she was trying to set up an appointment for an interview with me this afternoon."

"Just what we needed," John said. "How did Charlene take the news, by the way?"

We'd barely had a chance to chat since breakfast started. "She's convinced he's innocent," I said. "On the plus side, Eli is coming to help out with the *Summer Breeze* today."

"Good thinking," he said.

"It was Adam's idea," I told him.

"Did Charlene find out anything else about who was looking to buy Cliffside?" he asked. I'd told him about the call last night when I went up to bed.

"I didn't ask," I told him. "Too many other things going on."

"No kidding," he said, glancing at the laundry room door. "And I haven't even called the insurance company yet."

"Let's get through breakfast and the rooms, and then we'll deal with it."

"Aren't you glad we have such a relaxing, glamorous life?" he asked with a grin.

"At least we won't die of boredom," I replied.

"And at least the company is good," he said, sweeping me into an embrace that made me—if only for a moment—forget about everything else that had happened.

And that's when Bridget walked in the back door—at the same time that Gwen started down the stairs from her room.

TEN

Bridget had just closed the door behind her when Gwen got to the bottom of the stairs. Despite sharing dark hair and willowy figures, they could not look more different; while Bridget wore a navy pantsuit and looked like she was ready for a client meeting, Gwen was dressed in a crinkled cotton skirt and an oversized wool sweater, her unruly hair caught up in a loose, artsy bun.

"I was hoping I'd run into you," Bridget said, sweeping a critical eye over her daughter.

"Going to try to persuade me to leave Adam and fly back to California with you again?" Gwen asked.

"I went to your gallery yesterday," my sister announced.

Gwen looked surprised. "Why?"

"I wanted to see your work, of course," Bridget said. "I can tell you've been putting a lot of time and effort into it."

Not exactly the compliment an artist wanted to hear, I thought, cringing inside.

"Gee, thanks," Gwen said frostily, and turned to me. "Do you need me to take care of the rooms today?" she asked.

"I think my mother offered to do it," John said. "You want to take the day off?"

She nodded. "I sold three more paintings yesterday, and I'd like to finish a few more."

"Three paintings? That's great!" I said.

"Congratulations!" John added.

"All to the same person, and she's thinking of commissioning another one," Gwen answered, and for the first time since our discussion yesterday, I sensed a slight thaw.

"Don't you think you'd sell more if you got into one of the mainland galleries?" my sister piped up.

"I've tried that route," Gwen said, and the temperature in the kitchen dropped again. "It wasn't very effective. Besides," she said, casting her mother an icy glance, "I thought you wanted me to go to business school."

Bridget threw up your hands. "Just trying to help," she said. "But I can see when my opinion isn't wanted."

I almost choked; if that were the case, she would have shut up a long time ago. Gwen gave her a look that could have taken paint off a wall. "Right. See you later."

"Are you sure you don't want some breakfast?" I asked as my niece marched toward the door.

"No thanks," she said, without looking back. "I've lost my appetite."

Bridget, John and I watched her go, and then my sister turned to me. "She's touchy. Always has been.

Once she gets an idea in her head..." She shook her head.

"I wonder where she gets that from?" I said dryly.

"The difference," my sister continued, as if I hadn't spoken, "is that she's not practical. She has no common sense."

"You know, I think this is between you and Gwen," I told her. "If you have an issue with her, you can take it up with her. I don't want to be in the middle."

"But you've put yourself in the middle." Bridget frowned. "That's the problem."

"Look," I told her. "I have a relationship with my niece; I love her. But what she does is her choice, and always has been-- not mine. If you have a problem with her decisions, talk to her—but please leave me out of it."

Bridget started to say something else, but John cut her off. "Natalie's right, Bridget. She hasn't tried to influence your daughter. All of Gwen's decisions have been hers alone. It's not fair to put Nat in the middle."

Bridget tightened her lips. "I can see you're all in league against me," she said. "I never should have let her come here. Just because you all feel comfortable throwing your lives away doesn't mean it's okay for my daughter to do it, too."

"Throwing our lives away?" John asked. "Is that really what you think of what we're doing here?"

She got up without answering. "I'm going to have a conversation with my daughter," she said.

"Somebody needs to talk some sense into her—and I can tell no one here is capable of it." She stormed out the door, half-slamming it behind her, leaving John and me alone in the kitchen. Even though I loved my life, tears of anger and humiliation stung my eyes. How dare my sister say such things to me—and to John?

"Wow," John said after a long moment. "Nat. I'm so sorry."

"I'm sorry you had to hear that," I told him.

"I'm not," he said, closing the distance between us and taking me into his arms. "I didn't realize what it was you have to deal with; now I have a better idea. I'm so sorry, honey," he said, squeezing me tight.

Something inside me loosened at his touch. "I can't believe I let her get me so upset," I told him.

"Family can do that. I can see why you moved across the country," he said. "She goes for the throat. I'm not even related to her, and I'm upset."

"You don't think we've wasted our lives, do you?"

John took me by the shoulders and looked into my eyes. "Is that a serious question?"

I shrugged. "It's just…"

"No," he said with conviction. "We have not wasted our lives. We are living full lives, doing what we love to do, in a wonderful community in a beautiful part of the world. What would you do differently? Work in a corporate office 60 hours a week and live in a high-rise somewhere?"

"Of course not," I said. "I'd hate that. "It's just…"

"Just what?"

I sighed. "Something about Bridget makes me question everything I've done."

John grinned. "Family does that," he said. "We all fall into those old patterns."

"You don't seem to with Catherine," I pointed out.

"I still have to work at it," he said. "When she gives me one of those looks...I feel like I'm five years old and got caught stealing a cookie from the Chips Ahoy bag. It all comes rushing back."

"Chips Ahoy?"

"She wasn't much of a baker," he said. "But when that happens, I remind myself that I am here, with you, living the life I want to. With free access to the cookie jar—and much better cookies."

I laughed a little bit, and wiped at my eyes. "Even so. Do you think she's right, and that I've influenced Gwen?"

"I think you've given Gwen room to discover her passions," he said. "You have been supportive, but haven't suggested she do anything. The choices she's made are hers alone; you didn't talk her into anything."

"That's not what Bridget thinks," I said.

"What your sister thinks doesn't matter to me," he replied. "And I hope you can find a way for it not to matter to you. Besides," he said, "we've got bigger fish to fry."

"Like what?" I asked.

"Like getting Charlene's boyfriend off the hook—

if he deserves to be," John said. "And calling the insurance company about the laundry room ceiling—and looking to see how bad the room upstairs is."

"And doing publicity damage control," I added, thinking of Stacy's request for an interview. "And saving that whale."

"Not to mention keeping your sister and your niece from strangling each other. Good thing you picked such a menial, unchallenging job," John said with a crooked grin.

I laughed, feeling lighter. "Thank you," I told him.

"Any time," he said, kissing me lightly on the forehead. "Now," he said. "Do you want to be in charge of breakfast cleanup, or calling the insurance company?"

"Breakfast cleanup for sure," I said. "I just need something that doesn't require brainpower for a few minutes."

"Good luck," he said with a final peck on the forehead, just as Eli knocked on the back door.

"Thanks so much for coming to help," I said as I poured Eli a cup of coffee and settled him at the table. John had taken the gray kitten down to his workshop and planned to call the insurance company from there. "I saved a few cookies for you," I told Eli, putting a few of my cookie bars on a plate.

"Promise you won't tell Claudie?"

"Promise," I said as he bit into the first cookie, looking dreamy. Although Eli's wife Claudette was an amazing bread baker, she was not particularly gifted in the pastry department, as everything she made was sugar free. Although she was more than amply proportioned and Eli was thin as a rail, she still kept him on a tight dietary leash. "Why don't I go get Martina and you two can hash out the details?" I suggested.

He reached for another cookie. "This tour group isn't having the best week, is it?"

"No," I said. "And it's bad luck for them, too; there's a journalist and a would-be investor aboard. Although with the captain gone, I'm not sure if the first mate was still planning on expanding."

"Were they buying another boat?"

"That was the theory," I said. "I don't know, though; it may be dead in the water." I winced as soon as I spoke.

"The deal's not the only thing dead in the water," he replied, saying what I was thinking out loud. "Did you know this wasn't the captain's first time on the island?"

"Captain Bainbridge? I'd heard rumors."

"Ayuh," Eli said. "He sterned for me one summer when I was lobstering, years ago. Came up from Boothbay Harbor. Went by the name of Bridges then, though. Carl Bridges."

"Charlene said he looked familiar. And that explains why he decided to make the island his home base; he knew about it from his time here."

"He was always looking for ways to make money," Eli said. "Not the most ethical way necessarily, either. Got caught up in a robbery—one of his girlfriends took the fall—and I caught him pulling up Tom Lockhart's traps one day."

"I'm surprised Tom didn't kill him then," I said.

"He caused quite a stir on the island that summer, as I recall. Quite popular with the ladies—a good-looking young man from away always is on the island."

"Did he date anyone in particular?" I asked.

"Lorraine Lockhart, as I recall. She was pretty broken up about it when he left after a season."

"Lorraine? I thought she and Tom had been together forever?"

"Not quite. Of course, she took up with Tom soon after Bridges left, and you know how that turned out."

"Yes," I said. The two had been married for years, and had children. "I had no idea the captain had such an interesting history. I wonder why he changed his name?"

Eli shrugged. "We'll probably never know. Now...where's that first mate? Although I guess she's the captain, now."

"I'll go get her," I said, and headed out of the kitchen, still considering what Eli had told me. Carl and Lorraine...was one of them still carrying a torch for the other? Was Lorraine the reason Carl had come back to the island? I turned the corner, deep in thought, and almost bumped into Nan and Gayla.

"Lots of untapped potential. If you'd like, we can arrange…" Gayla was saying. She trailed off when she saw me.

"Excuse me," I said. "Sorry to interrupt. Have you seen Martina?"

"I think she went upstairs for a minute," Nan said, pushing up her wire-rimmed glasses. "Poor thing. This trip has not at all gone as she planned."

"Murphy's Law," I said. "Although I feel a bit worse for the captain, to be honest—and Alex."

"I heard they arrested him this morning," Nan said. "What's next? There's almost no crew left on this tour. I hope they're planning a refund—or at least a big discount to the passengers."

"I'm sure Martina will make sure everyone is taken care of," I said. As I spoke, Martina came around the corner. "Just who I was looking for," I said brightly. "Eli's here; I was hoping to introduce you," I told her.

"Terrific," she told me, looking relieved. "We'll be ready to head out in an hour," she told the two women with a bright, confident smile. As she followed me into the kitchen, I relayed what Nan had told me. She groaned. "This whole second boat thing was a mistake," she said, her confident facade sagging. "I knew it from the beginning. Now, not only are we not going to get the second boat, but the whole business is going to be torpedoed."

"You never know how it's going to turn out," I told

her. "And if worse comes to worst, you can always rebrand the company and start fresh."

"But how am I going to make the payments on the boat without income?" she asked. "I'll have to build our reputation all over again, from scratch."

"I'm sure you'll pull through," I said in an encouraging tone of voice. "This is my friend Eli," I said, introducing her to my old friend as we walked into the kitchen.

Martina gave the old boatwright a weary, grateful smile. "I hear you're the most experienced sailor on the island. Thank you so much for coming to help out," she said.

"My pleasure," he said, nodding toward where the *Summer Breeze* gleamed in the morning light. "It'll be a joy. She's a beauty."

"I'll finish making lunch while you get acquainted," I said. As the two of them headed out into the cool morning air, already talking about currents and sails, I began assembling lunch: rare roast beef sandwiches on fresh Little Notch bakery bread, slices of blueberry pie, and salt and vinegar potato chips. I was slicing the last sandwich when John walked in the back door.

"What did the insurance company say?"

"They're sending an adjustor next week."

"Next week? That's a long time to wait. What do we do in the meantime?"

"I have a call in to see if I can make it faster. Hope the ceiling doesn't completely cave in, I guess," John said. "Good thing we're short one guest, or we'd be sleeping in a tent in the yard."

"I suppose that is a very faint silver lining," I said as I put the last sandwich into its box and fit it into the padded cooler.

"When do they leave?" John asked, looking at the stack of assembled lunches.

"In an hour or so," I told him. "Eli and Martina are down on the *Summer Breeze* getting it ready.

"Did your sister ever come back?"

"Not that I've seen," I said. "But I found out something about the captain from Eli." I relayed what he'd told me about his connection to Lorraine.

"That explains why he looked familiar," John said. "His name was different then; close, but not quite the same."

"Bridges. I wonder why he changed it?"

"It might be worth looking into," John suggested.

"You think Lorraine may have had something to do with what happened to him?"

He sighed and ran a hand through his sandy hair. "Somebody did him in, Nat. Maybe Lorraine wasn't the only one he was connected to romantically. Or maybe there was jealousy."

"You're thinking Tom?" I said. I could not imagine the head of the lobster co-op tying an anchor to a man's leg and dropping him into the Gulf of Maine. "He did go after Tom's traps, according to Eli."

"Even if they weren't involved—and I hope they're not—maybe they know something we don't," he said. "It's worth talking to them. If Catherine's doing the rooms, maybe you could swing by and talk to Lorraine; I'll see if I can connect with Tom."

"I did promise Charlene I'd take some cookies down to the store," I mused. "And pick up the grocery order."

"And if you're not here, Bridget can't corner you," John pointed out.

"Will you take care of the kitten?" I asked.

"I'll keep her in the workshop with me," he said. "And I'll even start dinner."

"What would I do without you?" I asked, grinning at my handsome husband.

"Let's hope you never have to find out," he said as I pulled my cookie cookbook out of the shelf. "Still no binder?" he asked.

"Missing in action," I told him. "On the plus side, I'm having to experiment with new recipes."

"We'd better find that binder," he said. "I don't think I can survive without your Wicked Blueberry Coffee Cake."

"Better to lose the binder than our mailing list, I guess."

"I'm not so sure about that," he said darkly as I leafed through the cookbook for another recipe. I decided on raspberry oatmeal bars; I had just made jam last week, and although my pantry was running low, I had enough eggs and butter for the recipe. I'd drop the bars by the store, say hi to Charlene, and then pick up my grocery order.

As I pulled the oats out of the pantry, Catherine walked into the kitchen.

"Hey, Mom," John said. "I was just on my way down to the workshop. Thanks for taking care of the rooms today."

"And thanks for putting up with my sister," I added.

"Natalie," she said, giving me a pitying look. "However did you survive growing up?"

"That bad?" John asked with a wry grin.

"You would think Cranberry Island was some hotbed of sloth and iniquity, to hear her talk," she said. "And that you had lured her daughter into a den of vice."

"Did Bridget really say that?" I asked.

"Well, maybe the words were a little bit milder," she confessed, "but she's pretty adamant about taking her daughter back to what she calls 'civilization.' Of course, I understand on some level," she said, sliding her eyes at John. "When you have a child who's bright with lots of potential, it's hard when they take a path other than the one you'd envisioned for them."

"Subtle, Mom," John said. "Have you recovered from the disappointment yet?" Although his voice was light, I could hear a strained undertone. It looked like John wasn't as sanguine about his job choice as he'd let on, I realized.

"John," she said, "I long ago realized that no one knows your path better than you." She walked over and put an arm around him. "You have a varied career, you live on a beautiful island, and you've got a terrific, patient, wife."

"Patient?" John winked at me. "Let's not go too far, Mother."

She smiled. "The point is, when you're a driven person with an only child, sometimes it's easy to find yourself living vicariously. It can be hard to let go of those expectations."

"What exactly were you expecting me to do?" John asked, raising an eyebrow.

"Nothing too outlandish. President of the United States would have been fine." She winked at him. "Seriously, though," she said. "There comes a point when you have to realize your children are wiser than you are—at least in terms of their own destiny. Bridget just hasn't gotten to that point yet."

"Do you think she will?"

"I hope for both their sakes she does," she said.

"Gwen thinks I'm on Bridget's side," I told Catherine.

"Why?"

"Because I asked her if she was sure she was doing the right thing."

"Nothing wrong with checking in," she said. "But if I were you, I'd leave it and let the two of them work it out."

"It would be a lot easier if Bridget were still in California," I said darkly.

"Fortunately for you, you've got a murder and an arrest to keep you occupied," Catherine said glibly.

"Not to mention a full inn. I'm planning on taking care of the rooms."

"Thanks. It should be easy," I said. "No need to change sheets yet—but Gayla and Herb's room flooded last night; if you could check and make sure things are drying out okay, that would be good."

"How?"

"Overflowing bathtub," John said. "We had to move them to Bainbridge's room." The police had cleared us to use it, and the Fowlers had taken it reluctantly—after demanding a discount.

"Are the floors okay?"

"They're not in great shape," John admitted. "Neither is the laundry room ceiling."

"It's been some week, hasn't it? On the plus side, I don't see how it could get much worse."

Unfortunately, she was wrong.

ELEVEN

Once the guests headed out for the day on the *Summer Breeze*—Nan and Stacy seemed concerned at first, but Eli quickly won them over with his charm—I spent a meditative hour making raspberry bars. Eli had promised he would chart the location of the entangled whale if he saw it; I hoped it had broken free, or that Adam and Alex's efforts would be successful in helping free it.

As I mixed the dry ingredients together, I wondered about Captain Bainbridge—or Carl Bridges—and his connection to the island. Most people who came back reminisced about their childhood memories, but despite his time sterning with Eli, the captain had never mentioned that he'd been on Cranberry Island before. Something seemed strange there; I was hoping Lorraine could fill me in on what she knew about him.

My thoughts turned to Alex as I kneaded butter into the dry mixture. I had told them I'd seen Alex coming back at 2 a.m., because it was true. Was it because of that that the detectives had arrested him? And what did they think was his motive was for killing the captain?

I threw my mind back to the captain's comment to Martina about trouble with Alex. I was going to have to ask Martina about that; I was guessing there was more to the relationship between Bainbridge and Alex than met the eye.

I patted the dough into the pan and reached for a jar of raspberry jam, spreading the garnet-colored jam over the golden crust, then sprinkled the remaining dough crumbles over the top. I was just sliding it into the oven when Gwen came in, looking haunted.

"Is she here?" she asked in a furtive voice, her eyes darting around the kitchen.

"No," I said. "I thought she was with you."

"I sent her to the mainland on the mail boat to look at galleries," Gwen said, depositing her art bag on the table and heading to the fridge. "I didn't wait for the ferry, though, and I was afraid she might turn back."

"Why did you send her to look at galleries?"

"So she'd feel she had some control," Gwen said as she pulled out a container and opened it up. "What's this?" she asked.

"I don't know," I said, glancing at the contents of the unfamiliar Tupperware. "Maybe it's Catherine's; I don't recognize the container."

"It's gross enough to be Catherine's," Gwen said as she tucked it back into the refrigerator. "Probably gluten-free cabbage casserole, or something."

"There's left-over strata, some fruit salad, and

some coffee cake—the cake's next to the cookie jar," I told her."

"Sounds good," she said, grabbing the container of strata from the fridge and reaching for a plate. "By the way," she said as she spooned out a large helping, "I'm still mad at you for butting in."

"I know," I said, relieved that at least the fury that had accompanied my niece out the door that morning seemed to have dissipated. "I'm sorry you felt I was interfering," I told her. "Your mom and I have a long history; even now, she can make me second-guess myself."

"No kidding," Gwen said. "Imagine having her for a mother!"

"She loves you," I told her. "And she's right; it's not my job to tell you what to do."

"When have you ever told me what to do?" Gwen asked, and something inside me relaxed a little. "You've listened to me, you've given me advice when I asked—and okay, maybe you told me doing huge oils for that awful gallery owner on Mount Desert Island wasn't the best idea."

"Yeah—I really influenced you there, didn't I?"

"I wish you had," she said ruefully. "Those paintings were awful."

I shrugged. "It doesn't hurt to try something new. But I'm glad you're doing what you love."

She sighed as she slid the strata back into the fridge and reached for the fruit salad. "Maybe my mom can set me up with a mainland gallery. If that will keep her satisfied with me being here, it might be worth it."

"And you never know," I said. "It could be profitable; they get a lot more traffic in Northeast Harbor, and there are some pretty ritzy visitors."

"If nothing else," she said, "I have an afternoon off." She looked at me a little bit guiltily; she had been rather absent the last few days, although it was understandable. "Not from work, I mean."

"Catherine's got the rooms and I've got dinner," I said. "I think you deserve a little time to yourself."

"Actually, Adam and I are planning to meet with some scientists from College of the Atlantic," she said as she spooned a few scoops of cut fruit into a small bowl. "He's hauling traps this morning, but someone's coming out to the island this afternoon to show the lobstermen how to tag the whale if they see her…"

"I just hope it doesn't get caught up on other traps," I said. "I can't imagine what it would be like to drown," I said, shuddering—and then remembered that Captain Bainbridge had done just that. "By the way," I said. "Apparently the captain spent a summer sterning with Eli several years back."

"Why didn't he mention it?"

"I don't know," I said. "He and Lorraine apparently had a summer romance, too; I'm hoping I can ask her a bit about him today."

"Why wouldn't he tell us he'd been on the island before?" She sliced off a hunk of coffee cake and added it to her plate. Again, I wondered how she ate so much yet stayed so thin; whatever miraculous metabolism she had inherited clearly hadn't come to me. "Are you thinking somebody he knew on the island might have something to do with what happened to him?" she asked.

"That's a very good question. I'm exploring all options," I said. "You know Alex was arrested, right?"

She almost dropped her plate. "What?"

"Adam didn't tell you?"

"I barely saw him today," she said. "I spent the whole morning fending off my mother. When did this happen?"

"First thing this morning," I said. "I was fixing breakfast."

"How is Martina going to handle the boat on her own?"

"Eli's helping her," I said.

"Good thinking."

"It was Adam's idea, actually," I told her, and she smiled.

"He is awesome, isn't he? Regardless of what my mother thinks, I'm glad I'm marrying him."

"Don't tell your mom I said so, but so am I," I told her. "And I hope I'm not interfering by saying so."

Gwen walked over and gave me a big hug. "I love you, Aunt Nat!"

"I love you too," I said. "Thanks for putting up with me."

"Are you kidding?" she said. "Thanks for putting up with me!"

I was just slicing the raspberry bars, which were looking decadent, when John walked into the kitchen, looking like an L.L. Bean cover model in faded jeans and a plaid shirt that was dusted lightly with sawdust. A simple wedding band glinted on his left hand, and I had to resist the urge to pinch myself. "How's it going?" I asked, feeling slightly better just looking at my handsome husband.

"Well, I found out a little more about why they arrested Alex this morning," he said as I removed the first bar from the tray. "Those look and smell amazing," he said.

"You're welcome to try one," I told him as he came up next to me, bringing a whiff of his woodsy scent. "It's a new recipe; I still can't find my binder."

"That could be a problem," he said, biting into the bar. His eyes closed, and he let out a moan. "Oh, these are terrific. When you do find the binder, put this recipe near the front."

"I hope I can," I said as I began transferring the rest of the bars to a container. "But tell me about Alex."

"Well," he said, "the fact that he didn't make it back to the inn until 2:00 in the morning was certainly a factor," he said, "but apparently he and the captain had a bit of a blow-out after that whale expedition."

"Was it because he was getting too close to the whales?" I said. "I wasn't too thrilled with it, either, but he seemed to want to impress the investor."

"That was it," John said. Apparently Doreen overheard them talking on the back porch once they got back. She said Alex threatened to run the captain over with a boat himself if he didn't back off from the whales. Said something about him already having done enough damage—and that he was going to have to pay for it some day."

"Ouch," I said. "But he didn't damage the whales; he got too close, but the boat never made contact. Have they questioned Alex about it?"

"He said he was just angry that the captain was threatening the whales—that he actually never intended to hurt him."

"What about his late-night return from Charlene's?"

"He said he couldn't sleep, so he went for a walk."

"If it were during the day, half the island would be able to give him an alibi, but there were probably no witnesses after midnight, unfortunately."

"Even if they did, they'd have to cover a two-hour span," John told me. "Did you hear any boats or anything when you came down to check on the kitten?"

I shook my head. "But somebody must have made it out to the *Summer Breeze* and back, and I doubt they swam. Do they really not have anything else in the history between Alex and the captain? That kind of seems like a weak motive."

"Apparently Doreen thought his threat sounded pretty convincing," John said. "And with the late arrival back at the inn…besides, there really aren't any other suspects."

"What about Martina?" I asked. "She was kind of nervous about expanding the business."

"It's possible," he said. "Who else?"

"Maybe someone on the island," I suggested.

"Like Lorraine, you mean? Don't you think she'd be over that by now? It must have been what—fifteen years ago?"

"Or Tom," I pointed out.

"We don't even know if they knew he was here," John pointed out.

"She would recognize him," I said. "Fifteen years isn't that long. Besides, do you really think Alex would have killed the captain?"

"I don't know him well enough to have an opinion," he said.

"Charlene thinks he's innocent," I told him.

John gave me a wry smile. "She's also half in love with him," he pointed out.

"I won't argue that," I said. "But I don't think they've done a whole lot of digging. There might be more history between the captain and some of the tour guests than we know."

"You think?"

"I think it's worth looking into, anyway," I said. "And it might be worth talking to Stacy to see if she's dug up anything on the captain or the history of Northern Spirit Tours."

"That's risky, though," John said. "We don't want to dig up any more problems for her to write about."

"If anything, it might take her mind off of what Gayla keeps telling her," I said.

"What do you mean?"

"She was going on about the murders at the inn, the ghost...all kinds of juicy tidbits this morning."

"How does she know all of that?" he asked.

"I don't know, but I don't like it," I said. "By the way, we need to get flyers out for the murder mystery event we're planning this fall." Bookings were usually slower once summer passed, so we were experimenting with ways to drum up more business. "They're supposed to be delivered today. Would you mind printing out labels while I'm at Lorraine's?"

"Sure," he said, "but why are you headed to the Lockharts' house?"

"I told Charlene I'd try to find out what happened to Captain Bainbridge," I said. "I have to start somewhere."

"Speaking of Charlene, any word on Smudge?"

"Smudge?"

"The kitten," he said, looking a little bit embarrassed.

"You two seem to be getting along famously," I said as I fitted the cover on the container of raspberry bars. "She's asking around…unless you'd rather I keep it quiet?" I added with a grin.

"Of course not," he said. "I don't want to steal someone's kitten. But if she needs a home…she's good company in the workshop."

"Biscuit begs to differ, I'm afraid." I still hadn't seen her since she stalked out of the kitchen earlier.

"She'll get over it," he said.

"Just like Bridget's gotten over Gwen moving to Maine," I said with a grin.

"I forgot about that. How's that going?"

"Bridget's off on the mainland scouting out galleries."

"And Gwen?"

"We talked this morning, and we're good again. For now, anyway."

"At least something's going right," he said as I grabbed my windbreaker from the hook by the door. "Are you taking the van?"

"I've got to pick up groceries, so yes," I said. "Do you need it?"

"I've got to take some more toy boats over to Island Artists, but I can use *Mooncatcher*. See you later this afternoon?" he asked.

"I look forward to it," I said, walking over to give him a quick kiss that morphed into a rather longer kiss. I did love my life on Cranberry Island, I decided as I waved goodbye to my handsome husband and prepared to head out into a beautiful morning. Besides, what else could possibly go wrong? I thought to myself as I opened the front door of the van and rolled the window down, enjoying the cool sea breeze as I backed out of the driveway.

Ha.

TWELVE

I stopped by the Lockharts' house first; I had to pick up the inn's grocery order from the store, and even though I carried a cooler in the van for that purpose, I liked to take the food straight back to the inn. Lorraine and Tom had recently moved to one of the old sea-captain's houses overlooking the harbor. Bright red geraniums that had miraculously escaped the attention of Claudette's goats Muffin and Pudge flanked the white-painted porch, and ruffled curtains framed the sparkling windows.

Lorraine's son Logan answered the door, a dollop of what looked like green frosting on his nose. "Hi, Miss Natalie," he said. "Did you bring us cookies?"

"Not today, I'm afraid," I said; the raspberry bars were for Charlene to sell at the front counter. "But what's your favorite?"

"Chocolate chip," he said.

"I'll make some this week and take them down to the store," I told him. "Is your mom home?'

"She's in the kitchen. We're making cupcakes for my birthday!" he announced.

"Who's there, Logan?" Lorraine called from somewhere near the back of the house.

"Miss Natalie from the Gray Whale!" her son called back.

"Invite her in!" Lorraine said brightly, and I reflected that she didn't seem terribly broken up about the loss of her former flame. Did she even know? I wondered as I followed Logan through the house to the Lockhart's cheerful, if small, kitchen.

Although the counters was covered in mixing spoons and batter-splattered bowls, there was a happy air to the old kitchen. Children's artwork covered the old Frigidaire fridge, and jars of sea glass and shells were lined up on the window sill, gleaming in the sun.

"It smells delicious in here," I said, inhaling the vanilla-scented air.

"We're making Logan's favorite recipe," Lorraine told me. "His birthday is tomorrow."

"Happy Birthday!" I told the brown-eyed boy.

"Can I get you a cup of coffee?" Lorraine asked as she applied frosting to a cupcake. She was a pretty, curvy woman in her mid-thirties, with glossy brown hair swept up into a clip and big coffee-colored eyes. Right now, there were shadows under her eyes, though, and I could see why. A few feet away from her, Logan grabbed a plastic jar of sprinkles and shook it over an already-frosted cupcake, causing a small blizzard of blue sugar to fall to the floor. "Careful!" Lorraine said. "Gentle, and try to keep it on the plate."

"Lady doesn't seem to mind," I said, watching as

the family beagle licked up the fallen sprinkles and a stray dollop of frosting from the hardwood floor. "And yes, I'd love some coffee, if you have some made. Thank you."

"Let me just finish frosting these last three cupcakes so that Logan can decorate them." Lorraine gave him a stern look. "Carefully."

"Yes, Mom," Logan said.

"Why don't I pour us some coffee while you finish up?" I asked.

"That would be great. The mugs are in the cabinet above the coffee maker; black for me, please," she said. "After all these cupcakes, I don't need any more sugar," she said, patting her slightly padded waist line as I poured us some coffee. She frosted the last cupcakes and rinsed her hands as I doctored my mug. "Remember," Lorraine reminded her enthusiastic son, "the sprinkles go on the cupcakes, not the dog."

"I know," Logan said, biting his lip with concentration as he picked up the jar of green sprinkles.

"Let's go out on the porch," Lorraine suggested. "I need a break from the sugar; besides, it might be better if I just don't watch."

I laughed and followed her out to the front porch. As we settled ourselves onto two rockers, she breathed a tired sigh, then took a sip of her coffee and turned to me. "It's been a while since we've had a chat," she said. "How are things at the inn?"

"We've had a bit of excitement the last few days—

I'm sure you've heard."

"Tom mentioned that there was an incident, but didn't say what—and I've been too busy getting ready for Logan's party to get out much. What's going on?"

"Captain Bainbridge appears to have been murdered," I said, watching her face.

She froze for a moment, the coffee cup halfway to her lips. "Oh, God," she said, and the cup started to shake in her hand. She put it down quickly, sloshing some of the brown liquid onto the wicker table. "Why didn't Tom tell me?" She wrapped her arms around herself and began to rock back and forth. "How?"

"Someone tied him to the anchor and dropped him overboard," I told her.

"Oh, God," she said. "That's awful."

"I'm sorry to have to break the news. I didn't realize until today that he used to stern for Eli," I said, introducing the topic cautiously. "I understand you and he knew each other, too."

"Yes," she said. "He spent a summer on the island a long time ago—probably fifteen years, now. I didn't recognize him at first when he came back—different last name."

"Were you friends?"

She gave a low laugh. "Yes—we dated for a bit, too. He is—was—a handsome man. Oh, Carl," she said softly. "Who did you make so angry?"

"What makes you think he made someone angry?" I asked.

"That was how he was," she said. "Such a strong

personality; he did what he wanted, and sometimes there was hell to pay." She looked at me. "I'm surprised he lasted with Eli as long as he did." Her eyes seemed unfocused, as if she were watching a replay of something that had happened long ago. A small smile twitched on her mouth, and then her face crumpled, and she let out a sob that seemed to come from deep inside. "I just can't believe he's gone." .

I reached out to touch her shoulder as she sobbed. We sat together for several minutes, until it passed, and she swiped at her eyes. "Are you okay?" I asked. "Do you need to lie down? I can keep an eye on Logan if you want."

"I'm fine," she said, sitting up and waving me away.

"I'm so sorry for your loss," I said.

"He's not mine anymore," Lorraine said, with something that sounded like a pang of regret. "Never really was. Still, it is sad...he was young." She picked up her coffee and took a mechanical sip, her eyes far away. "Do they have any idea who did it?"

"The police arrested the naturalist this morning," I told her.

"Alex?" She blinked. "That doesn't seem right. I only met him twice, but he was so nice!"

"I know. Charlene is devastated." I took a sip of my coffee. "Do you have any idea if maybe he still had some old connections the island?"

Lorraine turned to me. "You mean you think he might have been killed by a local?"

"I have no idea what happened," I told her. "I was just hoping you might be able to tell me a little more about him—and his time on the island. He was all business at the inn; I don't know much about him, to be honest."

"But that was years ago," she said, puzzled.

"You're right," I said, backing off. "Did you get a chance to talk to him? Maybe he said something that could point us in the right direction?"

"I only saw him briefly twice," she said, looking away from me. "It stirred up old things that should have stayed buried." The bitterness in her voice was barely masked.

Strange, I thought, that he should choose to base his tours here, then.

She glanced back toward the house. "It really isn't relevant now, anyway; I'm married with kids. Our lives had moved on."

"He never married, did he?"

"I don't think so," she said. "Or if he did, he must have divorced; he told me he was still single."

"It must be a real shock."

Lorraine's hand leapt to her mouth, and she let out another sob. "I'm sorry," she said, putting down her coffee and swiping at her eyes. "I shouldn't be so upset…after all, it's not like we were close."

"It's always upsetting when someone you were once close to dies," I said, reaching out and touching her shoulder again.

"He came over twice," she said. "He stopped by the

house the day before the tour started, and came over for coffee...the kids were at school." She flashed me a guilty look. "I never told Tom about it."

"You were just catching up with an old friend," I suggested. "I'm sure it's fine."

She shot me a look that suggested otherwise. "You're right, of course." She sniffled and wiped her eyes again, and I began wondering exactly what exactly they discussed over coffee. "He just...things seemed to be going so well for him, and now this."

"Did he tell you how the business was going?"

"It seemed to be booming," she said. "He was negotiating the purchase of a second boat, and looking to expand the business to the Caribbean."

"How long had he owned the company?"

"About five years, he said. Before that he was involved in some Japanese company."

"Japanese company?" I asked. "He didn't mention that."

"I think he captained a boat he was part owner of," she said. "I don't know what it was called...*Kobe Maru*...something like that."

Interesting, but I didn't see how it related to his death.

"Why did he change his name?"

"I think he must have thought it sounded more captain-like," she said with a wry smile. "He told me it was for professional reasons."

"Did he say what made him decide to base tours out of Cranberry Island?" I asked.

"It's closer to open water than the mainland," she said. "Not so far to get to the whales—and the accommodations are a little less expensive," she said. "Plus, we've got that island mystique…"

I knew it well; that's what had drawn me to buy the Gray Whale Inn a few years back. "Did he mention visiting anyone else when he was here?"

She shook her head. "He was only here for a summer," she told me. Tears welled up again. "I'm sorry…it's still just so hard to believe he's gone."

"Mommy?" Logan stepped out onto the porch, covered in green frosting. "I had an accident with the sprinkles."

Lorraine swiped at her eyes again and stood up, taking a deep breath. "What happened?" she asked Logan in a bright voice.

"I dropped the whole thing on the floor, and Lady ate all the sprinkles."

"I'll be right in," she said. "Give me just a moment, okay, sweetie?"

"It's really messy," he warned her.

"I know," Lorraine said. "Give Mommy just a moment."

"Why don't you take a few minutes?" I said. "I'll go help."

"Are you sure?" Lorraine asked, looking at me red-eyed.

"Of course," I said, heading into the house as Lorraine dabbed at her eyes. "Take your time."

Logan wasn't kidding about the mess. Lady was

busy licking up the floor; her muzzle had turned blue-green, and there were so many sprinkles the kitchen floor looked like a technicolor beach.

"Do you have a broom and dustpan?" I asked Logan as I grabbed Lady by the collar and escorted her to the back yard.

"Right here, he said, opening the pantry door and reaching for the broom.

"Wait!" I said as he yanked it from the rack on the door. The broom lurched sidewise, knocking off the mop and the duster, which slid into the cleaning supply shelf, sweeping the motley assortment of bottles onto the floor and causing Lady to start barking at the back door.

"Why don't you go out back and keep Lady company?" I asked, surveying the mess—the cap had come off the window cleaner, and blue fluid was mixing with the blue and green sprinkles to create a lurid pattern on the floor.

"Okay," he said, and opened the back door. Lady came skidding into the kitchen and promptly galloped through the blue puddle, spreading the mess further. "Lady!" I chased her down and grabbed her collar, and promptly sent both of them to the back yard. There were times when I regretted not having children; as I surveyed the chaos Logan had created in less than five minutes, I reflected that this was not one of them.

I had just finished mopping up the last of the sprinkles and was putting the broom back on its rack when a letter caught my eye. "I'm sorry I had to leave in such a hurry. Know you are in my heart...always. I love you. Carl."

I glanced toward the front door, then picked up the letter. "I can't marry you now—but someday, I promise, you will be Lorraine Bridges."

"Everything okay in here?"

I dropped the letter back on the counter and stepped away from it as Lorraine walked down the hallway to the kitchen. "I just finished sweeping up," I said. "Are you doing any better?"

"Yes," she said. "Sorry about that. Silly of me. I mean, he was just a summer fling."

"It's okay," I said, thinking that from what I'd read, it sounded like a lot more than a summer fling. "Grief is a funny thing. How did you two end up drifting apart?"

She shrugged. "He got a job overseas. We just kind of...lost touch." There was a sadness in her eyes I'd never seen before.

"And then you met Tom," I said.

"Yes," she told me. "It's for the best, really," she said, her eyes drifting to the back yard, where Logan was running around with Lady. "I have a good life."

"Yes," I said, taking in the sunny kitchen with its rows of lumpy cupcakes, the cheerful drawings on the fridge, the jars of sea glass on the windowsill. I knew she and Tom had had problems—he had had a fling with another woman a few years back—but overall, they seemed to have smoothed things out, and the kids certainly seemed happy. "You've made a good life for yourself, Lorraine."

"Last week I was happy," she said. "But sometimes things happen that get you to thinking about the road not taken..." She shrugged. "It doesn't matter now. He's gone. And besides, I made my decision a long time ago."

"I'm so sorry, Lorraine," I said, reaching out to touch her arm.

She looked at me with welling eyes. "I hope they find out who did that to him. He wasn't perfect, but was a good man. He didn't deserve to die that way." A tear rolled down her cheek and she swiped at it.

"I hope they find out too," I said. "If anything comes to you—anything he said, or anything you may have seen—let me know, and I'll tell John."

She nodded. "I will."

"And I hope the party goes well tomorrow," I told her, looking out the back door to where Logan was romping with Lady.

Lorraine's eyes followed mine, and her face softened into a smile. "I'm sure it will," she told me. "He's getting a light saber. How long do you think before he whacks his brother over the head?"

I laughed. "Might want to start a betting pool," I suggested. "Seriously, though," I added. "If you need to talk—or need anything at all—I'm here."

"Thanks, Natalie," she said, her sad eyes crinkling at the corners as she gave me a wan smile. "Want a cupcake?" she offered.

I looked down at the virulently green frosting and smiled. The cupcakes looked pretty appalling, but the vanilla scent in the air was too tempting to ignore. "Why not?" I asked. "But only if you can spare one."

"The less sugar in the house, the better," she said, handing me a lopsided cupcake. "There are ten boys coming over tomorrow. Every cupcake that gets eaten before that is one less cupcake I may have to scrape off the walls."

I took a bite; despite appearances, it was delicious. "This is great," I said. "What makes the frosting so good?"

"A bit of almond extract," she said. "But don't tell Logan. He thinks he hates nuts." She looked out at her son, who had turned on the hose and was spraying Lady as the beagle rolled in a patch of bare dirt, creating a muddy mess. "I can't wait until he starts school," she groaned.

"I can only imagine," I said, feeling grateful for my niece, Gwen. Not only was I not officially her mother, but she was well past the green cupcake stage.

Although they were pretty tasty, I had to admit.

I pulled up outside the Cranberry Island store a few minutes later, still thinking about Lorraine and her former flame. She seemed terribly upset over the loss of an old boyfriend. Had Tom's dalliance a few years back made Lorraine question her decision to marry him…or maybe reignited interest in an old lover? Was there more to her meetings with the late captain than she had told me? And had Tom found out about it—or read the old love letter she'd left on the kitchen counter?

Although I couldn't imagine the charismatic co-op president tying Captain Bainbridge's ankle to an anchor chain, somebody had, and I couldn't rule out the possibility of it being Tom. I stepped out of the van, grabbed the container of raspberry bars and headed for the wooden porch that stretched across the front of the store. The rose bushes, I noticed, appeared to have been paid a visit by Claudette's goats in the recent past, which was unfortunate, since their pink blooms were usually beautiful. The notices taped to the mullioned windows fluttered as I opened the door. The overstuffed couches in the front of the store were filled with islanders, which was no surprise after yesterday's discovery.

"Good morning, Natalie," Emmeline Hoyle said, fixing me with bright eyes. "A bit of excitement out at the inn, eh?"

"Not at the inn, actually," I corrected her.

"But one of the guests," she said.

I shrugged. "Accidents happen."

"That's not what Gertrude Pickens thinks," Emmeline said. "Big article in the Daily Mail…someone tied him to an anchor and threw him overboard, apparently. And I heard there was a police launch out by the inn this morning."

"I'm sure we'll read all about it tomorrow, then," I replied. I was surprised they hadn't heard about the arrest. On the other hand, since Charlene was usually the main conduit for all island gossip, it made sense. She wasn't going to be talking about Alex being implicated. Gertrude Pickens, I knew, wouldn't be quite so circumspect.

Charlene, I noticed, was not a part of the conversation. My friend was behind the counter, staring down at a copy of the Daily Mail with dark-circled eyes.

She hadn't bothered with eyeliner or mascara—never a good sign—and her caramel-colored hair was pulled back into a ponytail.

"Good to see you all," I said with a smile, "but I've got to run." I had taken a step toward the door when Emmeline said, "Did you hear about the new hotel going in?"

I stopped short. "What?"

"Contract was signed for Cliffside this morning," she announced. "Going to be a 100-room luxury hotel. Tennis courts, swimming pool, full-service restaurant, boat service to the mainland…the works."

"I'd heard it was under contract, but thought the hotel was just a rumor. Who bought it?" I asked, feeling like someone had dumped a bucket of ice water over my head.

"Some operation out of Portland, I hear,"

Emmeline told me, confirming what Charlene had said. "I have a few calls into my real estate friend in Bar Harbor. I'll let you know if I find out anything else."

"Thanks," I said, trying to imagine what the island would feel like with a luxury hotel on it. What would that mean for the Gray Whale Inn? I wondered—or the island as a whole? Where would they put the tennis courts? I'd have to ask Catherine if Murray knew anything about the sale.

But I didn't have time to worry about that now. I walked over to where Charlene was staring at the paper, feeling my heart go out to her. She and Alex hadn't been together long, but I knew she was smitten with him—and her relationship history had not been a happy one. "How are you holding up?" I asked in a quiet voice, aware of the lull that had fallen over the front of the store—what we often called the island's living room—as I spoke.

"He's not in here yet," she said tonelessly, pointing to an article on the captain's death, "but he will be tomorrow."

"Have a raspberry bar," I said, pulling the lid off the bar cookies.

"No thanks," Charlene told me.

And that's when I knew for sure she was in trouble.

"Did you get a chance to talk to him?" I asked.

She shook her head. "I don't know who his first phone call was to, but it wasn't to me."

"He told me to tell you he loves you," I said.

She brightened for a moment, then slumped again. "Just my luck. I find the perfect man, and he's arrested for a crime he didn't commit."

I grabbed my friend's hand, and she looked up at me. Dark circles ringed her eyes, and she was pale. "Are you sure he's innocent?" I asked.

"Yes," she said, with no trace of doubt.

I glanced over my shoulder to where the islanders were gathered, talking quietly among themselves again. "Then what was he doing for two hours after he left your house two nights ago?"

She blanched. "I don't know," she said. "But I know he's not a murderer."

"All right then," I told her. "We need to figure out where he was that night."

"I'm going to visit him as soon as I can," she told me. "I'll ask."

What he told her and the truth might be two different things, but I let it ride. "In the meantime, did Alex tell you anything about Bainbridge's relationships with the rest of the crew—and the guests?"

"I've been thinking about that," she said. "I know things were a bit dicey with Martina sometimes— they had different visions for the company. Bainbridge wanted to borrow heavily to expand, and she was nervous about it."

"Were they co-owners?"

"Yes, but Bainbridge held the majority of the

company, so he could outvote her."

"Well, that's one motive," I said. "I wonder who inherits the captain's share of the company?"

"How do we find that out?" she asked.

"I don't know yet," I told her, "but I'll work on it. Anything else? Girlfriends, wives, boyfriends…"

"I got the impression he might be a girl-in-every-port kind of guy," Charlene said.

"You know he used to date Lorraine, right?" I asked.

She blinked at me. "What?"

"His last name used to be Bridges," I told her. "Eli said he worked for him one summer."

"Wait…" Her eyes got big. "Oh my gosh, you're right! I didn't recognize him!"

"Lorraine did, "I commented.

"I'll bet she did," Charlene said. "She started dating Tom not long after Carl took off; she was pretty devastated at the time. I had no idea he was the same person; why did he change his name? And why didn't he tell anyone who he was?"

"That's an interesting question, isn't it?"

Before Charlene could answer, the phone rang. She answered, then handed it to me.

"Hello?" I said.

"Natalie? It's John."

I could tell by the tone of his voice that there was a problem. "What's wrong?"

"The health inspector's here," he said.

"What? She was just here last month!"

"Someone called her," he said. "And there's some stuff in the fridge I've never seen before."

"I'll be right there," I said.

"What's wrong?" Charlene asked when I hung up the phone.

"Somebody called the health inspector," I told her.

"Why?"

"I don't know," I said. "But I'm heading home to find out."

"What about your grocery order?"

"I'll pick it up later," I said, and hurried out of the store.

Both John and the inspector looked grim when I hurried into the kitchen of the Gray Whale Inn ten minutes later.

"What's up?" I asked.

"Unfortunately," the inspector said, pushing her glasses up on her nose, "we got a phone call indicating there might be some violations."

"Violations?" I asked.

"Did you put this in the fridge?" John asked, pointing to an unfamiliar Tupperware container on the counter.

"No," I said. "Do you think maybe it belongs to one of the guests?"

"It was in your refrigerator," she informed me. "And I found a dead rat under your sink. I'm afraid

146

I'm going to have to close down the kitchen."

I felt faint. "Close us down? A rat in my kitchen?"

"I suspect it was planted," John said. "It looks like it died in a trap, and then someone hid it under the sink and called in an anonymous tip."

"I'm willing to accept that explanation," the inspector said. "But the laundry room ceiling is a problem. As is this," she said, pointing to the Tupperware on the counter.

"What's in it?" I asked.

"Something green and slimy," John said.

I turned to the inspector. "I've got an inn full of guests...if we get all of this taken care of today, is there any way we can keep the kitchen going?"

"What are you going to do about that ceiling?"

"I talked to the insurance company, and they moved things up; the insurance adjustor is coming out today," John said. "In the meantime, if we seal it off with a tarp, will that work?"

"I can come back and check later this week," she said, "but I'm afraid you'll have to stop preparing food until I'm able to clear you."

I looked at John. "Is there any way you could make it back tomorrow morning?" he asked, giving her the full benefit of his green eyes.

"I've got a very busy schedule this week," she said, but I could see her softening.

"Please," John said. "I know you've got a ton on your plate, but we have a journalist here...it could make or break the inn."

She pulled up the calendar on her phone. "Well, I suppose I might be able to fit you in."

"I can pick you up on the mainland in my skiff if that will make it easier. In fact, I'd be happy to take you back now, so you don't have to wait for the mail boat."

She let out a sigh, but I could tell the concept of a few minutes alone with John was a pretty strong inducement. "I suppose that would be okay."

"I'll take you back now then," he said. "What time should I get you in the morning?"

"Would nine be too early?" she asked.

"That would be perfect," John said.

"Well," she said, turning off her phone. "I suppose we're done here. It does look like someone tried to sabotage you," she said, looking at the Tupperware on the counter. "And I guess it wouldn't hurt for you to serve muffins and coffee in the morning. No real cooking, though, until we've cleared you."

I wasn't sure why muffins didn't count as "real cooking," but I wasn't going to argue. I suspected her leniency had more to do with my husband's green eyes than the health department's rules. Thank goodness Biscuit wasn't in her usual place by the radiator. "Thank you," I said. "I really appreciate it."

"Nat just made up a new recipe: chocolate caramel bars," John said, pointing to the cookie jar. "You want one for the road?"

"I really shouldn't," she said, eyeing the jar longingly. "But it has been a while since lunch."

John opened the cookie jar and offered her one, and she accepted with a shy smile.

"Check on Smudge, will you?" John asked in a low voice, coming over to give me a quick kiss on the forehead.

"Still in the workshop?" I asked.

He nodded. "She looks a little listless; I'm a bit worried about her. And the insurance adjustor should be here in an hour," he said.

"Good. The sooner I can get the laundry room cleaned up, the better."

"I'll help you when I get home," he said, and gave my shoulder a quick squeeze before turning back to the inspector. As she followed him out of the inn toward the dock, I leaned against the counter and breathed a sigh of relief, then picked up the offending Tupperware. It had a green lid, and the contents appeared to have once been a pasta salad. I threw it out, then called Spurrell's to make dinner reservations for the entire tour group.

"What's going on?" Martha Spurrell asked.

"I have a kitchen malfunction," I told her.

"We've got a pretty busy night."

"Is there any way you can make it work? I'm desperate."

She sighed. "I guess I can squeeze in another couple of tables on the dock—the weather is supposed to be good. I guess that's one good thing about having a new restaurant on the island," she said, sounding gloomy. "Overflow."

"Are you talking about the new hotel? What have you heard?"

"Nothing good, I'm afraid," she said. "The last thing we need is a Chi-Chi resort. I know it's good for the island economy, but it's not good for island life."

"Are you sure it's a go?"

"I heard the contract has been signed. I think there may be an option period, but I can't think why it wouldn't go through."

"Who bought it?"

"Some firm out of Portland," she said. "It's called MCG or something. Not even a human being." She sighed again. "I guess we can't stave off progress forever."

"Maybe it'll be better than we think," I suggested, trying to sound optimistic.

"We'll see," she said gloomily. "In the meantime, I have you down for seven. Will that work?"

"Absolutely," I said. "You're a lifesaver," I told her.

"Speaking of lifesavers, too bad the captain didn't have one," she said. "I heard someone tied him to an anchor and threw him overboard," she continued, demonstrating how efficiently news travels on a small island. "Any word on what's going on with that?"

"They arrested someone this morning," I told her, "but I think they have the wrong person. Which reminds me—did you know the captain spent a summer on the island about fifteen years ago? He went by the name of Bridges."

She was quiet for a moment. "That was a long time ago. Anyway...I'll look for your group around 7."

"Thanks again. See you later on!" I hung up the phone, then turned to the laundry room. I wanted to cover up the falling ceiling, but the insurance adjustor wasn't due for another hour. First I would check on Smudge, I decided, and then figure out what I was going to bake for tomorrow morning. What I was really in the mood for was my Wicked Blueberry Coffee Cake, but with my recipe binder MIA, I was going to have to come up with something else to make instead.

The breeze off the water was fresh when I opened the back door and headed down to the carriage house, looking out at the blue water and the craggy gray and green mountains of the mainland beyond. The schooner was gone, as if it had never been here, but I looked at the cold water where it had moored and shivered. The sea was beautiful, but it was deadly...as Carl Bridges—Bainbridge—had recently discovered. I averted my eyes and focused on the beach roses blooming on the path, inhaling their deep, winey scent, and let my eyes stray to the few purple lupines that still bloomed in the meadow near John's workshop.

As I opened the door, the smell of roses was replaced by the clean smell of fresh wood, along with the faintest whiff of John's masculine scent. Several of the toy boats that John sold at Island Artists were lined up, waiting for paint, alongside a few beautiful, miniature wood buoys he'd been testing out at the shop this year. His most recent work, a mermaid sculpture that seemed to have formed itself naturally from a huge piece of driftwood John had found down by the pier, was in the center of the room; he'd sent early photos to the New York gallery that sometimes showed his work, and he already had several interested buyers.

That income would certainly help if they shut down the inn's kitchen, I thought gloomily as I ran my hand over the mermaid's silky gray tail, rimed with the suggestion of sea foam.

"Here, kitty, kitty," I called, looking around the stacks of wood for the kitten. I found her in a nest of blankets in the corner under a window. She meowed faintly as I knelt down to check on her. Her food and water bowls looked untouched, and when I picked her up, she felt limp in my hands.

"Poor baby," I said, tucking her against my chest. She let out a raspy purr, sounding like a sick outboard motor. I hurried back to the inn with her and searched for advice on my laptop.

Smudge sat in my lap as I flipped through web pages. Subcutaneous fluids would be ideal—or kitten milk replacement—but I was woefully unprepared for sick kittens. I left a message for Claudette, who had nursed kittens in the past, and found a recipe for chicken and yogurt. I tucked the kitten in near the radiator to keep her warm and grabbed a tub of yogurt and some leftover chicken from the fridge. As I measured the yogurt out into the blender, Biscuit meowed at me from the steps.

"Oh, no...Biscuit..." I put down the yogurt and headed toward her, but she had spotted the kitten. Before I could reach her, she had leaped up to the kitten's bed. "Be nice," I warned—but to my surprise, Biscuit wasn't hissing. As I watched, she nosed the listless kitten, who started purring. "She may be sick," I said, picking up Biscuit. "I don't want you to catch anything if she is." I put my chunky orange tabby down on the floor and turned back to the counter, but before I'd taken two steps, Biscuit was back up and nosing at the kitten again.

"I'm going to have to lock you up upstairs, my friend," I warned her as I put her on the floor again. Biscuit looked up at me and meowed, then started sniffing in the direction of the kitten again. I watched, but instead of jumping up, she sat down at the base of the radiator, as if guarding Smudge. "Are you going to stay there?" I asked.

She gave me an inscrutable look from her green eyes, and after a moment, I turned back to my improvised kitten chow, keeping an eye on Biscuit as I worked.

I put the yogurt and chicken into a blender and pulsed it a few times, then poured the resultant sludge into a bowl and grabbed a spoon. I gave Biscuit a little on a saucer—no need to make her jealous—and then offered the spoon to the weak kitten.

For several seconds, she just sniffed at it, and I was afraid it was going to go nowhere. But then her little pink tongue came out and she lapped up the soupy liquid. I refilled the spoon; she emptied it four times before she turned her head away. I tucked her in to be sure she was warm, then wrapped the bowl in cling film and tucked it into the fridge. I'd have to get rid of it before the health inspector returned, I thought to myself, and glanced back at Biscuit and Smudge. I'd have to relocate them, too…but not right now.

As both cats settled in for a snooze—Smudge in her bed, Biscuit in a puddle of sunlight beneath her—I surveyed the contents of my pantry. I knew I had fresh blueberries in the fridge…and that no coffee cake would come close to my favorite. I was in the mood for cobbler, now that I thought of it, but muffins would be more easily eaten. What about Blueberry Cobbler Muffins? That would work…while John was on the mainland, he could pick up some smoked salmon, bagels and cream cheese. Coffee, muffins, and lox and bagels…it didn't involve cooking, but would still be a full breakfast. I picked up the phone to call John's cell, hoping he was still in range.

He answered on the second ring. "Hi, sweetheart."

"How'd it go with the inspector?"

"She was very understanding," he said. "I just dropped her off."

"Are you still in Northeast Harbor?"

"I was just about to cast off. What do you need?"

"Bagels and smoked salmon." I explained what I was thinking.

"Good thinking," he told me when I'd outlined my breakfast plan.

"Also, Smudge isn't doing too well," I told him, glancing over at where she was nestled into her bed. "I'm wondering if we should take her over to a vet on the mainland this afternoon."

"What's going on?" he asked.

"She's listless. I just got her to eat a little bit of soupy kitten food, but she's not looking too good."

"When is the *Summer Breeze* supposed to be back?"

I glanced at my watch. "A couple of hours," I said.

"I'll check with the vet here," he said. "If we need to, I'll bring her back over this afternoon."

"Thanks," I said. "Martha Spurrell is going to make room for everyone at the pound at 7, and I'm going to get started on the muffins. I appreciate you using your powers of persuasion to keep the inspector from shutting us down."

"I didn't do anything," he protested.

I grinned. "Right. See you soon!"

Once I hung up with John, I called the store to check on Charlene. Her niece Tania answered.

"Hey, Tania. Is Charlene around?"

"She headed over to the mail boat," she told me.

"What's she doing?"

"Going over to visit with Alex."

"Poor thing," I said. My friend had not been lucky in love the last few years.

"She seemed a bit more chipper, actually. Said she's got an idea."

"Really?" I wondered if she'd heard something since our conversation. "Well, tell her to call me when she's back."

"Will do," she told me, then added, "You don't really think he did it, do you?"

"Your aunt thinks he's innocent," I replied, dodging the question. It seemed to satisfy her.

"Oh—I heard something about the captain this morning," she told me as I was about to hang up. "I don't know what it has to do with anything, though."

I stood up a little straighter. "What was it?"

"The rumor is that he spent a summer on the island about fifteen years ago and made off with 50,000 dollars in diamonds from some summer people."

"What?" Eli hadn't mentioned that. "Whose diamonds? Where?"

"Cliffside, I think, " she said. "Marge O'Leary told me about it. Said he was seeing some girl who cleaned houses on the island, and talked her into it. Only she was the one who took the rap for it."

Lorraine? I wondered. Or someone else? "I'm going to have to ask Eli a few more questions when he gets back," I told her. "Maybe that's why he changed his name. Do you think this might have to do with what happened to him?"

"You never know," she said. "I'll see what else I can find out."

"Please do," I said. "I've got to run...but thanks for the update."

"Anytime, Natalie," she told me, then hung up.

I found myself deep in thought as I put the flour canister on the counter and retrieved the blueberries from the refrigerator. A diamond theft at Cliffside. Who had been staying there? I wondered as I measured out blueberries and tossed two sticks of butter into the microwave to soften. The recipe reminded me of my Wicked Blueberry Coffee Cake recipe, only in muffin form. It only took a few minutes to whip up the muffin batter and fold in the blueberries. My mouth watered as I mixed the streusel and then spooned the batter into the muffin cups, sprinkling some of the butter/brown sugar mixture on top. Things might not be going great today, but at least I'd have something delicious to dig into later.

When the muffins were in the oven, I checked on Smudge and tried to get her to eat a little more. She declined the chicken/milk slurry, but was willing to take a few droppers full of cream before drifting back off again. I hoped John called soon. I stroked Biscuit's head—she was being remarkably well behaved—and sat down at the kitchen table, pulling up a search engine on my laptop as the smell of muffins filled the kitchen. First I typed in "Carl Bridges Maine," but nothing came up. When I typed in "Captain Carl Bainbridge," though, there were a number of links to the Northern Spirit Tours web site. But another link came up, too...one from the Society for Animal Welfare. His name turned up on a page linked to the Whale Most Wanted List; I clicked on it, but the link was broken. Had he been reported for taking boats too close to whales? I wondered. I cruised the rest of the site, which seemed to be dedicated to calling out people who had caused damage to whales— Norwegian whalers and the U.S. Navy for starters— but there was nothing else about Bainbridge on the site. A few pages later, I found a picture of him on the deck of a ship that looked nothing like a schooner; he was flanked by two Japanese sailors, and the sun gleamed on his much younger face. I clicked on the web page, but it was in Japanese, and the web translator wasn't much help.

After searching for a few more minutes, I gave up and typed in "Jewel Theft Cranberry Island Maine."

Thankfully, someone at the *Daily Mail* appeared to have been uploading old editions, because I immediately got a hit. "Jewel Heist on Cranberry Island" read the headline. I scrolled through the document. Tania was right; the theft had been at Cliffside, and had involved a diamond tiara— although why on God's green earth anyone would need a tiara on Cranberry island was beyond me. The newspaper was dated around fifteen years ago—right around the time Captain Bainbridge—or Carl Bridges—was working for Eli.

Apparently the visitors were a wealthy society family from Boston—the Henrys, up for a summer family retreat on the island. There was no explanation as to why Margot Henry had brought a tiara to a rugged Maine Island for a family vacation, but evidently she had gone looking for it one evening before dinner and discovered it missing. A local woman was implicated, according to the article—Jenna Spurrell. I knew one Jenna; Jenna Pool, Martha Spurrell's daughter, who had married a local lobsterman a few years back and still helped out at the lobster pound. Captain Bainbridge had cut quite a swathe on the island during his short tenure as Bridges, it seemed. I searched other articles, looking to see if Jenna had been convicted, but couldn't find anything about it. I'd have to ask Charlene. It certainly wasn't something I was going to ask Martha Spurrell about.

The timer beeped, and I pulled the muffins out of the oven. They looked delicious; the streusel topping glistened, and they were studded with dark berries. I had just set them on the cooling rack, resisting the urge to test one, when the phone rang.

"I just talked with the vet," John said.

"And?"

"She's worried about whether Smudge is eating and drinking enough…it could be fading kitten syndrome. Did you get anything down her?"

"I did," I told him.

"She wants to take a look at her, but gave me some stuff in case we can't make it back today," he told me. "I told her Jan was going to be back at the inn in a few hours; she told me keeping the kitten warm and hydrated is the most important thing."

"Should we take her in this afternoon?" I asked.

"I've got time," he said. "I think we should. She's awfully sweet."

"Even Biscuit seems to be warming up to her," I told him, looking over at where my plump tabby had curled up. "Are you sure?"

"Absolutely," he said. "We'll just fill a hot water bottle to make sure she stays warm on the way."

"I'll try to get a little more liquid into her. By the way—did you know Jenna Pool was under suspicion for jewel theft about fifteen years ago?"

"How do you know about that?" he asked. "She went to trial, actually. They never found the tiara—without the evidence, they couldn't convict her. It was pretty traumatic, though."

"I heard she might have been seeing our good captain," I said.

"I thought he was dating Lorraine."

"Evidently he was busy while he was on the island. And there's a rumor he's the one who put Jenna up to stealing the jewels."

"How do you find all this stuff out?" he asked.

"Tania," I said.

"She's learning from her Aunt Charlene, I see,"

John said.

I laughed. "See you in a few?"

"I'm on my way," he said. As I hung up the phone, the door opened; it was Gwen.

"Is my mom here?" she asked, looking worried.

"No," I said. I hadn't seen Bridget, so she was probably still on the mainland. "You're safe. I assume your mom's still out; the next mailboat isn't in for another hour."

She let out an exaggerated sigh and collapsed into a chair. "Adam spent half the day on the phone calling anyone he could think of. The best vessel for the job is down in Cape Cod; it's going to take a while to get here."

"What about the Coast Guard?"

"They don't have a boat to spare," she said. "Adam's been talking with College of the Atlantic to see if maybe there's something we can do in the meantime; they're sending GPS trackers and training the lobstermen to tag the whale if they see her."

"I hope we manage to find her in time," I said.

"Me too," she said. "If it gets caught up on gear and can't make it to the surface for air..." She shuddered, as did I—we were both thinking of the captain, I knew. As I rinsed the beaters, trying not to think about it, Gwen spotted the kitten. "How's it doing?"

"She, actually," I said. "John named her Smudge. She's not doing very well, unfortunately; John's going to take her to the vet in a few minutes, but I'm trying to keep her hydrated. Want to try to get a little bit more cream down her while I wash up?"

"Of course!" she said, and I retrieved the bowl of cream from the fridge and handed it to her along with the eyedropper.

"The health inspector came today and shut us down," I informed Gwen as she gathered the kitten into her lap.

"What?"

"Someone planted a dead rat under the sink," I told her as I swirled soapy water around in the mixing bowl. "And put a Tupperware of something gross in the fridge."

"What are you going to do?" she asked, looking up.

"The inspector's coming to reinspect tomorrow," I said. "We'll take everyone to Spurrell's tonight and do a simple breakfast tomorrow. She likes John, thankfully; with any luck we'll be up and running tomorrow."

"Don't let Gertrude Pickens get wind of this," she warned me. "It will be all over the paper."

"Just what we need. A new hotel going in, a murder at the inn…it's not been the best week."

"At least your mother's not in town trying to break up your engagement," she said.

"She's my sister," I reminded her. "And she's convinced I'm trying to replace her as your mother."

"That's ridiculous," she snorted. "You've never once criticized my choice of clothing or recommended I look into corporate law."

"I think that may be part of the problem," I told her. "I've been encouraging you to adopt my slacker ways."

Gwen rolled her eyes as she introduced the dropper into the kitten's mouth. "Seriously?

"Yes, seriously."

"All you've done is give me the freedom to be myself. I've found the love of my life, I'm pursuing my life's passion, I live in one of the most beautiful places in the world...what more could I want?" Her voice wobbled a little bit. "I just wish she could see that. I always feel like I have to be some superwoman to earn her approval; it's like my choices disappoint her."

"I know the feeling," I said as I rinsed the bowl. "I always felt like whatever I did wasn't quite good enough. I remember having teachers a few years after they taught your mom, and always got the feeling I didn't quite measure up. I did okay, but I was never quite the shining star she was."

"I think I gave up after a while," she said, then looked up at me. "You don't think I'm doing all of this to...rebel against her, do you?"

"What do you mean?"

"I'm doing the exact opposite of what she wants me to do. Am I doing it for me, or just to spite her?"

I put down the bowl and looked at her. "What does your heart tell you?" I asked quietly.

"I love Adam," she said, looking down at the kitten

as it lapped at the eye dropper. "And I love painting...it makes me feel alive. I can't think of anything I'd rather do."

"So there you have it," I told her.

"Aunt Nat, I love my mom...but sometimes I feel like you're the mother I was supposed to have," she said. As soon as the words left her mouth, there was a movement at the end of the kitchen, and something that sounded like a sob. The door to the kitchen was swinging slightly, and my heart contracted.

"What was that?" Gwen asked.

"I'm afraid it might have been your mother," I told her.

"Oh, no," Gwen said. She handed me the kitten and hurried after her.

Bridget still hadn't come up from the carriage house when dinnertime rolled around, and there was no sign of John, who'd taken Smudge to the vet on the mainland. I was about to head out the door when the phone rang.

"How's it going?" John asked when I picked up.

"My sister heard Gwen say she wished I were her mother and hasn't come out of the carriage house all afternoon," I said.

"That good, eh?"

I sighed. "How's the kitten?"

"The vet's running some lab tests, but says it's good that she's eating. She sent some saline and syringes with me; hopefully Jan can help us with them. We need to keep her warm, fed, and hydrated, and she'll call when she has the results."

"Was she optimistic, then?"

"She was," he said. "We just have to keep an eye on her."

"That's some good news, at least," I said. The phone beeped. "I've got another call. Are you on your way back?"

"Heading over now," he said. "Take the call; I'll see you soon!"

I clicked over to an anxious-sounding Charlene. "Natalie," she said. "I got to talk with Alex today."

"I heard you were over on the mainland," I replied, watching out the window as the tour group headed up the hill. They were walking the half mile to the town dock; it was a beautiful evening. "How's he doing?"

"Not well," she said. "But he has some ideas on who might have done it."

"Who?"

"Well," she said. "Apparently Bainbridge and Martina were romantically linked a while back— maybe even engaged. The captain called it off not long ago...said he didn't want to mix business and personal life."

"A little late once you're already dating, but I guess I can understand it," I said. "Hard feelings?"

"Well, she wasn't happy with where he was taking the business...and she wasn't too happy about the way he was cozying up to Stacy."

"The journalist?"

"Alex and Martina surprised them kissing in the galley the other day," she said. "He said Martina looked like she wanted to grab the cleaver right then."

"Did he tell the police about it?" I asked.

"Yes," she said, "but they didn't sound convinced."

"I wonder what the terms of his will are?" I asked.

"Apparently they came up with a business agreement not long ago. They set it up so that if either one died, the partner got the business."

"No family to leave it to?"

"I got the impression they set it up while they were together, and he hadn't gotten around to changing the paperwork."

"Hard to work with an ex," I mused. "She certainly would have a motive."

"And another thing," she said. "He said Bainbridge had made a lot of enemies. He had some unsavory history; he wouldn't tell me more, though."

Because it might incriminate him? I wondered. "Apparently he was loosely linked to a jewel theft at Cliffside about 15 years ago." I told her what I'd learned about his relationship with Lorraine—and potentially with Jenna Pool.

"I remember that," she said. "They never found the tiara—and they couldn't convict Jenna. Not enough evidence."

"Did she incriminate the captain?"

"No, but he left the island right after they arrested her. Broke Lorraine's heart. I never made the connection before...do you think that's why he took off?"

"And maybe why he changed his name?" I suggested.

"It's worth looking into," Charlene said, sounding much more hopeful. "We'll get Alex out of jail...I just know it."

I hoped she was right.

Spurrell's Lobster Pound was humming when I got there twenty minutes later. The insurance adjustor had come on the second-to-last mail boat, and spent twenty minutes inspecting my laundry room and the room above it, whose floors were warped. "Lots of damage," he said, chewing on the end of his pen. He was pale and thin, with an Adam's apple that bobbed disturbingly. I got the impression this was the first time he'd been out of his office for months. "Going to be expensive to fix. Hope you don't have mold issues."

"That's why I have fans going," I told him, pointing to the two room fans we'd set up to dry the place out.

He made another note on his tablet. His Adam's apple bounced up and down as he said, "Well, we'll see what the company says."

"They'll cover it, right?"

"I don't know," he said. "I haven't submitted my report."

I offered him cookies and a ride back to the mail boat, but he declined. I got the feeling he thought I might be trying to ply him with favors.

"When will I know the results?"

"We'll call you," he said.

"When?"

"Within two weeks," he said, and set off up the road. I sighed. I guessed it could be worse.

Now, at the lobster pound, I tried to put thoughts of insurance companies out of my mind. Jenna Pool had already seated the tour group at a long table on the dock outside the low-slung shingled building, and the enticing scent of cooking lobster and baking bread made my stomach growl. Eli was regaling the group with tales of his time on the island, and the whole table seemed enchanted—Stacy was scribbling notes wildly, and even Nan was smiling. Martina, on the other hand, looked tense; her foot tapped a nervous rhythm on the boards of the dock, and her eyes flicked to me. I viewed both Martina and Stacy anew; they were seated as far as possible from each other, I noticed. They resembled each other slightly—both had shiny black hair, but while Martina's was pulled back into a neat ponytail, Stacy's was long and loose. They both shared high cheekbones and dark eyes, and could have been sisters…if I didn't know Lorraine, I would have said the captain definitely had a 'type.'

"How's it going?" I asked as Eli finished telling a story about a gear war that had gone on a few years ago.

"This man is just a treasure," Stacy said, looking up at me with a big smile. "I could write a whole book on him!"

"I'll bet," I said.

"Hi, Natalie," Jan said. "How's the kitten?"

"Could be better," I said. "John took her to the mainland for tests. We might need your help injecting her with saline later."

"Happy to assist," she told me. "Any word on that whale with the gear attached to it?"

"Nobody can get here for a while, I'm afraid. Adam Thrackton—he's a local lobsterman—is trying to work with College of the Atlantic."

"Good," she said. "With all those lobster traps and fishing lines out there," she said, gazing out at the buoy-studded water, "it's a minefield. Can you imagine being trapped underwater and not being able to breathe? What an awful way to go," she said in a low voice. Of course, we all thought of what Martina had pulled up with the anchor the day before.

"Well," I said, anxious to change the subject, "hopefully he'll have good news for us. How was your day?"

"Fun!" Lizzie said. "Only Liam almost pushed me over the side of the boat."

"Did not," Liam protested.

"It scared me. I didn't want to end up like Captain Carl."

"Enough," Yvette said with a strained smile. "Why don't you work on your coloring pages?"

"Or I could tell you a story," Eli suggested with a twinkle in his eye. "I know a lady who found a baby seal and raised her in her laundry room!" he said.

Both kids lit up immediately, and I shot him a grateful smile.

"A baby seal?" Lizzie asked. "I saw a skunk lady the other day, but I'd rather see a baby seal."

I didn't linger to find out what a "skunk lady" was. With things at the table under control again, I drifted to the back of the restaurant, where Martha was busy ringing up orders. "Thanks so much for fitting us in," I said.

"We look out for each other," she said with a smile, but she looked tired.

"Is Jenna here?" I asked.

"She's in the kitchen," Martha told me as she rang up another order. Her graying hair was caught up in a tight bun; it looked like she hadn't had time to touch up her roots, since the white streak was about an inch wide. I touched my own hair; I hadn't started coloring it yet, but my "natural highlights" were becoming a bit more numerous lately.

"I heard your daughter knew the captain," I said as I pushed a lock of hair behind my ear.

Martha froze. "What makes you say that?"

"He used to be Carl Bridges," I said.

"Bastard," she muttered under her breath. I was taken aback; I'd never heard her utter anything close to an obscenity.

"He set your daughter up, I hear."

"Cost us tens of thousands in legal fees. And the thing is? I think he sold the damned thing and walked off with the profits."

"So she did take it?"

She narrowed her eyes at me. "He talked his way into the house while she was there. He talked her into looking at the family's jewelry box—just to see—and must have palmed the tiara. I promise, Jenna had nothing to do with it.

"I won't say anything," I told her. "It was a long time ago. Besides, like you said...we look after each other."

"Thanks." She gave me a grateful smile. "She was totally enamored of him," she told me. "I told her to tell the police, but she refused. Said he was coming back to the island, and they were going to be together."

"But he didn't."

She sighed. "Of course not. Men like him never do. Just leave a trail of broken hearts in their wake."

"And big legal bills," I added. "Do you think Jenna would talk to me about him? About who might have wanted him to..."

"To die?" She snorted. I could see the worry lines in her face; I wondered how many of them had been carved by her daughter's relationship with the late captain…and the fallout. "Fifteen years ago, I would have topped the list, to be honest. But I don't think she has any idea who would have wanted to kill him. I'm not sure she knew he was on the island."

"Still," I said. "She might remember something. The tour naturalist is in jail for murder."

"I heard. The one Charlene's sweet on."

"Yes," I said.

"Women are always so gullible," she said, stabbing a check onto a spike.

"Maybe," I admitted. The thought had crossed my mind. "But it sounds like there were a lot of people who might have wanted him dead. It might be nice to at least consider possibilities…after all, she might be right."

"She might be," Martha said, "but I wouldn't count on it. I'll talk to Jenna, see if she's up for talking about it. It's a little embarrassing, still, I think, and now that she's married…"

"I get it," I told her. "Thanks."

"Any more news on the hotel going in?" she asked.

"With everything going on, it kind of slipped my mind," I confessed.

"Mom!" The call came from the kitchen.

"I'd better go," Martha said.

"I'll take care of the bill for the table," I told her.

"Expensive."

"I know. But it's part of the deal."

"I'll discount it," she told me.

"You don't have to. I really appreciate you fitting us in on such short notice."

"We look out for each other, remember?" she reminded me with a wink as she disappeared back into the kitchen, her no-nonsense rubber-soled shoes squeaking on the wood floor.

It was turning dark by the time we started back toward the inn. I'd treated myself to a bowl of clam chowder and Martha's excellent lemon fool for dessert. The bill was high, but thanks to Martha, was less punitive than it might have been; I left a big tip, though. If I didn't get my kitchen up and running soon, we were going to have a hard time paying the bills, I thought as the sun painted the sky gold, orange, and a deep, beautiful blue.

"It's chilly," Stacy said, pulling her cardigan tighter around her.

"It is," I said, falling in beside her. "How's the article coming?" I asked.

"It's coming along well," she said. "The trip's been more exciting than I thought. Can you hang back with me for a moment?" she asked in a low voice.

"Sure," I said, slowing down and letting the rest of the group drift by. "What's up?" I asked.

"Two things," she said. "First, someone was rifling through your desk the other day."

"What?" I almost stopped. "Who?"

"I imagine one of the guests. They heard me

coming; by the time I got down the stairs, they were gone.

She shrugged. "It could have been. I got the impression that whoever it was didn't want to be found out."

"Thanks for telling me," I said, resolving to look through my desk when I got back to the inn. "What's the other thing?

Stacy lowered her voice further. "Someone further down the hall from me at the inn left the room at around 1 a.m. the night the captain died."

"How do you know?" I asked.

"I was up doing research for my article. I heard the door open and close, and the creak of footsteps."

I thought of Alex, and scanned the guests; that left Nan, Doreen, and the Fowlers. "Did you hear them come back?'

"Yes," she said. "About an hour later."

Enough time to get out to the schooner, kill the captain, and come back, I thought. But why would any of them want to kill Captain Bainbridge? "Did you tell the police this?"

"I did," she said, "but they arrested Alex, so I don't think they're really looking into it."

"Do you think he did it?" I asked—I'm not sure why. Probably because I was nervous about it myself.

"He had a beef with the captain, but I don't think he'd stoop to murder."

"What kind of beef?"

"Bainbridge was involved in some activities Alex

considered…unsavory."

"Why didn't he say something about it?"

"If anything, it would incriminate him more, wouldn't it?" she asked.

"What kind of activities?"

"Let's just say he was involved in some politically incorrect industries," she said vaguely.

"Is that why he changed his name?"

"You know that?" she asked, surprised.

"I do. I hear you and the captain might have been…involved."

She gave a low chuckle. "Oh, yes. Martina walked in while he was putting the moves on me. I let him go a bit—easier to get information that way."

"I thought you were writing a travel article?"

"Sort of," she said, and my antennae pricked up. Was she going to write bad things about the tour— and the inn? I hoped she didn't find out about the health inspector.

"So, what was he involved in?" I asked. But before she could answer, Nan doubled back to us. In a loud voice, she asked, "What are you two gossiping about?"

"Just wondering what it's like to live on an island," Stacy lied smoothly. "Getting some background information for the story."

"Going to feature the inn?" Nan asked.

"We'll see how the article turns out," Stacy said vaguely. I didn't know if that was a good thing or a bad thing.

***

The first thing I did when I got back to the Gray Whale Inn was excuse myself and look through my desk, which was in the front hall by the door. I could tell immediately that Stacy was right; when I opened the file drawer, which contained guest addresses and information, I could tell something was wrong. Although I kept most of the information on my laptop, I had made files for each guest, including addresses and any unusual preferences.

Somebody else had been digging through them. Several pages were misfiled, and several were jammed into one manila folder in the front. I closed the drawer and sat back in my chair, feeling both angry and violated. Someone had gone through my guest files. My recipe binder was missing. And the health department had come based on an anonymous tip.

Was someone on the tour trying to ruin my business?

THIRTEEN

I was still reorganizing the files when Catherine walked up to me, looking elegant as always in slacks and a fuzzy pink cashmere sweater I didn't recognize. "That's where you've been hiding," she said.

"I wish I *could* hide," I told her.

"Sounds like things between you and Bridget aren't going too well."

"They're not," I agreed.

"She told me about everything this afternoon," Catherine said. "It can be hard for parents to let go."

"She's talking to you about it?" I asked.

Catherine nodded. "Wondering where she went wrong. I keep telling her she hasn't gone wrong, but she's still too caught up in thinking her daughter's choices are a reflection of her."

"And studying art on a Maine island isn't exactly high on Bridget's priority list." I grimaced. "Thanks for trying, Catherine," I said, then added, "The health inspector came this morning, by the way. The kitchen is closed because someone called in an anonymous tip; and it looks like someone rifled through my desk."

"Ouch. And I know one of the bathtubs

overflowed, too. Whose room was it?"

"Gayla and Herb Fowler," I told her.

"Those two. Nothing's right for them."

"I had to put them in the captain's former room; they weren't happy about that. It wouldn't surprise me if they called the inspector, but that doesn't explain this," I said, pointing to the files.

"Think it might have anything to do with the new hotel going in?" Catherine asked. "Maybe someone wanted your guest list?"

"I guess that's possible. What do you know about the hotel?" I asked as I shoved another page into a file.

"Murray mentioned it. He's looking into the investors."

"Why?"

"He doesn't like outsiders having such a big impact on the island," she said. "He's made a few offers over the years, but the seller wouldn't budge on the price."

"I heard they're going to put in a huge building," I said.

"If they do, it'll change things around here," she said.

"Not for the better, I'm afraid," I told her.

"People probably said that when you opened the inn here," Catherine pointed out with a smile.

"True," I said. "But I didn't add tennis courts, a swimming pool, and boat service."

"Who knows? Maybe it won't go through."

"They've already had an architect out looking at it."

"Even if they did, Murray said they still have to get a permit, and since they're on the shoreline, they may run into some difficulties."

"Who approves the permits?"

"The code enforcement officer," she said. "Murray's asked him to give him a call when they submit the plans."

"I guess if anyone can scuttle it, Murray can," I said.

"I'll see what he can do," she said with a grin, then came over and squeezed my shoulder. "Don't worry too much about Bridget. You've been just what Gwen's needed; don't back away from her just to appease your sister."

"You don't think I've been too forward?"

"You've treated her like a young adult who is making her own decisions. If she needs you, you're there for her, but you don't try to railroad her. That's what a good mentor does."

"Thanks," I said, feeling relief. "It's hard to know what's right and what's wrong sometimes."

"Isn't being an adult fun?" she said with a grin. She adjusted her pearls and turned to go when something she said struck me. "Does Murray know the investors in Cliffside?" I asked.

"I don't know," she said.

"Ask him," I said. "If it's related to what's going on here," I said, waving at my messed-up files, "I want to know."

"I'll ask," she said. As she spoke, the phone rang. I reached for it; it was Charlene.

"How are you doing?" I asked.

"I was just talking with Eli," she said. "He was out early the morning the captain was found."

"How early?" I asked.

"Like around 2 in the morning early," she said. "He couldn't sleep, so he decided to go work on one of the boats."

"At two in the morning?" I asked.

"I know. Anyway," she said, "He saw a skiff headed toward the inn."

"Where was it coming from?" I asked.

"The other side of the island," she said.

"Does he know if it went to the inn?"

"Unfortunately, no; it went around the point, and he didn't follow it. But at least it's something, right? I told him to tell the police."

"Did he see the skiff come back?"

"Unfortunately not."

I sighed. Nothing seemed to be coming together. Lorraine had a motive—as did her husband, Tom, now that I thought of it—and both of them lived on the other side of the island. I couldn't imagine either of them being killers, but I'd been wrong before. Despite Martha's assertions that her daughter was over it, Jenna Pool was a possibility, too…I hadn't gotten a chance to talk to her last night, but I would. Who else? The first mate? I needed to find out more,

I realized...I had nothing but dead ends.

"Natalie?"

"Sorry," I said. "Woolgathering. Hey—I asked Catherine to talk to Murray, but see if you can find out anything about the new inn going in, okay?"

"Why?"

"Someone went through my files and called the health department on me," I said. "I'm wondering if it's related to whoever's buying Cliffside."

"I'll see what I can do."

I hung up a few minutes later and finished reassembling what was left of my file drawer. I was just putting the last pages back in when John walked in, cradling the kitten.

"How is she?" I asked.

"Doing better," he told me. "She's dehydrated and has a little stomach bug, but the vet says if we can keep her warm, fed, and hydrated, we've got a good shot."

I walked over and petted the kitten's head; she was snuggled into John's chest. "She looks exhausted. How did you keep her warm?"

"I tucked her into my jacket, against my chest," he said, then looked at the open file on my desk. "What's going on here?"

I told him what I'd discovered.

"Someone's trying to mess with us," he said. "First the health inspector, and now this..."

"My recipe binder is missing, too," I reminded him.

"And there's the overflowing water, too," he said.

"The Fowlers said they didn't do it," I told him.

"But their door was locked. If not them, then who?"

"Their room has an adjoining door to the next room. That's where Yvette's family is staying."

"Maybe one of the kids slipped in and played with the faucet," he suggested.

"Or maybe Yvette and Carson have something to do with the purchase of Cliffside."

He sighed. "Let's not think about it anymore tonight," he said. "It's been a long week. I put the salmon in the fridge and the bagels in the bread basket. I vote we go upstairs and snuggle this kitten."

I grimaced. "I got the plastic up on the ceiling in the laundry room, at least—still waiting to hear from the insurance company. Anything else we need to do before the inspector comes back tomorrow?"

"I'll do a last check in the morning. Right now, I think we both need some sleep." The kitten meowed as if in agreement.

"Let me check on Gwen first," I suggested. I had picked up the phone to call Adam when headlights flashed from the top of the hill outside. I recognized the growl of Adam's truck.

"Looks like she's back," John said. We stayed downstairs long enough to say hi to my niece and her fiancé, then headed upstairs together.

***

The one benefit of not having a functioning kitchen was a slightly later wake-up time. Despite the events of the last week, I felt relatively refreshed as I turned off the alarm and tiptoed into the bathroom, leaving John and Smudge curled up together. Biscuit had declined to come upstairs, which was probably for the best, as we were still waiting on results from Smudge's tests.

I ground French Roast coffee and poured it into the coffee maker, looking out the window at the sloping green lawn and the dark blue water below it; the sun was already up, and the tide was high. My eyes swept over the remaining lupines in the field by John's workshop. There was something yellow in among the flowers. Probably a bag blown in off the water, I thought as I filled the coffee maker with water and reached for the bag of bagels.

By the time the guests came down for breakfast, I had a pretty display of smoked salmon, sliced tomatoes and fresh bagels, along with a tray of blueberry cobbler muffins and some fruit. I had just finished setting up the coffee when I noticed that the roses in their little vases were looking a bit limp. I gathered the vases and took them to the kitchen, then headed out the back door to snip some fresh flowers.

The beach roses were brilliant and numerous, if thorny. I snipped a few, inhaling their sweet, wine-like fragrance, and put them in my basket, then glanced over at the lupines. The bag seemed awfully large, now that I was closer. I walked closer, and suddenly felt a chill that had nothing to do with the breeze off the water.

It wasn't a bag. It was Stacy Cox. The reporter was lying spread-eagle in the middle of the lupines, her eyes wide and staring, her tongue sticking out.

I dropped the basket and stepped back, feeling sick to my stomach. After a moment, I forced myself to look again. There was a thin red line around her throat…someone had strangled her.

I was about to turn and run back to the inn when something caught my eye. A note, about a foot away from the body. It was slightly crumpled, but I could read it. *I know something about Bainbridge, but no one else can know I told you. Meet me at midnight behind the inn.*

Someone had lured her with the promise of a scoop. But who?

I paused, surveying the scene; something glinted in the sunlight on the path a few feet away from Stacy. I squatted down to look at it: another hairpin. I'd have to mention it to the police, I thought as I looked back at the young journalist's frozen features.

My heart went out to Stacy…she had just been doing her job. I averted my eyes from her contorted face and headed up to find John.

I hated to wake him, but I didn't really have a choice. Smudge was snuggled in next to him; I wished for a moment I hadn't gone out to snip flowers. On the other hand, it was better for me to find her than the guests.

"John."

He sat up right away. "What's wrong?" he asked as Smudge looked up at him and let out a small meow.

"Somebody killed Stacy Cox. I found her in the lupines by your workshop."

"How do you know someone killed her?"

"She was...strangled, I think." I shivered. "Her tongue was sticking out. It was horrible."

"Are you okay?"

"I'm fine," I said. "But it looks like whoever murdered the captain is still on the loose. And we've got to let the police on the mainland know."

John swung his legs over the side of the bed and reached for his jeans. "Call the mainland; I'll head out back."

"How are we going to hide it from the guests?"

"I don't know that we can," he said.

I sighed. "At least this means Alex is off the hook."

"Not necessarily," John pointed out.

"You think there may be two murderers?"

"They won't rule it out," he said as he slung on a green T-shirt that brought out the color of his eyes. Even with Stacy lying dead in my back yard, John still made my heart skip a beat. "But it is a mark in his favor."

"Poor Stacy," I said. "Oh—there's a note next to her on the ground."

He raised a sandy eyebrow. "You didn't touch it, did you?"

I shook my head. "All I did is look at it. Promise. Anyway, the note said whoever wrote it had information on Bainbridge, and to meet outside the inn at midnight."

"Sounds like Stacy had some inside knowledge someone else was worried would get out."

"Like what?"

"She's a journalist," John said. "I'm guessing she uncovered something someone thought was dangerous."

"I thought she was a travel journalist!"

"Might want to check her out," he said, one hand on the doorknob. "I'll head down and guard the body if you'll call the detectives."

"Got it," I said. "And I might do a little research on Stacy before breakfast."

"Might be worthwhile," he said. "We should probably feed the little one, too," John suggested.

I scooped her up off the pillow and snuggled her into my chest. "I'll take her down with me," I told him as she purred against me.

I spooned some of the cat gruel into a bowl for her—and a bowl for Biscuit, who had taken up residence on the radiator and eyed me with disdain—and watched with relief as the little kitten lapped it up. She seemed to be turning the corner, thankfully.

As I stood up, my eyes were drawn to John's shingled workshop—and the dead woman in front of it. She was so young—only in her mid-thirties. A few years younger than me. Why had she died? Had Martina's jealousy won out? If so, why kill her now, when the captain was dead? Had she seen or heard something she shouldn't have?

And what would the health inspector think of a dead body on the premises? I wondered, then chided myself. There was more at stake than my kitchen. Having a murderer on the loose was a bigger issue than my kitchen troubles. I called the dispatcher and gave him the details. "This means Alex must be innocent, right?" I added at the end.

"This only means there's another homicide," he said.

"What are the odds that there are two murderers on one island?" I asked.

"We'll send someone over," he said shortly, and hung up the phone.

Disgruntled, I pulled out the laptop and ran a search on Stacy Cox. She had a few travel articles, yes—but they dated from five years ago. Her most recent articles were exposés on companies who had polluted waterways or secretly disposed of contaminated fill.

So why was she doing a story on Northern Spirit Tours?

I glanced out at John, who was standing guard, and looked at my watch. Fifteen minutes to breakfast. Enough time to see if there was anything of interest upstairs. I pulled a pair of yellow gloves out of the laundry room and hurried up the stairs, grabbing the skeleton key from under the front desk along the way. That, at least, hadn't been stolen.

As it turned out, I didn't need it; the door was ajar.

My skin prickled as I pushed the door the rest of the way open, half-expecting someone to jump out at me. Which was ridiculous, really, since whoever had killed Stacy was hardly likely to be hanging out in her room eight hours later—assuming the deed was done at midnight.

Whoever it was had been here, though. The desk was a blizzard of papers, and the drawers were on the floor. I took a few steps forward and leafed through the pages. Most of them were on Captain Bainbridge—or Carl Bridges, as he'd been known before. That secret had been uncovered by Stacy, at least.

I looked closer at the papers. There was a registry for a boat called the *Kobyashi Maru*, based out of Japan. Carl Bridges was listed as part owner. Why was she concerned about that? I wondered. Then I picked up the next piece of paper—about the Sea Shepherd, an anti-whaling boat, trying to prevent the *Kobyashi Maru* from taking whales off the coast of Iceland.

My stomach curdled. No wonder she was along for the tour; she seemed to have been doing an expose on Carl's secret ownership of a whale boat in Japan. I looked through a few more pictures; there was one of him helping haul a whale carcass onto the back of a ship. Of course he wasn't worried about getting too close to the whales. He wasn't concerned about conserving them at all, from the looks of it.

There was plenty of incriminating evidence about the captain in Stacy's room. But if he was already dead, why break in and sift through it? Unless they were looking for something specific—something that was no longer here. Like her laptop, for instance; there was no sign of it.

Beside the unruly pile of papers was a black and white composition book; I'd seen her carrying it around with her and taking notes. I flipped through it. "Whale breaching through the dark water," read one entry, and "Captain Bainbridge schmoozing with potential investor Nan McGee." I flipped through to the end—the last few pages were torn out. I caught a few partial words and a number on the remnants of the torn pages—"saw M" and "199," but that was all that was left.

Whatever the searcher was looking for had been written in that composition book, I suspected—and was long gone.

What had she seen? I wondered as I closed the composition book back up and scanned the room. I glanced at my watch—five minutes to go—and did a quick search of the rest of the room. A few toiletries in the bathroom, a bottle of Ibuprofen, and a book on the night table—a murder mystery by Sue Ann Jaffarian, ironically. A moment later, I let myself out of the room, leaving the door ajar behind me. I was just turning around when Nan McGee stepped out of the next room.

"You're tidying rooms on the early side," she remarked, glancing at my gloves. "You forgot to close it," she added, pointing to the still-open door.

"Just checking to make sure there wasn't another water leak," I lied.

"Does that happen often in old houses like these?" she asked.

"There's always something to fix, unfortunately," I said, peeling off my gloves and heading for the stairs. "Ready for breakfast?" I asked, hoping to change the subject.

"I hear the health department was here yesterday," she said. "I'm surprised you're allowed to cook."

"I've got bagels and smoked salmon, and everything should be cleared today. It was just a misunderstanding," I said with a forced smile, wondering how she'd heard about the inspector—or if perhaps she was the one who had placed the anonymous call. But why would she do that? Particularly if she was considering investing in the tour company that used my inn?

"What are your thoughts on Northern Spirit Tours?" I asked. "It's been kind of a crazy week, hasn't it?" And I hadn't even told her that Stacy was dead. Of course, there was always a possibility that Nan was responsible for killing the journalist. In truth, I didn't know much about Nan McGee. Had she killed the captain to drop the value of the tour company—and

190

then killed Stacy before she could write about it? A chill stole down my back at the thought that I might be alone with a murderer.

"It has been a bad week for the company," she agreed. "Fortunately, I'm researching a number of opportunities."

"All in the area?"

"I don't limit myself to one area," she said as I followed her down the hall. "But I do see a lot of potential in this part of the world. Beautiful, unspoiled…"

"Yes," I said. "I hope it stays that way. I'm kind of glad it's not close enough to the mainland to put a bridge in."

"There are other ways to increase traffic though," she told me as we walked down the stairs. As we stepped into the parlor, the police launch appeared at the dock. "Back to do more investigating?" she asked.

"It seems so," I said. "Actually, I found Stacy Cox dead this morning," I said, watching Nan's face.

Her eyes narrowed slightly. "This is a dangerous establishment you're running, it seems."

"It seems to have more to do with the tour than the inn," I pointed out.

"Maybe," she said. "Unless one of your staff is a mass murderer. How did she die, anyway? Someone drown her, too?"

"I don't think I'm allowed to say, actually. Breakfast will be out in a minute if you're hungry; there's coffee on the table."

I abandoned Nan and hurried into the kitchen, where I immediately pulled up her name on my laptop. Several entries came up; philanthropist in Boston, member of a prominent business family...and chair of the board of MCG Venture Capital.

The name rang a bell. It took me a moment to place it—and then I remembered. MCG was the name of the company looking into buying Cliffside.

I caught my breath. Nan McGee wasn't interested in investing in the Northern Spirit Tours—or at least only investing in the tour company. She was planning to buy Cliffside and turn it into a resort.

Was Nan the one who had let the bathtub overflow, and called the health inspector? Not to mention gone through my guest list files? It certainly would explain how she knew my kitchen was closed. Maybe she was planning on buying both Cliffside and Northern Spirit, I thought. But why commit murder just to decrease the value of an acquisition when you already had millions of dollars?

Unless the captain—and Stacy Cox—knew something about her she didn't want out.

I hurried to put together the breakfast platter, then headed into the dining room and laid them out, pouring Nan coffee. A moment later, Gayla and Herb came down, complaining about the overcast weather.

"Oh, good morning!" Gayla said as she rounded the corner and saw Nan sitting by the window. "Mind if we join you?"

"Sure," Nan said. I hurried over to fill their coffee as Nan filled them in on the police launch.

"What happened?" Herb asked.

"Apparently another one of the inn's guests was killed off last night," Nan informed them. "The journalist—Stacy Cox."

"What happened to her?"

"She won't say," Nan said, nodding toward me. "But the police are investigating, so I'm guessing it wasn't a heart attack."

"Are we safe here?" Gayla chimed in.

"I'm sure the police will be in to talk with everyone shortly," I said. "While you're waiting, though, breakfast is lox and bagels this morning, and I made a batch of Blueberry Cobbler muffins."

"Even with your kitchen closed?" Gayla asked.

I gave her a tight smile and retreated as the three of them launched into a lurid discussion of what might or might not have befallen Stacy Cox.

Once they were well underway, I hurried up the stairs, skeleton key in hand. I crept down the hall as quietly as I could and unlocked the door to Nan's room. If she was the one responsible for my guest files being ransacked, there should be some evidence of it here. I closed the door quietly behind me, glad to still hear the distant murmur of conversation, and headed for the desk.

At least she was orderly, I thought as I opened the drawers. I didn't like the idea of snooping, but I needed to know if she had stolen my files—or, now that I thought of it, my recipe binder. The standard notepad and pen were there, and her laptop was neatly closed on top of the desk, but there were no papers in the desk, or anywhere else.

Until I hit the night table. Inside was a folder with a valuation of Cliffside—and a copy of a site plan. Pools, tennis courts, a spa, a pier with shops—it looked like its own enormous, self-contained community.

I shut the folder and slid it back into the drawer, then did a quick survey of the rest of the room. No guest lists, no recipe binder—but I didn't need to find those to know I was harboring a future competitor.

A moment later, I closed the door behind me and headed downstairs, trying to stifle the urge to put bleach in Nan McGee's coffee.

Jan had arrived in the dining room by the time I got back. "Not good news this morning, eh?" she asked, nodding toward the police launch.

"I'm afraid not," I said.

"It's too bad. She was a nice woman," she said. "Nerve-wracking, too, though, I must admit. How's the kitten?" she asked.

"I think she's doing better, but when you're done with breakfast, I'd love it if you could take a look at her," I said, trying not to stare daggers at Nan McGee, who was deep in conversation with Herb and Gayla. Who were probably trying to interest her in some piece of Iowa farmland, I thought, gritting my teeth.

"I'd love to," she said. "She'd probably go for some

of this salmon if you're having a hard time getting her to eat. It's delicious."

"Glad you like it."

"And these muffins are to die for," she told me. "I would love the recipe, if you're willing to share."

"Happy to," I said, smiling, and a moment later, retreated to the kitchen.

Gwen had gotten up while I was up checking on Nan's room, and was now squinting out at the launch. Her hair was up in a loose, romantic knot on top of her head, and she wore a long, flowing skirt and a hand-painted tank top. "What happened?"

I filled her in on the details.

"That's horrible," she breathed. "At least they can't blame Alex for it."

"I asked the detective about that, but he seems to still think Alex is on the hook for the captain's death."

"So we've got two murderers on the island?"

"That's his theory."

"Who did it, do you think?" Gwen asked. "And I wonder who's next?"

"Hopefully we're done with murders for a while," I said. "And I have no idea who's responsible. But guess who's buying Cliffside?"

"Who?"

"The investor—Nan McGee. She's got the survey and plans for an enormous resort in her room."

"What's she doing here, then?"

"Sabotaging my inn and poaching my guest list, I suspect."

"Do you think so?"

"I do. I wouldn't be surprised if she caused that leak, either."

"But I thought she was looking to invest in the tour group."

"Maybe she's buying both," I suggested. "Starting her Maine coastal empire."

She was about to respond when Bridget showed up at the back door, looking pale. "Gwen," she said. "Thank God you're okay. I saw the police launch, and…" She shuddered. "I thought you'd be safe on this island, but people are dropping like flies."

"I'm fine," Gwen told her. "How did you sleep?"

"Not too bad," she said. "But I can't believe that woman died practically on my doorstep."

"Did you see or hear anything last night?" I asked.

"No," she said. As she spoke, one of the detectives knocked on the door.

"Come in," I called, and the detective let herself into the kitchen along with a cool breeze.

"Good morning," she said.

"Thanks for coming out," I told her with a smile. "Can I get you folks coffee, and maybe some muffins?"

"Coffee would be great. But I'm afraid I'm going to have to question your guests again," she told me. "And you."

"I figured as much," I said. "They're in the dining room, along with the coffee."

"Were you all here last night?" she asked, looking

at Gwen and Bridget.

"I was upstairs, asleep, and my mom was in the carriage house," Gwen answered.

She asked them a few more questions—when they got in, what they'd been doing, and if they'd heard or seen anything—the answers were negative—and then turned to me. "I have a few questions for you, too."

"I'll check on the guests," Gwen said, then turned to the detective. "How do you take your coffee?"

"Cream and sugar," she told her. "Thanks. Please let me know if there are any guests not at breakfast."

"I will," Gwen replied, heading into the dining room.

"May I?" the detective asked, gesturing to a chair.

"Of course," I said. "I hope you don't mind if I work while we talk, though," I said. "I've to clean the kitchen."

"No problem," she said. As I loaded coffee cups into the dishwasher, she asked me the standard questions—where I'd been, if I'd heard anything, etc. Since John had been with me all night, I wasn't too worried about my alibi, but I was curious what he was thinking.

"Are you thinking there may be two murderers, then?" I asked as I wiped down the counter.

"We can't rule anything out," she told me. "The murders were very different, after all."

"Still," I said. "What are the odds that there are two murderers at large?"

"We have to consider all options," she said. "Do you have any insight into who might have wanted to kill the captain—or Stacy Cox?"

"I do know that the captain had a bit of a shady past," I told her. "I'm sure you know his last name used to be Bridges; he worked on the island several years ago."

"We uncovered that," she said. "He was seeing a couple of young women, I understand."

"Yes," I said, impressed. "Do you think that might be connected? Or maybe that whoever killed Stacy also killed the captain?"

"Maybe," she said. "It's highly unlikely that there are two murderers on an island of this size."

"You're assuming there's only one murderer, then?"

"Not necessarily. We can't rule anything out."

"It may be that Stacy was writing something more than a travel article," I suggested, remembering the note I'd seen by her body—and the papers in her room. "And somebody didn't want something to get out. Her door is ajar, by the way; I peeked in, and it looks like someone ransacked her room."

"I know," she told me with a nod. "I've got detectives looking through it now."

"Back to your question," I said, "one of the guests was considering investing in the tour company; evidently she's also investing in a property on Cranberry Island. I know it's not murder, but someone's gone through my desk, ransacked my files, sabotaged my kitchen and potentially damaged the inn."

Her eyebrows rose. "Do you know who?"

"The logical choice would be the investor—Nan McGee," I said, "but the overflowing bathtub was in the Fowlers' room. I told him the details of what had happened. "The health inspector closed my kitchen because of the sabotage; she's coming back today."

"Did you keep the evidence?"

"I got rid of the dead rat someone planted," I told her, "but the Tupperware is still in the trash."

"Unfortunately, storing spoiled food in the fridge is hardly a crime," she told me, "or I'd be locked up for life. There's not much I can do about that, I'm afraid."

"I just wanted you to be aware of it," I told her. "If anything comes up in your questioning, please let me know."

"I will. Again…you didn't hear anything last night?"

"Nothing at all," I told her. "It was a shock this morning."

"I can imagine. I'm sorry it's been such a horrible week."

"Me too," I said, warmed by the sympathy. The detective had just turned to go to the rest of the inn when there was a knock at the door; it was the health inspector.

Perfect timing.

***

"What's going on here?" the inspector asked as I led her into the kitchen; the inn was buzzing with investigators.

"There was a death on the lawn last night," I said.

"Not food poisoning, I hope?"

"No," the detective said, walking up to her. "It was homicide, and poison wasn't involved."

"Who are you?"

"Detective Fleming," she said. "You must be the health inspector."

"Yes," she responded. "What is all this about?"

"Natalie was just telling me about the situation; it seems that someone has been sabotaging her inn. We have a suspect, and are investigating."

"What do you mean?"

"I can't give you details right now—it's an active investigation—but someone appears to be stealing her trade secrets and client list and attempting to paint the inn in a negative light."

"That's horrible!" she said.

"I'm not suggesting you not do your job, of course—like you, I take safety very seriously—but I just wanted to make you aware of the circumstances."

"Of course, officer," she said. "I'll keep it in mind."

"Let me show you what we've done," I said, sending Detective Fleming a grateful look and leading her to the laundry room first.

It was a short tour. "Well, you certainly have put

in an effort," she said when I closed the fridge. "It all looks good; and considering the extenuating circumstances the detective mentioned, I'll allow you to re-open. But I'm going to have to come back and inspect again soon."

"Thank you," I told her. "I can't tell you how much I appreciate it."

"I just can't believe someone stole your guest files."

"And my recipe binder," I said.

"Is it the same person who caused the water damage?"

"I don't know," I said. The Fowlers and the McGees had had "Do Not Disturb" signs on their doors all week, and I hadn't spent much time in their rooms. "All I can say is, thank you for your understanding."

"I'm not giving you a free pass," she warned. "I'll be back soon. But please let me know how it works out with the saboteurs. And I hope you don't lose any more guests."

"Me too," I said. "It's horrible; both victims were cut down way too young."

"And it's not the best business model in the world, for sure. On the plus side, at least you won't have a reporter talking about it to the world."

"On the other hand," I pointed out, "murdering a reporter at my inn is hardly a way to avoid bad press."

"I hope you survive all of this," she said. "It's hard to overcome negative PR."

"Thanks for the encouragement," I said as I

walked her out. Even though the health inspector had given my kitchen a pass, I felt worse than I had before she came.

It was hours before things settled down enough for me to reclaim my territory—my kitchen. Bridget, thankfully, had escaped to the mainland to "research" more galleries for Gwen, John was taking care of the rooms, and Smudge was sleeping peacefully in John's workshop, snuggled up to a hot water bottle; we'd taken a few minutes to inject her with saline, and she was looking better.

I was about to make a fresh pot of coffee and sit down on the porch when the phone rang.

"Someone killed the journalist," Charlene said into the phone. "Does that mean Alex is free?"

"Unfortunately not," I said as I grabbed the flour canister.

"Why not? Honestly. Do they think there are two murderers on the island?"

"I know," I said, "but I'm not in charge."

"Well, I'm sorry about Stacy, but I can't help feeling a little bit relieved. Maybe it's a good thing Alex is in jail; no one can accuse him of killing her. What happened, anyway?"

"I think she was strangled. I saw her right outside the house; she was going to meet someone, apparently."

"Poor thing. What was she working on?"

"I think she was doing an article on Bainbridge— he had ties to a Japanese whaling vessel, apparently."

"That doesn't make sense. He's already dead; who would want to stop her from publishing an article on him?"

"I suspect her death was related to something else," I said, thinking of the documentation I'd found in the reporter's room. Anyone trying to cover up his history would have taken the papers with them and destroyed them. "Is Alex holding up?" I asked, changing the subject.

"He is," she said. "I'm sick with worry about him, though. We haven't known each other long, but I really do think I'm in love with him."

I didn't know what I thought about that, but it wasn't worth discussing. "Has he told you what he was doing after he left your house?"

"He was out walking and thinking," she said.

I wasn't convinced, but I didn't say anything.

"How are you feeling about Cliffside, by the way?" my friend asked, changing the subject.

"I'm not thrilled," I confessed. "Catherine's asking Murray to talk to the code enforcement officer and see what can be done."

"She's got him wrapped around her little finger, doesn't she?"

"I'm not complaining," I said.

"Oh—I almost forgot to tell you. Tom and Lorraine had a big blow-out last night; apparently he spent the night at the co-op."

"What?" Had he discovered the love letter, too? And if he was at the co-op, I thought to myself, who would give him an alibi? "How do you know?"

"Adam found him there when he went in this morning," she said.

"Was anyone with him?"

"Why?" She paused and drew in a breath. "Are you thinking maybe Tom killed the journalist?"

"I'm not necessarily thinking that, but he's definitely linked to Bainbridge—or Bridges."

"You mean that old relationship the captain had with Lorraine?"

"Yes, and there may still have been some bad blood over those traps he pulled all those years ago. The journalist piece doesn't make sense, though—unless she was planning on publishing something that would be bad for the Lockharts."

"Now that I think of it, I did see her down at the Lockharts' a couple of days ago," Charlene said. "And apparently she was down at the pier asking questions, too."

"About what?"

"I don't know. Selene MacGregor at Island Artists mentioned that she was kind of nosy."

"I'll ask her, then," I said. "Any word on the kitten?"

"None yet," she said, "but I'll let you know."

I hung up with Charlene a moment later, slightly cheered by her improved mood, but still concerned about the fact that there were two unsolved murders at the inn.

As I filled the coffee pot with water, I turned the problem over in my head. It wasn't just logic that told me the two deaths were the work of the same hand; logic told me as much, too. But why?

I thought about what I knew of Bainbridge. He and Alex obviously had come to blows over the whales; but there was no way Alex could be responsible for what happened to Stacy.

And then there were the Lockharts. Why would Lorraine kill an ex-lover she was obviously still emotional about? And even if she had, why kill Stacy? Unless, I thought, thinking back to the kiss Stacy had told me about, she was jealous. But if Bainbridge was already dead, why go after Stacy? Unless Stacy knew who the killer was, it didn't make sense, I thought as I scooped fragrant coffee beans into the grinder and pressed down on the lid. Had Stacy been the second person out and about the night Bainbridge died? Had she spotted the killer? If she had, maybe that was why someone had gone through her room; looking for notes she might have made about the killer's identity. As much as it pained me to think either of my friends could be capable of murder, I couldn't discount Tom, either.

As I poured the coffee into the filter and turned the pot on, I reflected that Lorraine and Tom weren't the only ones Bainbridge had tangled with, though. If it was true that Martina had lied to me about the business, and that she knew she was going to inherit it, she had plenty of reason to do so. I thought back to the conversation I'd overheard after the whale outing; she'd told the captain she would take care of Alex in a tone of voice that made me shiver. Maybe she'd killed two birds with one stone—taking out both Alex and the captain. Had she killed Stacy out of jealousy...or because she suspected she was onto her?

And then there was Nan McGee, who was evidently ruthless in the business department. Had she done in the captain as an investment strategy? It seemed farfetched, but I couldn't discount it. It was always possible he had learned something about her shady deals—and told Stacy about them, too.

The jewel theft was another possible factor. Had Jenna harbored a grudge all these years...and taken the opportunity to avenge herself? Maybe she did Bainbridge in and then thought Stacy saw her...then lured her in to make sure the reporter didn't connect the dots.

The coffee pot had just finished brewing Gwen walked into the kitchen.

"How's it going?" I asked as I poured myself a mug. "I just made coffee."

"Thanks; I'll take a cup," she said. "John and I split the rooms, and I've got mine done," she said.

"Great."

"It doesn't take long when half of them have do-not-disturb signs," she said as she filled a cup with the dark brew.

"I know about the Fowlers, but who else?"

"The first mate—well, now the captain, I guess—and now the investor."

"Nan McGee. I believe she's the one buying Cliffside." I glanced up at the gap in my cookbook shelf. "I hate to say this, but let's go in anyway. I suspect she's the one who stole my recipe binder. Is she in the inn now?"

"No," she said, sipping her coffee. "I saw her walking up the main road with a few other guests a few minutes ago."

"Probably going to meet with her architect at Cliffside," I said, rolling my eyes. I put down my coffee mug. "Let's go."

Gwen smiled at me, and I followed her up the steps to Nan's room. I shivered at the sight of Stacy's door; the investigators had finished a little while ago. Ignoring the "Do Not Disturb" sign, my niece slid the skeleton key into the lock and pushed the door open.

"At least she's neat," I said, eyeing the carefully made bed and the clutter-free surfaces. The plans I'd seen the other day were no longer in evidence.

"Where do you think she'd hide it?" Gwen asked.

"I don't know," I said as my niece opened the drawers of the dresser. I hurried over and checked under the bed; together, we scoured the room. Unfortunately, though, either the investor wasn't hiding anything, or she'd taken it with her.

John was stepping out of Yvette and Carson's room when we closed her door behind us. "Man," he said. "I'm glad we don't have kids."

"That bad?"

"Goldfish crumbs everywhere," he said. "And it looks a little like a children's toy store exploded in the corner."

"No permanent damage?"

"Not that I could tell," he said, then realized which room we were coming out of. "Wait. I thought she had a do-not-disturb sign up."

"I was looking to see if my recipe binder had migrated to her room," I said. "Not to mention our client files."

"It's not in the kitchen somewhere?"

"No," I said. "And no Wicked Blueberry Coffee Cake until I track it down."

He bit his lip and scanned the other two do-not-disturb signs. "Have you been in the Fowlers' room?"

"Not since they created Niagara Falls, no."

"They were awfully protective of their things. I think it's worth a look," he said.

"Wait a moment. This is coming from Mr. Don't-Ever-Snoop?"

"We're talking about your coffee cake here," he said. "I'd say that constitutes extenuating circumstances. Are they here?"

"I saw them heading up the road behind Nan McGee," Gwen told him.

He hesitated for a moment, then said, "I vote we go in."

"Seconded," I declared, and Gwen slid the

skeleton key into the door. A moment later, it swung open.

"Wow," I said, surveying the mess. Clothes lay scattered across every surface, the sheets were a knot in the middle of the bed, and a sopping wet towel sat in the middle of my hardwood floor.

"I know they have a do-not-disturb sign, but I'm not leaving that there," I announced. When I picked it up, a white spot remained on the finished floors.

"That will come up, right?" I asked John.

"If not, I'll take care of it," he said. "Now let's find that binder."

Quickly, the three of us began moving clothes and opening drawers, searching for the missing binder. As I took on the night tables and John went through the dresser, Gwen walked into the bathroom.

"Ugh," she said. "It's like they had a toothpaste war."

"That's not the only thing in here," John said, pulling a wad of papers out of the bottom drawer of the desk. "Look familiar?"

"My client list," I said. "But why would the Fowlers want my client list?"

"Maybe they're the ones planning on opening the inn at Cliffside."

"But that was Nan."

"Nan may be the investor," he said. "Somebody's got to run it."

"They did follow her up the road," Gwen pointed out as she ran a hand under the mattress. "Wait a minute," she said, and pulled out a familiar looking three-ring binder. "This what you were looking for?"

"It is," I said, grimacing. "I think we need to have a talk with the Fowlers when they get back. This explains why they 'accidentally' left the water on; it was sabotage, after all."

"It looks like they're all here, but I think we need to put a lock on the front desk," John added, leafing through the papers. "This is a mess. Do you think they had a chance to copy them?"

"I hope not," I said. "I'm just glad we have it all back. I'm just not sure how we're going to explain how we tracked this stuff down."

"I vote you just say that you heard water running and were worried something might be overflowing, and happened to find your papers."

"Anything to link them to Bainbridge or Stacy?"

"No," John said. "But what would their motive be?"

I shrugged. "Maybe they didn't want McGee investing in the tour group instead of the inn," I suggested.

"And maybe Stacy saw something that would implicate the Fowlers."

"Someone from the second story did leave the inn the night he died," I said. "And I did see Stacy listening in on conversations more than once. Maybe she heard them talking about it."

"It's a reasonable motive. So we have another suspect," John suggested.

"We've got Martina, Nan, the Lockharts…"

"The Lockharts?" Gwen asked.

"Tom was sleeping at the co-op the night Bainbridge died," I said.

"Why?"

"Lorraine dated him a long time ago," John supplied. "They had an argument over it."

"So neither one has an alibi," Gwen said. "But I just can't imagine either of them being a killer."

"I doubt Lorraine would leave the kids at home in the middle of the night," I said.

"We still can't rule her out," John said. "As much as I'd like to. Any other potential suspects, Ms. Holmes?"

"The only other one I could think of was Jenna Pool," I suggested. "After all, he got her into hot water over a jewel theft about fifteen years ago, evidently."

"But why not kill him then?"

"He skipped town, then. Maybe she couldn't get to him."

"I wonder if anyone saw them together?" I mused. "I'll have to ask Charlene; if anyone knows or can find out, it's her."

"Anyone else on the list?" Gwen asked. "The Easter Bunny? Maybe Liam and Lizzie?"

"I'd like to put Doreen on the list, to be honest, but I'm sure she's allergic to death."

"Most of us are," John said. "Both crimes required some strength. Do you think Gayla and Herb could manage it? They're a bit older."

"Older doesn't mean weaker," I said. "Besides, they

could have worked together."

"That's true. What I can't figure out is, did they go to the boat in a dinghy with the captain?"

"If they knocked him out, they could have put him in the boat and then pulled him onto deck of the *Summer Breeze*...or someone could have gone aboard, pulled up the anchor, and then attached him to it."

"Or he could have gone to the schooner willingly...thought it was for another reason."

"Martina could have asked him to check something out," I suggested. "Although there was another skiff out that night...from the other side of the island. It could be unrelated...or it could be someone who's involved, or at least saw something."

"Has Charlene heard anything?"

"If she has, she hasn't told me, and I just got off the phone with her a little while ago."

"Surely someone would know who was out," John said. "Everyone seems to know everything on this island."

"Maybe it will come to light," I said. "In the meantime, are we done in here?"

"I think so," John said.

"Should we say something to them, or let them figure it out on their own?" I asked.

John chuckled. "What are they going to do, come and ask why the things they stole from the inn are missing?"

"Good point," I answered. "But I'm going to store

my binder upstairs while they're still here—and see if Murray can find out if the Fowlers are involved in Cliffside. I guess if they did kill Stacy to cover up their connection with Bainbridge's murder, it would make sense to go through her room and make sure she hadn't recorded the connection."

"Her laptop was gone, right?" Gwen asked. "Whoever went through her room stole it, presumably, but it's not here."

"Maybe they got rid of it and any other incriminating things so that the police wouldn't find it," John suggested.

"It's not here, though. So does that point suspicion away from the Fowlers?" Gwen asked.

"Just because it's not here doesn't mean they didn't take it. They could have gotten rid of it in the water, or tossed it off a cliff."

"Hopefully it will turn up," I said, "and we'll find something to exonerate Alex."

"Are you thinking he's innocent, then?" Gwen asked.

"I think it's highly unlikely that there are two murderers on Cranberry Island," I responded. "And it's hard to kill someone when you're miles away and locked behind bars. Maybe it's a good thing they arrested him after all."

"The murders could be related," John said, "but there are no guarantees."

I turned to look at my husband. "Really?"

"Correlation does not mean causation," he said.

I rolled my eyes. "Well, in this case, I think you're wrong. And I'm going to start by checking to see if Catherine's back, stopping in at Cliffside and heading down to the store and talking to Charlene."

"How will that help?"

"I don't know that it will, but I've got to do something," I said.

"I'll take care of dinner, then," John said. "At least we have the kitchen open!"

"Amen to that," I agreed as I hugged my binder to my chest and stepped out of the Fowlers' messy room.

Catherine wasn't home, so I hopped in the van and headed toward Cliffside. Sure enough, Nan was tramping around the grounds with the Fowlers, a stylishly dressed woman I didn't recognize trailing in her wake.

I pulled the van over and got out, hailing my guests. "Out for a hike?" I asked.

Nan looked startled, and Herb Fowler looked as if I'd caught them with their hands in the cookie jar. Gayla, on the other hand, pressed her lips together into a look of disapproval. "We're just taking a look at the place," she said.

"You must be an architect," I said, addressing the woman I didn't know.

"I am," she said, adjusting her rectangular glasses. "Do I know you?"

"No," I said, walking over and extending a hand. "I'm Natalie Barnes. I run the Gray Whale Inn. Congratulations on the commission to turn this place into a resort; when do you break ground?"

"Thanks," she said, shaking my hand. "Assuming all goes well with the permitting, we're thinking in another month or so, right?" she asked, turning to Gayla.

Gayla opened her mouth, but nothing came out.

"Get it going before winter starts," I supplied for her. "Good thinking." I turned to Herb and Gayla. "So is this why you flooded the room and sabotaged my kitchen? Trying to put me out of business?"

Gayla's eyes flicked to her husband, and after a moment's pause, she swallowed and said, "I don't know what you're talking about."

"Sabotage? What *is* she talking about?" the architect asked, looking confused.

"She's a bit histrionic," Nan said, stepping in. "Her guests have been dropping like flies; I'm sure it must be very upsetting to have her establishment linked with homicide in the news so often."

"Not as bad as ending up behind bars for homicide," I said lightly, staring at Gayla. "Well, I'll let you get on with things." I turned back to the architect. "Permitting moving along okay?"

"We're still working on it," she said, looking uncomfortable.

"Good luck," I said. "Do you have a card?"

"Why do you need a card?" Nan asked.

"Considering expanding?"

"You never know," I said with a grim smile. "Have a nice day."

"Any word on Stacy?" Charlene asked when I walked into the Cranberry Island store a few minutes later. Gwen was already there, sitting at the counter in the back. I walked past the overstuffed couches in the front of the store to join them. I was glad to see that Charlene looked better today; her hair was styled, and I could tell she'd put on lipstick.

"Not yet," I said.

"And no cookies, either," she said, glancing at my empty hands. "What kind of friend are you, anyway?" she said with a half grin.

"A friend with questions," I said, my recent encounter still on my mind despite that morning's tragedy. "About Cliffside, for starters. I haven't seen Catherine; do you have any idea where things are on permitting?"

"No, but I'll see what I can find out," she said. "But back to Stacy. I heard you found her."

"I did," I said, shuddering at the memory. I lowered my voice. "Someone had written her a note saying they had some information to share on Bainbridge—Bridges. It was right next to the body, but don't say anything; I don't think the police want that out."

"Do you think it was someone at the inn?"

"I don't know," I said, and went over the list of suspects I'd come up with earlier that day.

"Martina seems like the obvious choice," Charlene said. "You've got means—she had total access to the boat—motive, which she's got in spades, since she inherits the business and was jealous of Stacy—and opportunity."

"It would explain Stacy's murder, too," Gwen said.

"I guess," I said. "She told me she didn't know how the inheritance would work out. I don't know if she was lying or not, but I still feel like we might be missing something."

"Like what?"

"Someone saw a skiff out on the water the night the captain died. I don't know why, but I think it's got to be connected."

"The Lockharts?" Gwen looked appalled. "Do you really think Tom or Lorraine would do something like that?"

"I'd like to think they wouldn't, but we can't rule it out," I said.

"And then there's Jenna. She's a bit of a dark horse," Charlene said. "As far as I know, she didn't even know Bainbridge was here."

"She's so quiet, how would you know?" Gwen asked. "Although she did look pretty upset the other day when I was swinging by Island Artists with a couple of watercolor paintings."

"Did you talk to her?"

"Only briefly," she said. "She was arguing with her

mother about something; I saw them having angry words out by the end of the pier."

"What did she say when you talked to her?"

"She told me I was lucky my mother lived in California."

"Ouch," I said. "No idea what they were arguing about?"

She shook her head. "Nope."

"Think Jenna was getting involved with the good captain again?" Charlene asked.

My niece's hand leapt to her throat; she looked horrified. "But she's married!"

"Lorraine saw him, and she's married, too," I pointed out.

Gwen's eyes widened. "You think they were...together?"

"I think Lorraine was still carrying a torch for him," I said, remembering how upset Lorraine had been, and her regretful words about roads not taken. "And I know they talked. But I don't know that anything else happened. She and Tom did have an argument, though; he ended up sleeping in the co-op the night Stacy died."

"That's not good," Charlene said. "I don't imagine anyone else was with him?"

"Evidently not," I replied. "No alibi."

"Where was Jenna Pool?" Gwen asked.

"No way to know."

"Might be worth talking to her, don't you think?" Charlene asked.

"You're right, I think. I'll stop by there next," I said.

Charlene smoothed back a lock of her caramel-colored hair. "Want me to go with you?"

"I don't want her to feel like we're ganging up on her," I said. "But keep an ear out and let me know if you hear anything, okay?"

"Of course," my friend said. "Do you really think we'll be able to clear Alex?"

I put on what I hoped was an encouraging smile. "We'll do our best."

"Is it safe to go back to the inn?" Gwen asked as I turned to leave the store.

"If you're talking about your mom, she wasn't there when I left, but I've been gone a while."

"Maybe I'll just stay with Adam until she's gone back to California."

"She loves you, you know."

"I know. It's just...hard to be around someone who tells you you're doing everything wrong."

"Believe me," I told her as I slid off the stool and headed for the front door. "I get it."

Jenna Pool lived in a small, but tidy house tucked back in a copse of evergreens, just two houses down from Emmeline Hoyle. Pots of impatiens flanked the wooden steps leading up to a glassed-in porch in which a sea glass mobile—handmade, I was guessing—gleamed in the sun.

I knocked on the door. A moment later, there were footsteps, and Jenna came to the door. I knew she had to be at least 30, but she looked very young; something about her reminded me of a spooked deer. She was dressed in tight blue yoga pants and an oversized plaid flannel shirt that was off a button.

"Hi," she said, and I got a strong whiff of alcohol. "Is everything okay?"

"It is," I said. "I was just wondering if I could ask you a couple of questions."

Her bloodshot eyes darted away from me, and then back. "About what?" she asked, swaying slightly in the doorway.

"About Captain Bainbridge," I said quietly. "You knew him as Carl Bridges. I understand he made life very difficult for you."

She swallowed hard. "How do you know about that?"

"Eli recognized him," I said. "It sounds like he really left you in a terrible spot."

Her eyes welled with tears. "It shouldn't upset me so much, but it still does," she confessed. "I loved him so much. I still don't believe he was responsible for what happened. The suspicion here destroyed his career, so he had to find a job overseas...that's why he left. My mother still doesn't believe me...blames me for everything."

"From everything I've heard, it wasn't your fault," I said gently.

"I'm sorry," she said, opening the door wider. "I

shouldn't leave you standing out here on the porch. Come in," she said.

I followed her as she wove through the glassed-in porch and into the living room. Although it was small, it was well kept, with blue rag rugs, a slipcovered couch in the living room and several jars with sea glass on the windowsills. There was a big tumbler of what looked like Coke on the living room table, half-gone; something told me it was more than just a soft drink.

"Do you want a soda, or a cup of coffee, or tea?"

"A cup of coffee would be great," I said. I sat at the small kitchen table while fumbled with the coffee things, debating whether I should offer to help, but she managed with only a few extra grounds and some water on the floor. She got it started, then sat down at the table across from me. "Oops. I forgot my own drink," she said, and wandered back into the living room, returning a moment later with her giant glass.

"And thanks for talking to me."

"I still can't believe he's gone," she said. "I shouldn't have, I know… I'm married to Bill, but I think Carl was the love of my life. Everyone thought he set me up, and that I was stupid to still love him, but…I do."

"That's got to be really hard," I said.

"It is," she said, taking a big swig from her "soda" and giving me a strong whiff of what I suspected was rum. "And now he's gone," she continued, tears streaming down her face, "and we'll never be together."

"Did you see him when he came back to the island?"

"We got together once," she told me. "He came to the house during the day, while Bill was gone. He said he was so sorry for leaving…that he thought I hated him, and that's why he didn't come back." She rubbed at her eyes. "He said he thought I blamed him for everything. And now…now he's dead."

"I'm so sorry," I said, not sure what else to say. "Were you and he planning to still see each other?"

She nodded. "But now that awful man killed him, and we can't," she said. Again, I found myself wondering how much of this plan her husband had known about—and where he had been the night Bridges died.

"Was your husband with you the night he died?" I asked.

"I guess," she drawled. "He was here when I went to sleep, but I sleep pretty hard." Sleep, or pass out? I wondered. She squinted at me. "I thought the police said that naturalist killed him?"

"That seems to be the theory."

She gave me a confused look. "But he couldn't have killed that reporter, could he?"

"Not from jail," I agreed. I wanted to ask more about her husband, but decided to wait. "Is there anyone else you can think of who might have wanted to harm the captain?"

"That Martina woman was jealous," she slurred. "I

think she wanted him for herself. She didn't understand the history we had together."

"I heard something about that," I said, thankful that she'd broached the subject. "What happened with the whole tiara fiasco, anyway?"

"Carl talked me into giving him a tour of Cliffside when the owners were out on their boat. We....Well, we spent some romantic time there." She sniffled, then leaned forward, almost falling off her chair. "I'm not supposed to say anything, but I got...got pregnant. When he had to leave, my mother was furious with me."

"Had to leave?"

"He said he had signed up to crew some ship in Japan, and that he'd lay low until it all got worked out." She raised the tumbler to her lips. "I wanted to keep the baby and wait, but my mother insisted I have an abortion. Now I can't get pregnant...and the lawyers got all of my fund. If only someone hadn't stolen that tiara..." Her face crumpled. "He never would have left, and we could have had a family together."

My instinct told me that Carl Bainbridge had no interest in a happily-ever-after with Jenna. Although something and obviously brought him back to Cranberry Island. Was I wrong? I wasn't sure who I felt sorrier for: Jenna, or her poor husband, who was married to a woman who was obviously still in love with someone else. Had he taken care of his rival that night on the *Summer Breeze*?

"Who do you think took the tiara?" I asked.

"Lorraine Lockhart. She was jealous of me. She wanted Carl for herself."

"Did anyone suspect her?"

"I told them she did it, but no one believed me." She choked out a sob. "I was going to get married to Carl, go to college, have beautiful children…and now my whole life is ruined." The coffee pot gurgled behind her. "I think your coffee's done," she said, swaying in her chair.

"I'll get it," I told her. "Don't get up."

She swiped at her eyes. "You sure?"

"Positive," I told her. "Do you want one, too? You look like you've had a lot of…soda."

"Rum and Diet Coke," she clarified.

"Why don't you have a cup of coffee, instead? I'm worried about you."

She grimaced. "I guess, maybe."

I poured us both coffee and sat back down at the table, sliding a mug across to her. "You can still go back to school, you know."

"It's too late for me."

"No it's not," I countered. "It's never too late to pursue a dream."

"You think?" She gave me a skeptical look.

"I'm positive," I told her. "I switched careers in my thirties, and my life is so much better because of it."

"But I'm stuck out here on this island, and the nearest university is on the mainland!"

"Isn't there a community college in Ellsworth?

You could start taking a few classes there; you could knock out half your degree and still stay here. You don't have kids, so you don't have to worry about child care."

She pursed her lips. "I never thought about anything like that. Do you think?"

"I do think. You might even be able to do a few online," I suggested. "You might want to cut down on the rum and Diet Coke, though," I said with a smile. "But in the meantime...I promised I'd try to help Charlene out. I was hoping you could tell me something...anything...that would help us figure out what happened to Bainbridge."

She took a sip of coffee, sloshing a good bit of it onto her sweater. "I don't know," she said. "My husband, for sure, if he knew about us."

FOURTEEN

I leaned forward. "Did he?"

"I don't think so,"

"It's hard," I agreed. "I know he knew Lorraine Lockhart," I said, and her mouth twisted into a grimace, "but I can't imagine she would have done that to him. I mean, she's got a life now…a family."

"People do funny things," I said. "What did you and Carl talk about when you saw him?" I asked.

"He said he was terribly sorry about what had happened, and that he'd find a way to make it up to me." Her eyes welled with tears again. "And now…he's gone."

"I'm so sorry," I told her, leaning forward and wondering if maybe, despite her sad story, it was Jenna who had done the captain in after all. But somehow I didn't think so; she seemed more crushed than angry, somehow. "It was a setback—a big one—but it didn't ruin your life. The captain may be gone, but you can still pursue your dreams."

"Do you think?" she asked a second time. "After all this time? My mother always kind of treated me like my future was over. She was so angry at me for letting myself get involved with him."

"We all make mistakes. But it's never too late," I said. "I'll go with you to check it out if you want."

She gave me a dubious look from bloodshot eyes. "Will you?"

"Of course," I told her. "Classes probably start in September; we'll head over one day. But in the meantime, can you think of anyone else here on the island who might have wanted to kill Bainbridge? I promised Charlene I'd help if I could."

"Well," she said, her voice slightly less slurred. "I guess my hubby wasn't too happy about him, but I don't think he had the guts to do anything. Besides, Carl was so much stronger than Bill."

"Where was he last night?" I asked.

"I don't know," she said. "We don't always sleep in the same room. Plus, I'd had a few drinks."

"So he could have been out."

"Yeah, but I don't think he has it in him. What about Lorraine Lockhart?" she suggested. "Or her husband, Tom?"

I'd had the same thoughts, unfortunately. "Whatever happened with Lorraine and Bridges, by the way? Do you know?"

"I know he was seeing her a bit on the side, way back when," she said. "I didn't know, but he was just doing it to be nice to her."

"When did you find out?"

"After he had to leave," she told me. "And this time, he told me she begged him to see her...he went to tell her he wasn't interested, but I think Tom found out."

"Why?"

"I heard he spent the night at the co-op. I figured he came home while he was there, or something."

"But why would Lorraine want to kill him?"

"I don't know. Maybe she didn't want him messing up her relationship. Maybe she found out about me. Maybe she was jealous." Her eyes widened. "Should I be worried?"

"I'm sure you're fine," I said, and hoped I was right. "Do you think there may be some other reason he went over to see Lorraine?"

"Maybe he knew something," Jenna suggested. "Who knows? Maybe the reporter found out Lorraine stole the tiara."

"It's a theory," I said. "Would she have had access to the house?"

"Everyone did," Jenna told me. "Those people didn't keep things locked up. It was only because I worked there that the police arrested me."

"I'm so sorry," I said. "Why do you think he came back to the island?"

"He was carrying a torch for me, of course," she said. "Only now…"

"I'm sorry," I said, reaching over and touching her hand. "But there's still hope."

"Really?"

"Really," I said. "Let me know when you want to go to look at the college. In the meantime, I think I may have to go talk with Lorraine."

As Jenna trailed after me to the door, Bill walked in, looking angry. He was a short, solid man, with none of the captain's handsomeness, and a ruddy face over ginger whiskers.

He squinted at me. "What are you doing here?"

"She stopped in to ask about the dead reporter," Jenna said.

His eyes narrowed. "Why?"

"I'm just trying to figure out what happened, that's all. Another guest turned up dead outside the inn. It's a bit distressing."

"What does Jenna have to do with anything?" he asked, coming and putting a protective arm around his wife.

"I was trying to find out if she knew of any other old island connections," I said.

"Like Lorraine Lockhart, you mean?"

"Yes, that name came up," I said, feeling suddenly defensive. "Do you know of anyone else?"

"I know I saw him and Lorraine canoodling the other day," he said. "And she's a married woman. No wonder Tom left her."

Canoodling? Jenna's face hardened, but she said nothing. I knew Tom had had his own lapse in judgment in the past, but I decided not to bring that up. "What do you mean, canoodling?"

"Kissing, hugging…you know."

Jenna looked down, but I could feel her practically bursting to talk.

"When was this?" I asked.

"A couple days before he died," he said. "They were out on the path by the cliffs. Thought no one could see them, but I spotted them on my way to town. Good thing I wasn't on the mail boat, or the whole island would have known." He grunted. "Probably did Bridges in when she realized he wasn't serious. And then took care of that reporter so that her husband wouldn't find out."

"Did the reporter know?"

He shrugged. "Reporters find things out, don't they?"

"Natalie was talking to me about community college," Jenna said, changing the subject.

"What about it?"

"I'm thinking of taking some classes."

"Is it going to take too much time away from your work?" Not the encouragement I would have hoped for.

"It's never too late," she said, lifting her chin.

"I bought the inn in my 30s," I piped up.

"I don't know. It's expensive. I'm not sure we can afford it."

"It doesn't have to be, and there's financial aid, too."

"We'll talk about it," he said, but I wasn't optimistic. "In the meantime, do you need a ride to work?"

"Sure," Jenna said meekly. "Let me just get cleaned up."

"I'll let you go, then," I said. "Think about the college thing. And if anything else occurs to you, let me know."

"I will," Jenna said as I let myself out the front door. I glanced back over my shoulder; Bill still had a protective arm around her. Someone had been in a skiff the night Bainbridge died; could it have been Jenna's jealous husband?

It was a definite possibility.

On the way to Lorraine's, I stopped by the store to check in with Charlene, who was working her way through a Snicker's bar and talking on the phone.

"What's up?" I asked.

"Alex's mother is trying to post bail," she said. "The attorney thinks with the second murder, it should be lowered."

"Does it work that way?"

She shrugged. "I have no idea, to be honest, but I hope he's out soon."

If there was another murder, it might be better for him to still be in jail, I thought, but let it pass. Hopefully the body count would stop at two. "What do you know about Jenna Pool's husband?" I asked.

"Bill? He's a nice enough man, but not a lot of imagination. Why?"

"He seems really protective of her," I said. "I found myself wondering if maybe he had something to do with the murders."

"Why?"

"Jealousy," I suggested. "Just ask around, will you?"

As she nodded, the bell rang. I turned to see Tom Lockhart's tall frame at the front of the shop.

"Here we go," Charlene murmured as he walked toward us. He looked haggard—kind of like he'd slept on the floor of the co-op for a bit—but still flashed us a smile.

"Hello, ladies."

"You look like you've been wrestling sharks or something," Charlene said.

"It's been a tough couple of days," he confessed.

Charlene offered him a cookie from the jar by the register; she'd given up on me and dumped in a package of Lorna Doones, it appeared. "It's on me today," she said. "You look like you need it."

"Thanks," he said, taking her up on it. As he bit into the shortbread cookie, my friend said, "I heard you and Lorraine had a bit of a tiff." I stared at Charlene, impressed at the way she got straight to the point.

"Well, you don't make it through a decade or so of marriage without a few dust-ups," he admitted. "Yes, we did."

"Was it about the late captain?" Charlene asked.

"What, are you telepathic?," he asked. "I have to admit I was a bit jealous. Bainbridge—Bridges—was a good-looking guy. I heard he and Lorraine met and talked, and well…" He shrugged. "I said some things

I regret. We spent a few days apart, and now we're making it up."

"You don't seem to torn up about his loss," I said.

"He was a bad egg," Tom said. "Set up poor Jenna all those years ago, and I got the impression from the reporter that there were a few other skeletons in the closet."

"The reporter?"

"Yeah. Real shame about her; she was a nice young woman. She came and talked to me a few days ago," he said, and now his face looked solemn.

"What did she ask you about?"

"The captain, of course. What happened while he was here—the whole theft thing, and if I had any idea what he had been doing since then."

"And did you?"

"No," he said, shaking his head. "She implied he'd been involved some unsavory businesses, though."

"Like whaling," I said.

They both stared at me. "What?" Charlene asked.

"He was part-owner of a Japanese whaling boat, I think."

"No wonder she was investigating him. Do you think someone else was involved in it? Someone who wanted to kill the story?" Tom asked.

"It's worth thinking about," I said. Privately, I was wondering about both Bill and Martina, but I still had to view Tom with suspicion --much as I didn't want to. Had he killed Bridges in a fit of passion? I hoped not, but I couldn't rule it out. If things had gone so badly with Jenna and the tiara, why would the captain ever come back to Cranberry Island? Unless he still had designs on Lorraine…

Too many strands, and none of them were weaving together properly. Before I could ask another question, the bells on the door jingled, and Gertrude Pickens walked in.

All three of us stifled a groan.

"I'm so glad to find you here," she said. "I got a phone call saying that there are problems at the inn; a health inspector shut you down, and now you've got two murders on the premises. That's got to be bad for business, don't you think?"

"What a nightmare," I said as I walked into the kitchen of the Gray Whale Inn a half hour later.

"What?" John asked, looking up from the kitchen table, where he was feeding Smudge.

"She's looking better, isn't she?" I asked, smiling at the little gray kitten. She mewled and then continued to eat while Biscuit looked on from the windowsill.

"Gertrude Pickens was at the store," I said. "She knows all about the health inspector, and I think she's going to do an article about the murders."

"Of course she is," he said. "It is news. But how did she find out about the health inspector?"

"Someone called," I said. "I have a guess who it might be."

"Our lovely guests the Fowlers?" he asked.

"Either that or Ms. McGee," I said. "She wouldn't say, of course."

"I've got news, too," he said. "They argued on the pier the other day. Tom said he should have thrown Bridges overboard years ago."

I cringed. "He didn't."

"He did," he said. "And she's not the only one who heard it. Apparently somebody else passed that little nugget on to the police."

"Do you think he would have done it?" I asked.

"I don't know," he said. "He's a passionate guy— but he's also a good person. I just can't see him doing something so cold-blooded. Or killing a young reporter."

"Someone did, though," I said, as I retrieved my recipe binder from its hiding place and leafed through it. "My money's on Martina."

"You think?"

"She didn't like how he was running the business. She now owns the whole thing. She was jealous of Stacy...plus, Stacy was probably writing a nasty article about her business."

"And it wouldn't be hard to get Bainbridge out onto the schooner the night he died."

"Or to slip out and do in Stacy," he added as I pulled a green bell pepper out of the fridge. "What are you making?"

"I was thinking of doing a King Ranch chicken casserole," I said. "I've got tortillas in the freezer and soup in the pantry, we've got plenty of chicken, and I could use the comfort food."

"Will the kids eat it?"

"I'll put some plain chicken aside for them just in case," I told him as I pulled a package of corn tortillas out of the freezer. There might be a murderer running around the inn, but people still needed to eat. I hoped Yvonne and Carson were keeping close tabs on Lizzie and Liam. "I was thinking of making Texas Sheet Cake for dessert, too."

"Feeling a little homesick?" John asked with a grin. "Not that I'm complaining, of course…in fact, I wouldn't object to a double batch."

"I think I'm just in the mood for comfort food," I said. "I don't miss Texas summers, but I do miss Tex-Mex."

"I'm glad you found that binder," he told me. "Although I still don't know how we're going to mention it to the Fowlers."

"They'll figure it out soon enough," I said as I put the chicken breasts into a pan with some water and transferred them to the stove to poach. "Maybe we should charge them extra."

"I wish we could charge them for damages."

"Have you heard anything from the insurance adjustor?" I asked as I turned on the oven and pulled a canister of flour down from the pantry for the Texas Sheet Cake.

"No, but I'm thinking maybe we should get in touch with an attorney."

"Are you thinking of charging them with vandalism or something? As much as it feels like the right call, I worry about the added publicity. Let's see what the insurance adjustor says first."

"Fine," he said, "but I don't like letting go without a fight."

"Me neither," I said, measuring the flour into a bowl and adding the other dry ingredients. "Is Catherine around? I want to ask her if she's talked with Murray about Cliffside."

Before he could answer, Bridget walked into the kitchen.

"Hi," she said shortly. The tension level in the kitchen shot up about 500%. I busied myself with adjusting the heat on the stove and glancing over my recipes.

"Hi," I said as I opened the fridge and grabbed a dozen eggs and a tub of sour cream. "John and I were just talking…have you seen Catherine?"

"No," she told me, stroking the kitten's head. "But I think I located some good gallery prospects for Gwen."

"That's nice of you," John said. "What did you find?"

As she pulled a wad of brochures from her purse, Catherine walked into the kitchen.

"I was hoping I'd find you here," my mother-in-law said. "Murray told me somebody applied for a permit to turn Cliffside into a resort. Guess who owns the company involved?"

Karen MacInerney

"Someone at the inn," I said, measuring out sour cream and adding it to the dry ingredients. "The Fowlers are the main people, but Nan McGee is backing them."

Her manicured eyebrows rose. "How did you know?"

"I saw them with the architect today," I said as I unwrapped two sticks of butter and plopped them into a pot. Once the butter melted, I'd add cocoa and water and let it cool a little before adding it to the other mixture; together, they made Texas Sheet Cake magic. I was salivating just thinking about it; thank goodness I'd found my binder. "It turns out the Fowlers were the ones who took my recipe binder and stole my client list."

"That's horrible!" Bridget said. "You should sue them."

"I was just talking to John about that," I said, checking on the chicken; when it was done, I'd let it cool, then shred it before sautéing onions and peppers and combining all three with the sauce. The final dish was like an enormous enchilada casserole, and always a big hit. "We could sue," I said, "but I don't know if it would be worth the bad publicity."

Bridget turned to Catherine. "Can they get the permitting through?"

"You should talk to Murray," Catherine said.

"I'm not familiar with the law here, but it wouldn't take long to read it," Bridget said. "I can't believe they're trying to run you out of business and steal

238

your client list. It's not right!"

I added cocoa and hot water to the melted butter and looked up at her. "I'm still not sure about suing, but if you can find some way to avoid the permit, that would be great."

"Some of the folks down at Island Artists were talking about protesting," John said.

"That's good, too, and may come in handy at a meeting to approve, but let me take a look at what's on the books, first," Bridget said, her pile of gallery brochures forgotten. "Can you introduce me to Murray?"

"Of course," Catherine said. "Maybe we can go over for cocktails this evening."

"Let's do it," my sister said.

"Come with me—we'll give him a call," Catherine said, and a moment later, John and I found ourselves staring at each other as his mother and my sister headed down to the carriage house together, still talking.

"What just happened?" John asked, still holding the kitten as I stirred the cocoa-butter mixture.

"I think we just found something else for my sister to chew on. And with her background, I can't think of a better ally to have."

"So maybe we need to worry less about the incoming hotel—for now, anyway—and figure out who's killing off our guests before we lose another one," he suggested.

I adjusted the heat on the stove. "I thought you

were the one always encouraging me to leave it to the police!"

"I talked with the detective, and she's not telling me much of anything, but I think she still thinks Alex did in Bridges," he said.

"Did you tell them about Martina?"

"Of course," he said.

I stirred the chocolaty mixture, inhaling the comforting scent. "What do they think happened to the reporter?"

"She came up here because things were getting hot down in Portland; she'd just unearthed some criminal connections with the mafia," he told me. "They're thinking her death was unrelated to what happened to Bridges."

I put down my wooden spoon. "Seriously?"

"Seriously," he told me.

"I don't buy that for a minute."

"It does seem awfully convenient," he said.

"I'm still putting my money on Martina," I said. "She's got means, motive, and opportunity."

"You think?" he asked. "She seemed pretty upset."

"I don't think it's Tom or Lorraine," I said, "although I haven't seen Lorraine again. I talked with Jenna, and I just can't believe she would have done it, but her husband Bill is a possibility. And why would Nan McGee or the Fowlers want him dead?"

"He was going to scuttle their deal? Maybe they were worried he'd invest in the tour instead."

"Maybe," I said.

"I hate to think it's one of the islanders," John told me, "but there was that skiff coming from the other side of the island the night Bridges died. Besides, why come back here if there wasn't still some connection to the past?"

"But Martina is the obvious choice," I objected. "She didn't like what Bridges was doing. I know Bridges told her to deal with Alex when he was giving him trouble." I remembered the coldness in her voice when she told the captain she'd "take care of him." "She benefits from inheriting the business. Stacy admitted to canoodling with him and being caught at it by Martina—and we know she and the captain were involved at some point. And I heard someone going up and downstairs the night Bridges died."

"Did we ever figure out what Alex was doing that night?" he asked. "We can't rule out the possibility that he was the one to kill the captain."

"You really think there are two killers?" I asked, watching as the first bubbles began to spring up around the edge of the pot. "I think we'd know if someone came from off-island to do in Stacy, don't you think?"

"One of the other guests?" John suggested. "Someone went through her room; maybe she was doing an exposé on Nan McGee's business?"

"I guess if she was, there would be no way to know. Whoever it was took everything related to it, and her laptop hasn't turned up, I'm guessing."

"Apparently not," John told me.

"So what now?" I asked.

"Martina's still out, right?"

"She is."

The mixture in the pot was boiling; I turned off the heat. After it cooled for a few minutes, I'd combine it with the other ingredients and tuck it into the oven; the chicken still needed some time, too. "This is on for another fifteen minutes or so. Unless you have any objections, I thought I might go and make sure there aren't any clogged drains in Martina's room."

He hesitated for a moment, then nodded. "Let's go. But we both need to wear gloves."

"Got it," I said, fishing two pairs of rubber gloves out from under the sink as he snuggled Smudge in next to the radiator.

Martina's room was as tidy as you'd expect it to be.

"Ship-shape," John quipped as he closed the door behind him.

"No surprise there," I said. "I just wish we knew what we were looking for."

"I think we'll know it when we find it," he said.

It didn't take long, actually. "She was setting him up," I said.

"What do you mean?"

I showed him a file with the name "Stacy" neatly printed on the front. Inside was a dossier on Captain

Bridges—or Bainbridge.

"Wow," John said. "It's got the whole tiara story, the whaling connections…"

"And apparently he was arrested for burglary down in New York," I said. "It didn't stick, but I can see why he'd change his name."

"Why give this to Stacy?"

"Revenge?" I asked. "Or to scare her off of him?"

"Maybe it was to scuttle the investment," he suggested.

"But that would destroy her stake in the business, too," I said. "Besides, if you're going to give her the file, why kill her?"

"Do you think maybe she used the note and the file to lure her?" he suggested. "I wish we had a copy of that note."

I looked at the front of the folder. "The handwriting wasn't this neat, but it could have been written in a hurry. Should we leave this here, or take it with us?"

"I'll take a picture," he said, "and we'll leave it here."

"I'll get my phone," I said, and hurried downstairs. We took a few photos and then scoured the rest of the room, but found nothing else of interest.

But what we'd found was intriguing enough.

Bridget burst into the kitchen just as I was frosting the cake, followed by Catherine. "It's not a done deal," she announced. "And I may have found an ordinance that prevents them building. Cliffside is a historic structure; if the board can get it approved as such, they can't do anything with it. Murray's willing to go to bat."

"Really?" I looked at Catherine. "You got Murray to go to bat against a developer?"

"He's not the one developing it," she pointed out. "If he's not profiting, why should someone else?"

That made more sense. I was about to answer when the phone rang. I picked it up: it was Charlene.

"They're not dropping the charges," she blurted.

"What?"

"They think the murders are unrelated, and Alex is guilty."

"John mentioned that might be the case," I said. "I'm working on it; we may have a lead." I glanced up at the clock. "I've got to get ready for dinner...do you want to come eat with us?"

"I can't eat. I can't think."

"Then come over and just be with us," I suggested. "I've got Texas Sheet Cake."

"I'm not hungry."

"It's chocolate," I said. "It's therapeutic. You'll see."

She let out a heavy sigh and said she'd walk over with Gwen in a little bit.

"What's going on?" Bridget asked.

"They still think the naturalist killed the captain," I said. "Charlene's coming over for comfort and cake."

"I think I was wrong about you living a quiet life up here," Bridget said. "I'm still worried about Gwen, though...where is she?"

"She's at the store with Charlene," I said. "They'll come over together."

"Good. I'm glad she's not alone." She shivered. "I hate to think of her on the island with a murderer."

"Charlene will look after her," I said soothingly.

But I was wrong.

The King Ranch Chicken casserole was a hit, as usual, and it was a good thing I kept back some sheet cake, or there would have been none left over. Just a bite of the fudgy, pecan-laced cake was enough to send me zinging back to my hometown of Austin...only the temperature outside was a lot more welcoming.

I was picking up the plates and still thinking about Stacy when I heard the two kids talking by the window.

"I told you she was right there," Lizzie said, pointing out toward the carriage house.

"You're making that up," Liam said.

"I am not. She had some kind of blue light on her face for a moment. It was her."

I walked over and set down the plate I was carrying, then squatted next to Lizzie. "Who did you see?" I asked.

"The bogeyman," Lizzie said.

"There's no such thing," Liam protested.

"When was this?" I asked.

"Last night," she said. "I couldn't sleep, so I was looking out at the moon. And that's when I saw here. She was right over there," she said, stabbing a finger toward the carriage house.

"Did you recognize her?" I asked.

"I told you. It was the skunk woman. Just like I saw at dinner the other day."

"Dinner the other day?"

"Lizzie," Yvette scolded. "Don't bother Miss Natalie."

"No, it's okay," I said. "When did you see her at dinner?"

"When we had that white soup," she said. "Over at the pier. She had that weird stripe on her head."

Stripe on her head?

"Like a skunk," she said.

My stomach dropped.

"You're sure you saw her?"

"I did," she said. "I was so scared when her face lit up that I went and hid under the covers. I tried to tell mom, but she didn't believe me."

"She's always talking about monsters, ever since she saw that zombie show."

I stood up, wheels turning in my brain. The hairpin on the deck of the ship. The hairpin on the floor outside Stacy's room.

They didn't belong to Martina at all.

FIFTEEN

I had just finished drying the last of the dishes when Charlene walked through the door.

"You don't look so hot," I said.

"I feel like I've been hit by a truck," she said, pushing back a lock of lank hair.

"I may have some good news...but first, where's Gwen?"

"She stopped by Island Artists; she'll be along in a few minutes."

"I thought you two were coming over together," I said, feeling a twinge of concern.

"What could happen?" Charlene asked, then bit her lip. "Good point. Maybe I should go back for her."

"I'll call her," I said, picking up the phone. Unfortunately, her phone was out of batteries or she was on the other line; it went straight to voicemail.

As I hung up, my sister walked into the kitchen. She saw Charlene. "Is Gwen upstairs?"

"She's coming in a few minutes," Charlene answered, a furrow between her brows.

"I have a bad feeling about this," Bridget said.

"You know what? I do, too," I said. "John should be here in a minute; Charlene, will you help clean up?

I'm going to run down to the pier and give her a ride."

"I'm going with you," Bridget said, and together we headed out to the van, shivering as a gust of chilled air blew in off the water. Both of us were jittery. I knew now that there was likely a murderer on the island—not just on the island, but on the pier, just down from Island Artists. I gunned the engine, and as we reached the crest of the hill, I felt my stomach clench; surely my niece would be just on the other side of the hill, clutching her bag of art supplies.

But she wasn't.

"I thought Charlene said she'd just be a few minutes behind," Bridget fretted.

"We'll find her," I said, more calmly than I felt.

She wasn't a few minutes behind. In fact, she was nowhere at all on the road home.

"Is there a shortcut?" Bridget asked.

"There's a footpath," I told her. "She may have taken it and stopped to do some sketches," I suggested as I pulled in at the end of the pier and cut the engine. I hoped I was right.

Selene MacGregor was rearranging some pottery mugs when Bridget and I knocked on the door of the little store. "Is Gwen here?" Bridget asked, breathless, when Selene unlocked the door.

"She left about half an hour ago," Selene said, looking surprised. "Is everything all right?"

"Where did she say she was going?" I asked.

"She said she had one more stop to make and that

she was heading back to the inn."

"Did she say what the stop was?" Bridget asked.

Selene shrugged.

"What did you talk about?"

"Her paintings, of course," Selene said, looking puzzled. "What's all this about?"

"Anything else?"

"Oh, all the goings-on at the inn, of course. I told her I thought there was no way Tom Lockhart would have done anything like that. And about that horrible case with the dead captain, all those years ago, when that poor naturalist got framed." Selene shook her head. "It wouldn't surprise me if her husband did him in. He's the jealous type."

"So you don't know where she went?"

"Sorry, I don't," she said. "Why are you so worried?" Her eyes grew big. "Wait. You don't think…"

"I'm sure she's fine," I cut in quickly. "Thanks."

"No problem," she said, and I could feel her eyes follow us as we hurried to the door.

"Now what?" Bridget asked.

"I think we need to check in at the lobster pound," I said.

"Why?"

"I think I know who killed the captain—and Stacy."

"What about Gwen?"

"I'm sure she's fine. We're just doing due diligence," I said, trying to remain calm as I hurried down the pier to the lobster pound, praying that Gwen would be there. Jenna was behind the counter, wrapping up silverware. She smiled when she saw me.

"Hi, Natalie. Thanks for stopping by today; I think you're right about taking classes."

"I'm glad," I said. "Hey—have you seen your mom?"

"She's not here right now," Jenna said. "Why?"

"Was Gwen here?" Bridget asked before I had a chance to answer.

Jenna shook her head. "I haven't seen her."

I felt a wave of relief. "Was your mom here?"

"She left about thirty minutes ago." Bridget and I looked at each other. The same time that Gwen left Island Artists.

"Did she say where she was going?"

"Home, I guess. I'll tell her you stopped by, if you want."

"No need," I said.

"Do you want to sit down for dinner?" she asked. "It's late, but we still have clam chowder."

"Not tonight," I said. "Thanks, though," and together, Bridget and I hurried outside.

"What was that all about? Where do you think she went?"

"I'm not sure," I told her, "but I think we need to stop by Martha Spurrell's house."

"Oh, God," Bridget breathed. "You don't think…"

"I don't know," I told her. "But we're going to find

out." Together, we hurried to the van. Even though it was high summer, I felt colder than I had all year.

As she buckled herself in and I pulled out onto the narrow road, Bridget turned to me . "You think she's the murderer, don't you? The woman at the lobster pound. Why?"

"I think she was avenging her daughter," I told her. "When Bridges came back into town, he stirred things back up with Jenna."

"So Martha murdered her?"

I nodded. "He really did a number on her daughter; I don't think she's ever recovered. And I think Stacy figured it out, so Martha had to get rid of her, too."

"And now Gwen?"

"We're going to make sure that doesn't happen," I told her as I turned down a small, wooded road and pulled up outside a small cottage with a stack of broken lobster traps in the side yard. Martha's beaten-up gold truck was parked crookedly in the driveway.

"What do we do?" Bridget asked as I walked up to the front door. "Shouldn't we strategize?"

"If she's got Gwen, we don't have time to lose," I said. "Why don't you wait here, and I'll go to the door?"

"No," she said. "I'm going with you."

Together, we hurried to the front door. I knocked, praying I was wrong. No one answered, but I heard something like a muffled cry from behind the door.

"That's Gwen," Bridget said, going pale.

I tried the door; it was locked. Not a good sign; almost no one on the island locked their doors.

"Let's go around back," she said. Together we rounded the house; the back door was locked, too.

"Gwen!" she called, pounding on the door. She looked at me, eyes wild. "Let's kick it in," she suggested.

"What?"

"I've never done it before, but I've seen it on TV."

"Why don't we break the glass and reach through and unlock it, instead?" I asked.

She gave me a blank, panicked look. I reached down and grabbed an egg-shaped granite rock and smashed the bottom pane of the door's window, then pulled my sweatshirt down around my hand and reached in to unfasten the deadbolt.

A moment later, we hurtled through the door into the darkened kitchen. It was neat and orderly—no surprise, since Martha owned a restaurant—but there was no sign of Gwen.

"Now what?" she whispered.

"Come on," I told her quietly. We'd already announced our presence with the pounding and the broken glass, but it felt right to whisper. Together we hurried out of the kitchen, searching the house. There was no more sound—and no sign of anyone.

"Where is she?" Bridget asked, almost in tears.

As soon as she spoke, there was another muffled cry; from below us.

The cellar.

"How do we get in?" my sister asked.

We walked back to the kitchen, where I'd seen a door I presumed was to a pantry. I grabbed the knob and pulled the door open; sure enough, wooden stairs descended into a dimly lit space.

"Don't you dare come down here," came a husky voice.

"Martha?" I asked. "Is that you?"

"Yes. And this is private property."

"You've got my daughter down there, don't you?" Bridget demanded, voice shaking.

I heard a whimper that sounded like Gwen.

The voice was cold and expressionless and carried a current of menace that made my hair stand up. "I said, go away."

My stomach plummeted. Were we too late?

"Let me at least talk to her," Bridget said, taking a step and motioning for me to stay. "Call the police," she whispered.

I didn't have my cell phone, but I spotted a phone across the kitchen. "We're not here to hurt you," Bridget said as I reached for it and dialed the inn, but no one answered. I tried the workshop next; John wasn't there. I hung up and dialed the inn again; if I called the mainland police, it would be at least 30 minutes before someone got here. Too long.

"Oh, God. No," Bridget said from down the stairs. I put the phone down and hurried over to the cellar door, looking down.

I was wrong about Martha not having a gun. She

was pointing it at my sister.

"Martha," I said.

Her eyes leapt up the stairs to me. "There are two of you. Damn. Can't you just leave me alone?"

"Is Gwen okay?" I asked.

"She's tied up in the corner," my sister answered, her voice shaky. "She looks bad, though. What did you do to her?"

"Shut her up," she said. "And now I have to shut you up, too. Christ. Why couldn't you leave it alone?"

"You don't have to do this," Bridget said, her voice steady. "I know what happened. I agree—the jerk deserved to die. If anyone had done that to my daughter…" She looked at Gwen. Her voice was firm, but I could see the tic in her left eye.

"Yeah, well, I can't have you blabbing it around. By the time I'm done, I'm going to have to start counting bodies on both hands."

"There's no need for anyone else to die," Bridget said calmly. "With good representation, you have a chance at a minimal sentence." She swallowed. "Or no sentence at all."

"Oh, that's right. You're a hoity-toity lawyer, aren't you? Well, I'm afraid I've done my research, and you're wrong. I'm in for the rest of my life, and I don't fancy a room with bars. I took care of what needed to be taken care of—the reporter was a nasty accident, but I don't regret it. In for a penny, in for a pound." Her voice was harsh. "Now get down here. Both of you."

My instinct was to flee and get help. But if I did, I'd be leaving both Bridget and Gwen at Martha's mercy...and I had no doubt she'd make good on her threat to kill them both.

"You don't have to do this," Bridget continued. "Seriously. You're making a big mistake."

"A boat accident will be just the thing," she said. "Maybe you went out together in a skiff, and it overturned in bad weather. There's a storm coming in tonight."

"But why would you be out in a skiff?" I asked. "It doesn't make sense."

"As long as it doesn't come back to me, it makes plenty of sense," Martha said. "Now here. Get downstairs next to Gwen here." Bridget hurried down the stairs to her daughter, who was curled in a corner with her hands duct-taped together in front of her. Her face was bruised, and her eyes wide like a deer's. Why had I ever invited her to Cranberry Island? I cursed my bad judgment. Without me, Gwen wouldn't be in this horrible situation.

"Are you okay?" she asked her daughter.

How had we gotten here? And more importantly, how could we get out of here?

Martha squinted at Bridget. "She's pretty, like you. A shame. But then our children's futures aren't always what we'd hoped for."

"I talked with your daughter today," I told Martha in a calming voice. "Just a little while ago. She's thinking of going back to college."

"How's she going to afford that? Her college fund got blown up by that man. So did my chance of having grandchildren. All so that jerk could walk off scot-free, with a bunch of diamonds." Her lips pulled back into a grim smile. Well, he's not walking anymore, is he?"

"When did you recognize him?" I asked.

"As soon as he set foot on the island," she said. "Same cocky walk. I'd know him anywhere."

"Yours was the skiff that was out that night," I said. "How did you get him out to the boat?"

"I left him a note saying I was Lorraine, of course," she said. "My daughter was enough of an idiot to think he came back for her, but I knew better."

"So you killed him."

"Knocked him out with a brick," she said. "Then I tied him to the anchor and towed the schooner's skiff back to the dock."

"Clever," I said. "Why did you have to kill Stacy?"

"She was asking too many questions about the tiara. Came by twice to ask about Jenna; she got wind of the fact that she was still in love with him. If I didn't do something, she was going to go to the police."

"But they already had Alex in custody," I said. "There was no way he could be accused of killing Stacy; wouldn't that just open things up again?" As I spoke, I moved over next to Gwen and glanced at Bridget. We exchanged glances just as we had when one of us would sneak out at night to raid the frozen

Snickers bars in the freezer. I would be the distraction; she would disable Martha.

My eyes were on the gun as Martha said, "I know. I thought about it, but I heard her asking around about where Jenna was the night the captain died. She knew it wasn't that naturalist." The gun was pointed at me now, not Bridget—right where I wanted it. "She started asking too many questions. It had to be done." She sighed. "And now I have to deal with you, too."

"Did Bridges tell you if he really did steal the tiara?" I asked, stalling for time as Bridget edged toward her.

"He took it, all right. Fenced the jewels, and then used some of the money to buy part-interest in some Japanese outfit, and the rest to start up his tour company."

"I can see why you were angry," I said. "Your daughter got left with huge legal bills and no college, and he walks off with enough money to start a new life."

She nodded. "You know what I'm talking about." She glanced at Gwen. "She's kind of like your daughter, isn't she?"

"She's my sister's daughter," I said, glancing at Bridget, who was only a few feet away from Martha, "but I love her very much."

"I just wish the two of you would stop fighting so much," Gwen piped up from where she was on the floor.

"It's not going to matter much longer anyway," Martha said. "You might as well make up now."

"How did you figure out it was Martha, anyway?" I asked Gwen.

"I remembered Lizzie talking about the skunk woman," Gwen told me. "I suddenly realized who it might have been."

I bit my lip; had Gwen just put Lizzie in danger, too?"

"You can't kill everyone," I reasoned with Martha, playing for time. As I talked, Bridget edged closer. I could see her scanning the cellar floor out of the corner of my eye. "Why don't you just pull a Bridges—change your identity and leave town?"

"If I had a diamond tiara, I might consider it," she told me. "But my whole life is here. The pound, my daughter...I've always lived on this island." She tightened her grip on the gun and glared at me. "I'm not going to let that man drive me out. He's ruined our lives enough already." She took a closer step to me and pushed the gun into my abdomen. Bridget, who had found an old baseball bat and had been advancing on her, stepped back. "Move over toward the others," she said, reaching for a roll of duct tape with the other hand.

"You're going to have to put the gun down to tie us up," I pointed out helpfully.

Martha looked at the gun, and then at me. "No I won't," she said. Before I could say another word, she lifted the gun and brought it down on my temple.

SIXTEEN

It was dark when I opened my eyes. "Gwen?" I called. "Bridget?"

"I'm here," Gwen said. "But I think Mom's still down for the count."

"How long have we been down here?"

"About an hour, I think. I have no idea what time it is, though. She knocked me out, too, before she tied me up."

I lifted my hands; they were taped together. "She said she was going to take us out after dark," I said. "We don't have much time to get out of this stuff."

"I never should have complimented that woman's clam chowder," Gwen said bitterly.

"Just because she's a murderer doesn't mean she's not a good cook," I pointed out. "But we should probably be worried about something other than chowder recipes. Did you notice anything sharp in here?"

"No," Gwen said, "but I've got an Exacto knife in my bag. Jeez…why didn't I think of that before? I'm an idiot."

"Panic makes it hard to think sometimes," I said. "Where is it?"

"I think it's in the corner there."

"Where's there?"

"Behind me," she said. "I'll see if I can scootch over there." There was a bit of grunting, as presumably she heaved herself across the concrete floor.

"Can you reach it?" I asked.

"I have the flap. I'm just trying to unbuckle it."

As she spoke, there was movement above us. "Hurry," I whispered as she fumbled with it in the dark. "Got it?"

"Yes," she said. "Ouch."

"Be careful," I warned her.

"I can't do it," she said. "Can you edge over here and hold it, so I can rub the tape against it?"

"Sure," I said, rolling toward her and maneuvering myself so that we were back to back.

"It's in my hand," she said. I fumbled for it, touching the sharp point and sucking in my breath before closing my fingers on the handle.

"I'll hold it," I said. "You rub the tape; that way I won't cut you."

She positioned herself against the blade and started rubbing, but she'd barely begun when the door at the top of the stairs swung open.

"Pretend I'm still knocked out," I whispered, and scooted back as best I could to where I'd been lying. The light flicked on, and I froze.

A chill ran through me as Martha clumped down the stairs. "Still out?" she asked.

"Yes," Gwen said. I heard a thumping sound, and

a whimper. "Don't kick my mother!" Gwen said.

"She's got to wake up," Martha said. A moment later, her foot slammed into my ribs. I whimpered, but didn't open my eyes. She kicked me again, harder.

"Why?" Gwen asked.

"I can't get them up the stairs," she said. "Too heavy." She kicked me again, but I kept my eyes closed.

"I'm sure they'll wake up soon," Gwen said. "Maybe another thirty minutes or so?"

"I don't have all night," she complained.

"I'm sure they'll be awake by then," Gwen said.

"She's moved," Martha said, nudging me with her foot.

"She's an active sleeper. Always has been," Gwen explained.

How long had we been gone? I wondered, feeling my heart pound in my chest. They must have noticed that we hadn't come back. Was someone searching for us? Even if they were, there was no way they'd know we were at Martha's house.

"I guess I'll give them a few more minutes," she said. "But if they're not up, you'll have to help me carry them."

"I will," she promised. To my relief, she clumped back up the stairs and turned off the light.

"What do we do?" Gwen hissed when the door had slammed shut.

"Let's get the tape cut first," I said. "Then we'll figure it out."

We moved back into position. It felt like hours, but it must only have been ten minutes before Gwen was freed.

She grabbed the Exacto knife from me and freed my hands, then went to work on her ankles. I borrowed the knife to free my legs, then sliced through the tape on Bridget's hands and feet.

"I'm worried about her," I whispered to Gwen. Her forehead was clammy to the touch. "She's been out a long time."

"What do we do when she comes back down?" she asked.

"I've been thinking about that," I said. "Let's put the tape so that it looks like it's still on. If only you are awake, she can't get us up the stairs alone, and she doesn't want to shoot us down here. If you're the only one awake, you can offer to help her move us. When she puts the gun down to pick up someone's legs or feet, say 'clear' and I'll tackle her."

"Are you sure?"

"Positive," I said. "I'll hold onto the knife. Did you happen to see anything else we can use as a weapon?"

"There are a bunch of boxes, but I didn't exactly have a chance to go through them. There's some laundry detergent by the washer and dryer."

"Liquid, or powder?"

"Liquid," she said.

"I just read something about detergent and eyes…it might be good to have around, just in case. Which direction?"

"To the left of the stairs," she said.

I fumbled my way over, trying not to make too much noise, and located the washer. The detergent was a large plastic jug, about half-full. "Got it," I whispered, and felt my way back to the area I'd come from. I loosened the lid and pushed it halfway behind a box; that way, it would be accessible, but not obvious to Martha when she turned the lights on.

All too soon, the door opened, and Martha's heavy tread landed on the top riser. I gripped the Exacto knife in my hand and tried to look like I was still unconscious; I could see the light through my eyelids.

"They're still out," Gwen said as she neared the bottom of the steps. "You really got them."

"Damn it," she said. "I don't have all night." She paused, and I imagined she was weighing her options.

"You said you were going to have me carry them with you," Gwen reminded her. And that's when I realized the error I had made. For Gwen to help her, Martha would have to cut the tape from her hands. And when she went to cut the tape, she'd realize that Gwen was already free.

I opened my eyes a little bit. Martha was standing turned half away from me, considering my sister. I cut my eyes over to the detergent; it was within reach.

"All right," she said. "I've got scissors down here somewhere." As Martha turned and walked over toward the washer and dryer, I tried to figure out what to do. She still had the gun in her hand. But she couldn't cut the tape off Gwen's hands and still hold the gun, could she?

I hated to wait a second longer, but it seemed like the best chance I'd have. My heart pounded as she knelt down by Gwen, the gun in her hand.

"Let me see your hands," she said. The scissors were in one hand, the gun in the other.

Gwen's eyes darted to me.

I grunted, hoping to distract her, and opened my eyes wide. "What are you doing?" I asked.

She glanced over at me. "Good. At least one of you is awake."

"Why don't you put down the gun so you don't accidentally shoot my niece?" I suggested.

"She's going to die anyway."

"I hope not, but if you do manage to pull it off, you don't want a mess to clean up down here, do you? Forensics, and all."

She grimaced, but looked like she was at least thinking about it. "You're probably right," she admitted, and put the gun down—but with her between it and me.

It was the only chance I was likely to have.

As Martha reached for Gwen, I launched myself across the cellar. At the same time, Gwen's hands snaked out from behind her and clamped onto Martha's wrists. But Martha was stronger than my niece.

"You little bitch," she hissed. As I barreled into

her, she wrenched her right hand free, and it darted toward the gun. Together, we landed on the concrete floor and rolled. There was an explosion from somewhere beneath me, and a searing pain slashed through my leg.

"Damn it!" she yelled, heaving herself on top of me. She pulled the hammer back on the gun and began moving it toward me. I grabbed her wrist, pushing her hand away from me.

"Gwen!" Bridget was waking up. "What's going on?"

"Mom..." Gwen gasped. "Aunt Nat's in trouble...help!"

I pushed away with all my strength, but Martha was stronger, and her arm lowered toward me, turning the gun toward me. My leg was throbbing—I could feel a warm, spreading wetness through my jeans—and my whole body had started to shake. The gun came closer and closer. As I watched, her thumb pulled back the safety. "No!" I yelled.

It was inches from my face when something loomed up behind her. "Leave my sister alone, you witch!" Bridget bellowed. Martha jumped, startled, and her arm wavered. I pushed the gun away just as Bridget brought down a broken chair on Martha's head.

"Are you okay?" Bridget asked, looking at my bloody leg, which was poking out from beneath

Martha's slack body. She was crushing the rest of me.

"Let's get rid of the gun and make sure she's out of commission first," I said, pushing Martha off of me. I took a deep breath as she rolled to the side.

"Gwen, get the gun and aim it at her," Bridget ordered. "I'm going to make a tourniquet."

Gwen, looking pale beneath her bruises, did as her mother told her, and Bridget ripped off her cardigan and wrapped it tight around my thigh.

"That's cashmere," I objected. "It'll ruin it."

"I've got six more sweaters at home," she replied. "I only have one of you."

When she'd tied the sleeves into a knot, she bent down and examined my leg. "It doesn't look like it went through the bone—you were lucky. It's pretty dirty down here, though; you're going to need to get that cleaned and stitched up."

I looked down at my leg; with the tourniquet on, the bleeding had slowed. My whole body was quaking, though, and I felt light-headed. "Why don't we get her tied up and call the police before we take on anything else?"

"Fine," she said. "But I'm going up to get you a blanket. You're in shock."

She trundled up the stairs, leaving me alone with Gwen and the supine Martha.

"Thank God your mom woke up when she did," I said. "It was about to go wrong fast."

"I'm just so glad you figured out I was here," Gwen told me. "How did you know?"

"You didn't come home with Charlene," I said. "And when I talked with Selene at Island Artists, I figured out what must have happened."

"How did you know it was Martha?"

"The hairpins," I said. "She's the only person I know who uses hairpins. They were on the boat, and I found one up in Stacy's room, too."

"I still don't understand why she did it," she said.

"Because he'd hurt her daughter and profited at her expense," I said. "And was trying to mess her life up again."

"But the only thing you had to go on was hairpins?"

"That wasn't the only thing. When Lizzie talked about the scary skunk lady, I figured it out; she's got that white streak at the part." I glanced over at the unconscious woman, her face slack and deceptively peaceful. "In her own way, she's as protective of your daughter as your mom is."

"And you," my sister said as she came down the stairs with a stack of blankets. "I am so thankful that you figured out what happened. Without you, I wouldn't even have a daughter."

"And without you, I'd be a goner," I replied.

"I called the police and found some duct tape on the kitchen table," she said. "John didn't pick up, but I left a message; I imagine he'll get it soon and come this way. In the meantime, I figured we'd get her trussed up while we wait for help."

I shivered under two wool blankets, pain radiating

up from my leg, as Gwen and her mother worked together to secure Martha's hands and feet. I pulled the blanket back to take a look, then regretted it; I hoped I'd be able to walk when this was all over. Bridget glanced over at me when she was done. "You don't look so good," she told me.

My teeth chattered as I tried to answer.

"Gwen, sweetheart, go make your aunt some tea. I'll keep an eye on Martha."

"Okay, Mom," she said, and headed up the stairs, leaving me alone with my sister.

She looked down at her feet and was quiet a moment. "I have an apology to make," she said.

"What do you mean?"

"I'm sorry I accused you of interfering and trying to replace me," she said. "I saw the other paintings in the galleries on the mainland, and none of them were as...as special as Gwen's. She does have a gift, and it wouldn't be right for her not to use it."

"No," I said. "I thought about it, and decided may you have a point. I probably did say too much to her. And if it weren't for my coming here, she wouldn't have gotten into this mess."

"She's where she belongs, Natalie," Bridget said. "At least for now. And I'm glad she has you looking after her."

"She's got both of us," I told her, feeling a warmth toward my sister I'd always longed for. "I never wanted to replace you. I couldn't if I tried."

Bridget gave me a smile, her face looking softer

than I'd ever seen it. "Thanks, Nitwit."

I rolled my eyes. "Really? Do you really want me to start calling you Bossyboots again?"

She laughed. "Considering the last few days, I can't complain if you do." She came over and hugged me while Gwen looked on, openmouthed.

"I'm going to have to get kidnapped more often," she said.

"Please don't," I said quickly.

"Absolutely not," Bridget chimed in. "What happened, anyway?"

Gwen sighed. "I thought it might be Jenna, so I made the mistake of asking Martha about her daughter, and whether she was still into the captain when he came back to the island. It's funny...all I did was ask about it, and she invited me for tea to talk more about it. As soon as we got here, she started questioning me hard...and then she must have decided I was a threat." She shivered, looking down at the prone woman. "I think she's not quite right."

"Since she was about to kill all three of us, I have to agree with you," I said.

"It's sad, though," she told me. "Bridges really did mess up her daughter's life. She was really only trying to look out for her. He came back and stirred things up for no good reason."

"Why did he come back, anyway?" Bridget asked.

"I think he was carrying a torch for Lorraine," I said. "Now that he'd built a business, he was trying to lure her back."

"I'll bet he used the proceeds of that tiara to fund it," Bridget said.

"We'll probably never know," I said. "I do know he wasn't a very nice man, though. He did some whaling after he left the island, and is part-owner of a Japanese whaling boat."

"How did you find that out?"

"Stacy was investigating," I said. "That's why I thought Martina was the murderer. The only thing that didn't make sense, though, was leaving all that info in Stacy's room; the bad press couldn't have been good for a nature tour company."

"So you think Martha went through her room?"

"I think she was making sure Stacy didn't have any notes pointing to her or her daughter as the killer," I said. "Stacy was starting to ask questions and make connections. She must have said something that spooked her."

"She was pretty easily spooked," Gwen said. "If she hadn't started going berserk on me, I wouldn't have thought anything of it." She frowned. "I feel bad for Jenna. She's not had good luck."

"No, she hasn't," I agreed. As I spoke, there was a hammering on the door upstairs.

"The reinforcements have arrived," Bridget said, and headed up the stairs.

"Aunt Nat," Gwen said, staring at me when she disappeared. "What happened?"

"I think she realized we both love you," I said. "And that it's not an either-or proposition."

"And she even thinks I'm in the right place," Gwen said. "Think it'll last?"

"We'll see when the adrenaline wears off," I told her, "but I'm hopeful."

"What about my engagement?"

I grinned at her. "Let's take one thing at a time, shall we?" As I answered, John's voice floated down the stairs to me...a moment later, he was hurtling down them, bringing a whiff of his woodsy, masculine scent. His tanned face looked pale. "Oh, my God...Nat, you're covered in blood."

"It's only a flesh wound," I said.

"A flesh wound that could have hit an artery," he said. "We need to get you to the hospital." He investigated the wound, sucking in his breath, and then pulled me up into his arms, burying his face in my hair. "You've got to stop doing this."

"I was trying to save Gwen," I said.

After a long moment, he released me gently and then looked over at Martha. "Why is she tied up?"

"She's the one who did in the captain," I said. "And Stacy."

"And almost you," he said, then turned to Gwen. "You've had a bad day, too; looks like we need to get both of you to the hospital."

"I'm fine," she said, touching her bruised face.

"What happened?"

"I didn't want to go downstairs, so she pushed me," Gwen said. "She gave Aunt Nat a few good kicks in the ribs, too."

Now that she mentioned it, I was feeling a little sore around the ribs when I moved; the pain in my leg had made me forget about that.

"The police are on their way. I asked them to send a paramedic, too," he said, and glanced over at Martha again. "Is she responsible for Stacy, too?"

"That's what she told us," I said, suddenly feeling very tired. "I'll give you the details later; for now, I'm just going to close my eyes."

"Natalie…"

I didn't hear the rest of what he said, because I either passed out or fell asleep.

"I am definitely not a fan of crutches… particularly not at low tide," I complained to John the next day as I clambered off the mail boat attempted to make my way up the gangway to the pier. I'd spent the night at the hospital on Mount Desert Island— the bullet, thankfully, had passed an inch away from an artery and had done mainly superficial damage— and had just been released from the hospital an hour ago. Making my way up the steep gangway felt a little like climbing Mt. Everest, and I was thankful that John was behind me in case I lost my balance.

"It's better than the alternative," he reminded me as he reached out to steady me. "And just think how fun the stairs will be when we get home."

Home. "I almost forgot Smudge…who took care of her last night?"

"Catherine did," he told me as I took another wobbly swing-step up the gangway. "She's doing better, and Biscuit is starting to warm to her. She likes the workshop; she's got a sunny spot by the west window where she likes to doze and keep me company."

"Still no word on who her owner is?"

"Nothing yet," he said. "That's one unsolved mystery."

"There she is!" I looked up to see Charlene, who was hurrying down the pier to greet me. She was looking like her cheery self again, with her caramel-colored hair coiffed and a sparkly red top. "John called and told me you got shot! How are you feeling?"

"I've been better," I told her.

"I'll make a batch of chicken soup," she said.

"Does it work for gunshot wounds?"

"We'll find out," my friend said as I lurched to the top of the gangway, breathing heavily. "You're awesome, by the way...thanks to you, they've dropped charges and they're letting Alex out today." She beamed. "I can't thank you enough. I'm headed over in a few hours to pick him up at the police station. I knew he didn't do it!"

"I'm glad it all got figured out," I said, feeling my thigh twinge from the effort to make it up the gangway. I looked down; the bandage was across the outside of my thigh. John called the place the bullet had gouged my new racing stripe, but I was afraid it wasn't going to be pretty. Oh, well. At least I was alive...and so was Gwen. I looked back up at Charlene. "How's Jenna doing, have you heard?"

"She's upset, but not as surprised as you'd think," Charlene told me as I stumped across the pier past Spurrell's Lobster Pound. A piece of yellow legal paper with "CLOSED UNTIL FURTHER NOTICE" scrawled on it was taped to the door.

"Maybe she'll take over the place," I said. "On the plus side, her mother can hardly complain about her daughter's legal fees anymore."

Bridget and Gwen were waiting next to the van at the end of the pier. Both of them threw themselves at me and embraced me in a three-way hug. "I'm so glad you're going to be okay," Bridget said as she released me. "What did they say?"

"Take it easy, keep it clean, and check back in a week," I told her. "Thank goodness I've got help," I said, smiling at Gwen.

"I owe you big time," she said.

"And so do I," said Bridget, who gave me a kiss on the cheek. "Let's get you back to the inn so you can rest."

It was a short ride, and I was glad to be sitting down. Catherine and Murray were in the kitchen waiting for me when they helped me through the door a few minutes later.

"How's it going?" I asked.

"Better for us than you," Catherine said. I would normally bristle at the presence of Murray Selfridge in my kitchen, but he was beaming at my mother-in-law so fondly I couldn't complain. "We do have some good news, though."

"What?"

"My dear Murray has hired an attorney to prevent the resort," she said.

"If I can't do it, why should they?" he asked.

SEVENTEEN

The next afternoon could not have been more perfect. I was on crutches, but they'd released me with a relatively clean bill of health and orders to relax, which meant fewer dishes for a while. Charlene sat with me at the kitchen table, looking happier than I'd seen her since the tour began; Alex was out of jail, and the charges had been dropped. I looked out the window, thinking of the team that was trying to free the whale from the fishing gear; they'd managed to locate it yesterday. Thankfully, the wind had died down, and the blue water was calm.

"That'll make things a lot easier," Charlene said as she finished off a scone.

"I just hope she survives until they get the gear off," I said.

"That won't be a problem. The marine entanglement team arrived this morning, located her and managed to put floats on her," she told me.

As she spoke, Alex pushed open the door. "Ready?"

"I'm coming," I said, reaching for my crutches and levering myself up off the chair.

Thirty minutes later, we were all on the Summer Breeze, Martina at the helm, Eli helping as first mate, and Alex scanning the water for signs of whales. Adam's boat, the Carpe Diem, flanked ours, with both Gwen and Bridget aboard, smiling—a small miracle. A little further on was Tom Lockhart on his boat, looking sunny; he and Lorraine seemed to have patched things up. I waved to Bridget, who had joined Gwen on the Carpe Diem.

"They're both smiling," I said. "It's a miracle."

"I talked to her a bit," Catherine said. "Also, I think your experience in Martha's cellar helped."

"Bonding through trauma," I said, and glanced back at Cranberry Island. "Any word from Murray on the Cliffside deal?"

"That's turned out to be an interesting situation," she said. "Murray called McGee and talked about his troubles with development on the island, and mentioned a piece of land out on Mount Desert Island he's been wanting to invest in. When he asked if she'd be interested in partnering with him, she said she was definitely interested."

"What does that mean for Cliffside?"

"Well, with the permitting issues, she's thinking of relocating the whole concept to the island; it's got better access to the park and the amenities of Bar Harbor."

"What about the architect's drawings?"

"The Fowlers paid for them," she said. "Nan and Murray will see if they're adjustable for the new site, or if they need to be scrapped; if they are, they'll pay for them."

"Will the Fowlers be involved if McGee buys the land on Mount Desert Island?"

"I doubt it," she told me. "McGee wasn't impressed by their sabotage efforts. Apparently they were downstairs going through your files the night Bridges died; they told McGee about it the next day."

"Well, that's one mystery solved," I said. "But they can still build on the island if they find funding."

"Yes, but the contract is contingent on funding," she said, "and they'll have to put it together quickly or back out."

"So there's hope after all. Plus, it keeps Murray busy building something other than a resort on Cranberry Island," I said. "Thank you so much, Catherine."

"It's the least I could do," she said. "I'm fond of the place, too. And it's not for sure yet, but he's pretty confident about it."

"Terrific news," I said. "Alex is out of jail, Cliffside is likely going to remain Cliffside, and Bridget and Gwen are actually talking to each other." I grinned. "Nothing like being held at gunpoint to encourage togetherness."

"Small steps," Catherine said, looking over at John fondly. "We all have ideas of what we think our children should be. It's hard to let go and realize that they don't really belong to us. They belong to themselves."

"You're right," I said, looking over at Gwen, her curly hair flying free in the wind.

"Don't worry about it, Natalie," she said, patting me on the shoulder. "Just love her, and let the two of them work it out on their own."

I turned and smiled at my mother-in-law. "Thank you," I said. "And thanks for not giving John too hard a time for moving to an island to become an artist and marrying a Texas innkeeper."

"I did at first," she confessed. "But I was wrong. I have to admit," she said with a sly grin, "it's turned out better than I expected."

I laughed. "I think it's turned out great. And I'm so glad you're here."

"Me too, Natalie," she said. "Oh, look! There's the whale! That looks horrible, doesn't it?"

She was right; the poor creature was attached to several orange floats. Alex had told me the practice was called "kegging;" it kept the whale at the surface, so that she was less likely to be caught underwater where she couldn't get up to breathe; it also helped rescuers track her. The tangle of lines stuck on the whale's fluke was readily visible; it seemed to have grown since last I'd seen them. A small inflatable boat idled near her, and a hundred yards farther on, a larger research vessel. Martina cut the engine, as did the two lobster boats behind us, and radioed the rescue boat.

"Stand by," they told us. "We've cut two of the ropes, but there's one more."

It was a long wait before the whale drifted close enough to the inflatable for the rescuers to reach her. We held our breath as the shorter of the two women reached over and hooked the last rope. She had just started sawing back and forth when the whale flapped its tail and struggled to dive. The woman almost lost her balance—I was glad she was wearing a life jacket—and pulled back just in time. The rope was sawed only partway through.

"So close," I breathed, watching the huge whale thrashing around in the water.

"I hope she doesn't overturn the inflatable," Catherine said beside me.

I was thinking the same thing. It took several minutes before she started to calm down. The inflatable nudged toward her again slowly, trying not to spook her. The rescuers looked tired; I wondered how long they'd been attempting to free her.

"I wish we could do something," I said. "I hate feeling so helpless."

"I know," she said. "It's kind of like being a mother." She gave me a sly smile. "Or an aunt."

After an interminable time, they managed to get the blade under the rope again. This time, as we watched, the rope came free, and the tangle of lines drifted off, away from the whale. A cheer went up from the boat as the whale slid through the water, then dove, lifting its tail into the water.

"She's free," Catherine whispered. I looked over at Gwen, who was beaming as Adam hugged her. At that moment, the whale breached through the water, coming down with a loud smack, and then rolled over before disappearing into the inky waves.

"Yes," I said. "She is."

Visit www.karenmacinerney.com to download a free copy of *The Gray Whale Inn Kitchen*, a collection of recipes from the first six *Gray Whale Inn* mysteries.

Karen MacInerney
Book List

The Gray Whale Inn Mysteries
Murder on the Rocks
Dead and Berried
Murder Most Maine
Berried to the Hilt
Brush With Death
Death Runs Adrift
Whale of a Crime

The Gray Whale Inn
The Gray Whale Inn Kitchen
Blueberry Blues, a short mystery
Pumpkin Pied, a short story

The Margie Peterson Mysteries
Mother's Day Out
Mother Knows Best
Mother's Little Helper (coming April 2017)

The Dewberry Farm Mysteries
Killer Jam
Fatal Frost
Deadly Brew (coming Fall 2017)

Tales of an Urban Werewolf
Howling at the Moon
On the Prowl
Leader of the Pack

For more information and to buy go to
www.karenmacinerney.com.

RECIPES

John's Beef Stroganoff

1 pound sirloin steak, cut into cubes
Kosher salt and black pepper (to taste)
2 tablespoons olive oil
1/2 onion, diced
2 carrots, diced
8 ounces cremini mushrooms, sliced
1/2 cup brandy
2 cups beef stock
2 tablespoons cornstarch
1/4 cup room-temperature sour cream
1 heaping teaspoon Dijon mustard
Minced fresh parsley

Season the steak with salt and pepper, then heat 1 tablespoon of the olive oil in a heavy saucepan over medium high heat. Add half the meat to the pan and brown it quickly (about 2 minutes). Remove the first batch to a bowl and cook the second half of the meat, then remove and set aside. Add the remaining olive oil to the pan and add the onion, carrots, and mushrooms. Sauté for about five minutes, or until the vegetables are golden brown. Turn off the heat; add the brandy and 2 cups of the stock. Stir, scrape the bottom of the pan, and turn the heat to medium-high. Cook 3 to 4 minutes, or until liquid is reduced by a third.

In a small bowl, mix the remaining 1/4 cup stock and the cornstarch with a fork. Pour the slurry into the saucepan and cook until the sauce thickens, about 1 to 2 minutes. Turn off the heat and stir in the sour cream and mustard, then add the beef and stir over low heat until the mixture is hot. Taste and adjust seasonings, then serve over cooked egg noodles and sprinkle with fresh parsley.

Serves 4.

Blueberry Cobbler Muffins

Muffin Batter

4 cups blueberries (fresh is best, but frozen is fine)
1 stick butter, softened
1 1/4 cup sugar
2 eggs
1 cup milk
3 cups flour
4 teaspoons baking powder
1 teaspoon salt

Streusel Topping

1 stick butter, softened
1 cup brown sugar
2/3 cup flour
1 teaspoon cinnamon
Dash of nutmeg

Preheat oven to 350 and line muffin tins. Cream together one stick of butter and sugar, then add eggs, milk, flour, baking powder, and salt. Fold in blueberries and pour into muffin tins. In a separate bowl, combine streusel topping ingredients with a fork or pastry blender; stop when the mixture is in pea-sized chunks. Sprinkle muffins with streusel topping, then bake for 25-30 minutes or until muffins spring back when touched.

Makes 24-36 muffins.

Oatmeal Raspberry Crumble Bars

1/2 cup packed light brown sugar
1 cup all-purpose flour
1/4 teaspoon baking soda
1/8 teaspoon salt
1 cup rolled oats
1/2 cup butter, softened
3/4 cup seedless raspberry jam

Preheat oven to 350. Grease an 8-inch square pan, then line it with greased foil. Combine brown sugar, flour, baking soda, salt, and rolled oats in a medium-size bowl, then rub in the butter using your hands or a pastry blender to form a crumbly mixture. Press 2 cups of the mixture into the bottom of the prepared pan, and spread the jam to within 1/4 inch of the edge. Sprinkle the remaining crumb mixture over the top and press lightly into the jam. Bake for 35 to 40 minutes or until lightly browned. Allow to cool before cutting into bars.

Salted Caramel Chocolate Chip Bars

1/2 cup caramel sauce, good quality or homemade.
2 1/8 cups flour
1/2 tsp. salt
1/2 tsp. baking soda
1 1/2 sticks unsalted butter, melted
1 cup light brown sugar
1/2 cup granulated sugar
1 egg
1 egg yolk
1 tsp. vanilla extract
2 cups milk chocolate chips
Fleur de sel or other coarse sea salt to taste

Preheat oven to 325°F/160°C and spray an 8-inch square baking dish with non-stick cooking spray. Stir together the flour, salt, and baking soda in a medium size bowl.

In the bowl of a stand mixer, add the sugars and the melted butter. And mix with the paddle attachment on low until combined. Increase the speed on your stand mixer by one and add the egg, yolk, and vanilla. Mix until creamy and smooth, then bring the mixer down to the lowest setting again and slowly add the dry ingredients. When everything is combined, fold in the chocolate chips.

Divide the cookie dough and spread half on the bottom of the prepared baking dish, then pour 1/2 cup caramel sauce over the dough and sprinkle on salt to taste (don't be too sparing). When caramel and salt have been distributed, put chunks of the remaining cookie dough evenly on top of the caramel sauce with a spoon. Use a spoon sprayed with cooking spray (or your fingers) to spread the cookie dough over the caramel until the caramel is covered, then sprinkle more salt on top. Bake for 30 to 38 minutes or until the cookie top is golden brown.

Yield: 16 2-inch bars.

Caramel Sauce

1 cup sugar
1 tablespoon corn syrup
1/4 cup water
1/2 cup heavy cream, heated
2 tablespoons unsalted butter, softened
1 teaspoon vanilla extract

In a heavy (preferably nonstick) saucepan, stir together sugar, syrup, and water until sugar is completely moistened. Heat, stirring constantly, until sugar dissolves and the syrup is bubbling. Stop stirring and let boil undisturbed until the mixture turns a deep amber (380°F on a candy thermometer). Remove from heat immediately; slowly pour the hot cream into the caramel. It will bubble up furiously.

Use a wooden spoon to stir the mixture until smooth, scraping up the thicker part that settles on the bottom. If lumps develop, return the pan to the heat and stir until dissolved. Stir in the butter; the mixture will be streaky but become uniform after cooling slightly and stirring.

Allow the sauce to cool for 3 minutes. Gently stir in the vanilla extract.

King Ranch Chicken Casserole

2 tablespoons olive oil or butter
1 onion, chopped
1/2 bell pepper, chopped
1 (10 1/2 ounce) can cream of mushroom soup
1 (10 1/2 ounce) can cream of chicken soup
1 (10 1/2 ounce) can Rotel tomatoes and chilies
1/2 cup chicken broth
2 cups diced cooked chicken (rotisserie chicken works great, or you can poach chicken breasts; I sometimes do this with a can of Hatch green chiles and some broth)
12 corn tortillas, ripped into bite sized pieces
2 cups shredded sharp cheddar cheese

Preheat oven to 325°F and spray a 9 x 13" baking dish with cooking spray. In a large saucepan, sauté the onion and pepper in the olive oil or butter until tender (about 5 minutes). Add soups, tomatoes, and broth, then stir to combine. Fold in the chicken until well blended.

Layer with 1/3 the tortillas into the bottom of the baking dish, then 1/3 of the chicken mixture, then 1/3 the cheese. Repeat layers twice more. Bake for 30-40 minutes, uncovered, until hot and bubbly. (Check at around 20 - 25 minutes; if cheese begins to brown too much, cover dish with foil.)

Texas Sheet Cake

Cake

2 cups all-purpose flour
2 cups sugar
1 teaspoon baking soda
1/2 teaspoon salt
1/2 cup sour cream
2 eggs
1 cup butter
1 cup water
5 tablespoons unsweetened cocoa powder
6 tablespoons milk

Icing

5 tablespoons unsweetened cocoa powder
1/2 cup butter
4 cups confectioners' sugar
1 teaspoon vanilla extract
1 cup chopped pecans (optional)

Preheat oven to 350, then grease and flour a 10x15 inch pan. Stir together flour, sugar, baking soda and salt until combined. Beat in the sour cream and eggs, and set aside. Melt the butter on low in a saucepan, then add the water and 5 tablespoons cocoa. Bring the mixture to a boil and remove from heat. Allow to cool slightly, then stir cocoa mixture into the egg mixture, mixing until blended.

Pour batter into prepared pan and bake in the preheated oven for 20 minutes, or until a toothpick inserted into the center comes out clean.

While the cake is baking, combine milk, 5 tablespoons cocoa powder and 1/2 cup butter in a saucepan. Bring to a boil, then remove from heat. Stir in the confectioners' sugar and vanilla, then fold in the pecans, mixing until blended. Spread frosting over warm cake.

A DEWBERRY FARM

Killer Jam

MYSTERY

Karen MacInerney

Chapter 1

I've always heard it's no use crying over spilled milk. But after three days of attempting to milk Blossom the cow (formerly Heifer #82), only to have her deliver a well-timed kick that deposited the entire contents of my bucket on the stall floor, it was hard not to feel a few tears of frustration forming in the corners of my eyes.

Stifling a sigh, I surveyed the giant puddle on the floor of the milking stall and reached for the hose. I'd tried surrounding the bucket with blocks, holding it in place with my feet—even tying the handle to the side of the stall with a length of twine. But for the sixth straight time, I had just squeezed the last drops from the teats when Blossom swung her right rear hoof in a kind of bovine hook kick, walloping the top of the bucket and sending gallons of the creamy white fluid spilling across both the concrete floor and my boots. I reprimanded her, but she simply tossed her head and grabbed another mouthful of the feed I affectionately called "cow chow."

She looked so unassuming. So velvety-nosed and kind, with big, long-lashed eyes. At least she had on the day I'd selected her from the line of cows for sale at the Double-Bar Ranch. Despite all the reading I'd done on selecting a heifer, when she pressed her soft nose up against my cheek, I knew she belonged at Dewberry Farm. Thankfully, the rancher I'd purchased her from had seemed more than happy to let her go, extolling her good nature and excellent production.

He'd somehow failed to mention her phobia of filled buckets.

Now, as I watched the tawny heifer gamboling into the pasture beside my farmhouse, kicking her heels up in what I imagined was a cow's version of the middle finger, I took a deep breath and tried to be philosophical about the whole thing. She still had those big brown eyes, and it made me happy to think of her in my pasture rather than the cramped conditions at Double-Bar Ranch. And she'd only kicked the milk bucket, not me.

Despite the farm's growing pains, as I turned toward the farmhouse, I couldn't help but smile. After fifteen years of life in Houston, I now lived in a century-old yellow farmhouse—the one I'd dreamed of owning my whole life—with ten acres of rolling pasture and field, a peach orchard, a patch of dewberries, and a quaint, bustling town just up the road. The mayor had even installed a Wi-Fi transmitter on the water tower, which meant I could someday put up a website for the farm. So what if Blossom was more trouble than I'd expected, I told myself. I'd only been a dairy farmer for seventy-two hours; how could I expect to know everything?

In fact, it had only been six months since my college roommate, Natalie Barnes, had convinced me to buy the farm that had once belonged to my grandparents. Natalie had cashed in her chips a few years back and bought an inn in Maine, and I'd never seen her happier. With my friend's encouragement, I'd gone after the dream of reliving those childhood summers, which I'd spent fishing in the creek and learning to put up jam at my grandmother's elbow.

It had been a long time since those magical days in Grandma Vogel's steamy, deliciously scented kitchen. I'd spent several years as a reporter for the *Houston Chronicle*, fantasizing about a simpler life as I wrote about big-city crime and corruption. As an antidote to the heartache I'd seen in my job, I'd grown tomatoes in a sunny patch of the backyard, made batches of soap on the kitchen stove, and even kept a couple of chickens until the neighbors complained.

Ever since those long summer days, I'd always fantasized about living in Buttercup, but it wasn't until two events happened almost simultaneously that my dream moved from fantasy to reality. First, the paper I worked for, which like most newspapers was suffering from the onset of the digital age, laid off half the staff, offering me a buyout that, combined with my savings and the equity on my small house, would give me a nice nest egg. And second, as I browsed the web one day, I discovered that my grandmother's farm—which she'd sold fifteen years ago, after my grandfather passed—was up for sale.

Ignoring my financial advisor's advice—and fending off questions from friends who questioned my sanity—I raided the library for every homesteading book I could find, cobbled together a plan I hoped would keep me from starving, took the buyout from the paper, and put an offer in on Dewberry Farm. Within a month, I went from being Lucy Resnick, reporter, to Lucy Resnick, unemployed homesteader of my grandparents' derelict farm. Now, after months of backbreaking work, I surveyed the rows of fresh green lettuce and broccoli plants sprouting up in the fields behind the house with a deep sense of satisfaction. I might not be rich, and I might not know how to milk a cow, but I was living the life I'd always wanted.

I focused on the tasks for the day, mentally crossing cheese making off the list as I headed for the little yellow farmhouse. There might not be fresh mozzarella on the menu, but I did have two more batches of soap to make, along with shade cover to spread over the lettuce, cucumber seeds to plant, chickens to feed, and buckets of dewberries to pick and turn into jam. I also needed to stop by and pick up some beeswax from the Bees' Knees, owned by local beekeeper Nancy Shaw.

The little beeswax candles I made in short mason jars were a top seller at Buttercup Market Days, and I needed to make more.

Fortunately, it was a gorgeous late spring day, with late bluebonnets carpeting the roadsides and larkspur blanketing the meadow beside the house, the tall flowers' ruffled lavender and pink spikes bringing a smile to my face. They'd make beautiful bouquets for the market this coming weekend—and for the pitcher in the middle of my kitchen table. Although the yellow Victorian-style farmhouse had been neglected and left vacant for the past decade or more, many of my grandmother's furnishings remained. She hadn't been able to take them with her to the retirement home, and for some reason, nobody else had claimed or moved them out, so many things I remembered from my childhood were still there.

The house had good bones, and with a bit of paint and elbow grease, I had quickly made it a comfortable home. The white tiled countertop sparkled again, and my grandmother's pie safe with its punched tin panels was filled with jars of jam for the market. I smoothed my hand over the enormous pine table my grandmother had served Sunday dinners on for years. I'd had to work to refinish it, sanding it down before adding several layers of polyurethane to the weathered surface, but I felt connected to my grandmother every time I sat down to a meal.

The outside had taken a bit more effort. Although the graceful oaks still sheltered the house, looking much like they had when I had visited as a child, the line of roses that lined the picket fence had suffered from neglect, and the irises were lost in a thicket of Johnson grass. The land itself had been in worse shape; the dewberries the farm had been named for had crept up into where the garden used to be, hiding in a sea of mesquite saplings and giant purple thistles. I had had to pay someone to plow a few acres for planting, and had lost some of the extra poundage I'd picked up at my desk job rooting out the rest. Although it was a continual battle against weeds, the greens I had put in that spring were looking lush and healthy—and the dewberries had been corralled to the banks of Dewberry Creek, which ran along the back side of the property. The peach trees in the small orchard had been cloaked in gorgeous pink blossoms and now were laden with tiny fruits. In a few short months, I'd be trying out the honey-peach preserves recipe I'd found in my grandmother's handwritten cookbook, which was my most treasured possession. Sometimes, when I flipped through its yellowed pages, I almost felt as if my grandmother were standing next to me.

Now, I stifled a sigh of frustration as I watched the heifer browse the pasture. With time, I was hoping to get a cheese concern going; right now, I only had Blossom, but hopefully she'd calve a heifer, and with luck, I'd have two or three milkers soon. Money was on the tight side, and I might have to consider driving to farmers' markets in Austin to make ends meet—or maybe finding some kind of part-time job—but now that I'd found my way to Buttercup, I didn't want to leave.

I readjusted my ponytail—now that I didn't need to dress for work, I usually pulled my long brown hair back in the mornings—and mentally reviewed my to-do list. Picking dewberries was next, a delightful change from the more mundane tasks of my city days. I needed a few more batches of jam for Buttercup's Founders' Day Festival and Jam-Off, which was coming up in a few days. I'd pick before it got too hot; it had been a few days since I'd been down by the creek, and I hoped to harvest another several quarts.

Chuck, the small apricot rescue poodle who had been my constant companion for the past five years, joined me as I grabbed a pair of gardening gloves and the galvanized silver bucket I kept by the back door, then headed past the garden in the back and down to the creek, where the sweet smell of sycamores filled the air. I didn't let Chuck near Blossom—I was afraid she would do the same thing to him that she did to the milk bucket—but he accompanied me almost everywhere else on the farm, prancing through the tall grass, guarding me from wayward squirrels and crickets, and—unfortunately—picking up hundreds of burrs. I'd had to shave him within a week of arriving at the farm, and I was still getting used to having a bald poodle. This morning, he romped through the tall grass, occasionally stopping to sniff a particularly compelling tuft of grass. His pink skin showed through his clipped fur, and I found myself wondering if there was such a thing as doggie sunscreen.

The creek was running well this spring—we'd had plenty of rain, which was always welcome in Texas, and a giant bullfrog plopped into the water as I approached the mass of brambles with their dark, sweet berries. They were similar to the blackberries I bought in the store, but a bit longer, with a sweet-tart tang that I loved. I popped the first few in my mouth.

I went to work filling the bucket, using a stick to push the brambles aside, and had filled it about halfway when I heard the grumble of a motor coming up the long driveway. Chuck, who had been trying to figure out how to get to the fish that were darting in the deeper part of the creek, turned and growled. I shushed him as we headed back toward the farmhouse, the bucket swinging at my side.

A lanky man in jeans and a button-down shirt was unfolding himself from the front seat of the truck as I opened the back gate. Chuck surged ahead of me, barking and growling, then slinking to my ankle when I shushed him with a sharp word.

"Can I help you?" I asked the man. He was in his

mid-forties, with work-worn boots and the roughened skin of a man who'd spent most of his life outdoors.

"You Lucy Resnick?" he asked.

"I am," I said, putting down the bucket. Chuck growled again and put himself between us.

"Butch Simmons, Lone Star Exploration," the man said, squinting at me.

"Nice to meet you," I said, extending a hand. Chuck yipped, and I apologized.

"Good doggie," the man said, reaching down to let the poodle sniff him. Usually, that was all the little dog needed to become comfortable, but something about the man upset him. He growled, backing away.

"I don't know what's gotten into him," I said, scooping him up in my arms. "Can I help you with something?" I asked again, holding the squirming poodle tight.

"Mind if I take a few pictures? We're surveying the property before we start the exploration process."

"Exploration process?" I asked. "Didn't anyone tell you?"

"Tell me what?"

He turned his head and spit out a wad of snuff. I wrinkled my nose, revolted by the glob of brown goo on the caliche driveway. "We're drillin' for oil."

Acknowledgments:

First, many thanks to my family, Eric, Abby, and Ian, not just for putting up with me, but for continuing to come up with creative ways to kill people. I also want to give a shout-out to Carol and Dave Swartz, Dorothy and Ed MacInerney, and Bethann and Beau Eccles for their years of continued support. Special thanks to the MacInerney Mystery Mavens (who help with all manner of things, from covers to concepts), particularly Kay Pucciarelli, Deborah Walker, Rudi Lee, Olivia Leigh Blacke, Edel Waugh, Priscilla Ormsby, Azanna Wishart, Georgette Thaler, Alicia Farage, and Norma Klanderman for their careful reading of the manuscript. What would I do without you??? Thank you also to ALL of the wonderful readers who make the Gray Whale Inn possible, especially my fabulous Facebook community at www.facebook.com/karenmacinerney. You keep me going!

About the Author

Karen is the housework-impaired, award-winning author of multiple mystery series, and her victims number well into the double digits. She lives in Austin, Texas with two sassy children, her husband, and a menagerie of animals, including twenty-three fish, two rabbits, and a rescue dog named Little Bit.

Feel free to visit Karen's web site at www.karen-macinerney.com, where you can down-load a free book and sign up to receive short stories, deleted scenes, recipes and other free bonus material. You can also find her on Facebook at www.facebook-.com/AuthorKarenMacInerney or www.facebook.-com/karenmacinerney (she spends an inordinate amount of time there). You are more than welcome to friend her there—and remind her to get back to work on the next book!

Made in the USA
Middletown, DE
29 January 2017